D0650534

"YOU'RE LUCKY
THIS TIME, GARRETT. . . ."

Morley Dotes chuckled. "You don't have anything weird. No vampires, no werewolves, no witches, no sorcerers, no dead gods trying to come back to life. None of the stuff you usually stumble into."

I snorted. Those things aren't on every street corner, but they're part of the world. Everybody brushes against them eventually.

I said, "I could have seen a ghost."

"A what?"

"A ghost. I keep seeing a woman that nobody admits is there. That nobody else sees. Unless they're pulling my leg. Which they probably are."

"Or you're crazy. She's a gorgeous blonde, right?"

"A blonde. Not bad."

"You're daydreaming. Your wishful thinking has gotten to you."

"Maybe. I'll know before I'm done."

But if I could have known then what I would eventually find out about my mysterious woman, and everyone else in that death-cursed mansion, I would have dropped the case immediately, grabbed a beer, and gone off to find some safer, saner company, someone like the Dead Man, for instance. . . .

OLD TIN SORROWS

A GARRETT, P.I., NOVEL

GLEN COOK

A ROC BOOK

ROC
Published by New American Library, a division of
Penguin Group (USA) Inc., 375 Hudson Street,
New York, New York 10014, USA
Penguin Group (Canada), 90 Eglinton Avenue East, Suite 700, Toronto,
Ontario M4P 2Y3, Canada (a division of Pearson Penguin Canada Inc.)
Penguin Books Ltd., 80 Strand, London WC2R 0RL, England
Penguin Ireland, 25 St. Stephen's Green, Dublin 2,
Ireland (a division of Penguin Books Ltd.)
Penguin Group (Australia), 250 Camberwell Road, Camberwell, Victoria 3124,
Australia (a division of Pearson Australia Group Pty. Ltd.)
Penguin Books India Pvt. Ltd., 11 Community Centre, Panchsheel Park,
New Delhi - 110 017, India
Penguin Group (NZ), 67 Apollo Drive, Rosedale, North Shore 0632,
New Zealand (a division of Pearson New Zealand Ltd.)
Penguin Books (South Africa) (Pty.) Ltd., 24 Sturdee Avenue,
Rosebank, Johannesburg 2196, South Africa

Penguin Books Ltd., Registered Offices:
80 Strand, London WC2R 0RL, England

First published by Roc, an imprint of New American Library,
a division of Penguin Group (USA) Inc.

First Printing, June 1989
10 9 8 7 6 5 4

Copyright © Glen Cook, 1989
All rights reserved

REGISTERED TRADEMARK—MARCA REGISTRADA

Printed in the United States of America

1

Just when you think you have it all scoped out and you're riding high, old Fate will stampede right over you and not even stop to say I'm sorry. Happens every time if your name is Garrett. You can make book on it.

I'm Garrett. Sitting pretty in my early thirties, over six feet, brown hair, two hundred pounds plus—maybe threatening to shoot up because my favorite food is beer. I have a disposition variously described as sulky, sour, sarky, or cynical. Anything with a sibilant. Sneaky and snaky, my enemies claim. But, hell, I'm a sweetheart. Really. Just a big, old, cuddly bear with a nice smile and soulful eyes.

Don't believe everything you hear. I'm just a realist who suffers from a recurrent tumor of romantic pragmatism. Once upon a time I was a lot more romantic. Then I did my five in the Fleet Marines. That almost snuffed the spark.

Keep that in mind, that time in the Corps. If I hadn't been there, none of this would have happened.

Bone-lazy, Morley would call me, but that's a base canard from a character without the moral fiber to sit still more than five minutes. I'm not lazy; I'd just rather not work if I don't need money. When I do, I operate as a confidential agent. Which means I spend a lot of time in the middle, between people you wouldn't invite to dinner. Kidnappers. Blackmailers. Thugs and thieves and killers.

My, the things kids grow up to be.

It isn't a great life. It won't get me into any history books. But it does let me be my own boss, set my own hours, pick my jobs. It lets me off a lot of hooks. I don't have to make a lot of compromises with my conscience.

Trying not to work when I don't need money means looking through the peephole first when someone knocks on the door of my place on Macunado Street. If whoever is there looks like a prospective client, I simply don't answer.

It was a false spring day early in the year. It was supposed to be winter out there but somebody was nodding. The snow had melted. After six days of unnatural warmth the trees had conned themselves into budding. They'd be sorry.

I hadn't been out since the thaw. I was at my desk reckoning accounts on a couple of minor jobs I'd subcontracted, thinking about taking a walk before cabin fever got me. Then somebody knocked.

It was Dean's day off. I had to do the legwork myself. I went to the door. I peeked. And I was startled. And, brother, was I fooled.

Whenever the big troubles came, the harbinger always wore a skirt and looked like something you couldn't find anywhere but in your dreams. In case that's too subtle, it's like this: I've got a weakness for ripe tomatoes. But I'm learning. Give me about a thousand years and . . .

This wasn't any tomato. This was a guy I'd known a long time ago and never expected to see again. One I hadn't ever wanted to see again when we'd parted. And he just looked uncomfortable out there, not like he was in trouble. So I opened the door.

That was my first mistake.

"Sarge! What're you doing here? How the hell are you?" I shoved a hand at him, something I wouldn't have dared do when I saw him last.

He was twenty years older than me, the same height, twenty pounds lighter. He had skin the color of tanned doeskin, big ears that stuck straight out, wrinkles, small black eyes, black hair with a lot of gray that hadn't been there before. No way to pin down exactly why, but he was one of the ugliest men I'd ever known. He looked damned fit, but he was the kind that would look that way if he lived forever. He stood there like he had a board nailed to his spine.

"I'm fine," he said, and took my hand in a sincere shake. Those beady little eyes went over me like they could see right through me. He'd always had that knack. "You've put on a few pounds."

"On in the middle, off at the top." I tapped my hair. It wasn't noticeable to anyone but me yet. "Come in. What're you doing in TunFaire?"

"I'm retired now. Out of the Corps. I've been hearing a lot about you. Into some exciting things. I was in the neighborhood. Thought I'd drop in. If you're not busy."

"I'm not. Beer? Come on back to the kitchen." I led the way into Dean's fiefdom. The old boy wasn't there to defend it. "When did you get out?"

"Been out three years, Garrett."

"Yeah? I figured you'd die in harness at a hundred fifty."

His name was Blake Peters. The guys in the company called him Black Pete. He'd been our leading sergeant and the nearest thing to a god or devil any of us had known, the kind of professional soldier that gives an outfit its spine. I couldn't imagine him as a civilian. Three years out? He looked like a Marine sergeant in disguise.

"We all change. I started thinking too much instead of just doing what I was told. The beer isn't bad."

It was damned good. Weider, who owns the brewery, had sent a keg of his special reserve to let me know he appreciated past favors—and to remind me I was still on retainer. I hadn't been around for a while. He was afraid his employees might go into freelance sales again.

"So, what're you doing now?" I was a little uncomfortable. I never had the experience myself—my father died in battle in the Cantard when I was four—but guys have told me they'd felt ill at ease dealing with their fathers man to man when that first happened. Black Pete hadn't ever been a friend; he'd been the Sergeant. He wasn't anymore but I didn't know him any other way.

"I'm working for General Stantnor. I was on his staff. When he retired he asked me to go with him. I did it."

I grunted. Stantnor had been a Colonel when I was in. He'd been boss of all the Marines operating out of Full Harbor, about two thousand men. I'd never met him, but I'd had plenty to say about him during my stint. Not much of it was complimentary. About the time I'd gotten out he'd become Commandant of the whole Corps and had moved to Leifmold, where the Karentine Navy and Marines have their headquarters.

"Job's about the same as it was, but the pay's better," Peters said. "You look like you're doing all right. Own your own place, I hear."

About then I started getting suspicious. It was just a niggling little worm, a whisper. He'd done some homework before he came, which meant he wasn't just stopping in for old time's sake.

"I don't go hungry," I admitted. "But I do worry about tomorrow. About how long the reflexes will last and the mind will stay sharp. The legs aren't what they used to be."

"You need more exercise. You haven't been keeping yourself up. It shows."

I snorted. Another Morley Dotes? "Don't start with the green leafies and red meat. I've already got a fairy godfather to pester me about that."

He looked puzzled, which was some sight on that phiz.

"Sorry. Private joke, sort of. So you're just sort of taking it easy these days, eh?" I hadn't heard Stantnor's name much since he'd retired. I knew he'd come home to TunFaire, to the family estate south of the city, but that was it. He'd become a recluse, ignoring politics and business, the usual pursuits of ranking survivors of the endless Cantard War.

"We haven't had much choice." He sounded sour and looked troubled for a moment. "He planned to go into material contracting, but he took sick. Maybe something he picked up in the islands. Took the fire out of him. He's bedridden most of the time."

Pity. On the plus side of Stantnor's ledger had been the fact that he hadn't sat in an office in Full Harbor spending his troops like markers on a game board. When the big shitstorms hit he was out in the weather with the rest of us.

A pity, and I said so.

"Maybe worse than a pity, Garrett. He's taken a turn for the worse. I think he's dying. And I think somebody is helping him along."

Suspicion became certainty. "You didn't just happen to be in the neighborhood."

He was direct. "No. I'm here to collect."

He didn't have to explain.

There was a time when we'd gotten caught with our pants down on one of the islands. A surprise Venageti invasion nearly wiped us out. We survivors had fled into the swamps and had lived on whatever didn't eat us first while we harrassed the Venageti. Sergeant Peters had brought us through that. I owed him for that.

But I owed him more. He'd carried me away when I'd been injured during a raid. He hadn't had to do it. I couldn't have done anything but lie there waiting for the Venageti to kill me.

He said, "That old man means a lot to me, Garrett. He's the only family I've got. Somebody's killing him slowly, but I can't figure out who or how. I can't stop it. I've never felt this helpless and out of control. So I come to a man who has a reputation for handling the unhandleable."

I didn't want a client. But Garrett pays his debts.

I took a long drink, a deep breath, cursed under my breath. "Tell me about it."

Peters shook his head. "I don't want to fill you up with ideas that didn't work for me."

"Damnit, Sarge . . ."

"Garrett!" He still had the whipcrack voice that got your attention without being raised.

"I'm listening."

"He's got other problems. I've sold him on hiring a specialist to handle them. I've sold him your reputation and my memories of you from the Corps. He'll interview you tomorrow morning. If you remember to knock the horse apples off your shoes before you go in the house, he'll hire you. Do the job he wants done. But while you're at it, do the real job. Got me?"

I nodded. It was screwy but clients are that way. They always want to sneak up on things.

"To everyone else you'll be a hired hand, job unknown, antecedents mostly unknown. You should use another name. You have a certain level of notoriety. The name Garrett might ring a bell."

I sighed. "You make it sound like I might spend a lot of time there."

"I want you to stay till the job is done. I'll need the name you're going to use before I leave or you won't get past the front door."

"Mike Sexton." I plucked it off the top of my head, but it had to be divine inspiration. If a little dangerous.

Mike Sexton had been our company's chief scout. He hadn't come back from that island. Peters had sent him out before a night strike and we'd never seen him again. He'd been Black Pete's main man, his only friend.

Peters's face went hard and cold. His eyes narrowed dangerously. He started to say something. But Black Pete never shot his mouth off without thinking.

He grunted. "It'll work. People have heard me mention the name. I'll explain how we know each other. I don't think I told anybody he's gone."

He wouldn't. He wouldn't brag about his mistakes, even to himself. I'd bet part of him was still waiting for Sexton to report.

"That's the way I figured it."

He downed the last of his beer. "You'll do it?"

"You knew I would before you pounded on the door. I didn't have any choice."

He smiled. It looked out of place on that ugly mug. "I wasn't a hundred percent sure. You were always a stubborn bastard." He took out a worn canvas purse, the same one he'd had back when, fatter than it had been before. He counted out fifty marks. In silver. Which was a statement of sorts. The price of silver has been shooting up since Glory Mooncalled double-crossed everybody and declared the whole Cantard an independent republic with no welcome for Karentines, Venageti, or what have you.

Silver is the fuel that makes sorcery go. Both Karenta and Venageta sway to the whims of cabals of sorcerers. The biggest, most productive silver mines in the world lie in the Cantard, which is why the ruling gangs have been at war there since my grandfather was a pup. Till the mercenary Glory Mooncalled pulled his stunt.

He's made it stick so far. But I'll be amazed if he keeps it up. He's got everybody pissed and he's right in the middle.

It won't be long before it's war as usual down there.

I opened my mouth to tell Peters he didn't need to pay me. I owed him. But I realized he *did* need to. He was calling in an obligation but not for free. He didn't expect me to work for nothing, he just wanted me to work. And maybe he was paying off something to the General by footing the bill.

"Eight a day and expenses," I told him. "Discount for a friend. I'll kick back if this comes out too much or I'll bill you if I need more." I took the fifty into the Dead Man's room for safekeeping. The Dead Man was hard at what he does best: snoozing. All four hundred plus pounds of him. He'd been at it so long I'd begun to miss his company.

With that thought I decided it *was* time I took a job. Missing the Dead Man's company was like missing the company of an inquisitor.

Peters was ready to go when I got back. "See you in the morning?" he asked. There was a whisper of desperation behind his words.

"I'll be there. Guaranteed."

2

It was eleven in the morning. They'd roofed the sky with planks of lead. I walked, though the General's hovel was four miles beyond South Gate. Me and horses don't get along.

I wished I'd taken the chance. My pins were letting me know I spend too much time planted on the back of my lap. Then fat raindrops started making coin-sized splats on the road. I wished some more. I was going to get wet if the old man and I didn't hit it off.

I shifted my duffel bag to my other shoulder and tried to hurry. That did all the good it ever does.

I'd bathed and shaved and combed my hair. I had on my best "meet the rich folks" outfit. I figured they'd give me credit for trying and not run me off before they asked my name. I hoped Black Pete was on the level and had left that at the door.

The Stantnor place wasn't exactly a squatter's shanty. I figured maybe a million marks' worth of brick and stone and timber. The grounds wouldn't have had any trouble gobbling the Lost Battalion.

I didn't need a map to find the house but I was lucky. The General had put out a paved private road for me to follow.

The shack was four storeys high at the wings and

five in the center, in the style called frame half-timber, and it spread out wide enough that I couldn't throw a rock from one corner to the other of the front. I tried. It was a good throw but the stone fell way short.

A fat raindrop got me in the back of the neck. I scampered up a dozen marble steps to the porch. I took a minute to arrange my face so I wouldn't look impressed when somebody answered the door. You want to deal with the rich, you've got to overcome the intimidation factor of wealth.

The door—which would have done a castle proud as a drawbridge—swung in without a sound, maybe a foot. A man looked out. All I could see was his face. I almost asked him what the grease bill was for silencing those monster hinges.

"Yes?"

"Mike Sexton. I'm expected."

"Yes." The face puckered up. Where did he get lemons this time of year?

Maybe he wasn't thrilled to see me, but he did open up and let me into a hallway where you could park a couple of woolly mammoths, if you didn't want to leave them out in the rain. He said, "I'll inform the General that you've arrived, sir." He walked away like they'd shoved a javelin up his back in boot camp, marching to drums only he could hear. Obviously another old Marine, like Black Pete.

He was gone awhile. I entertained myself by drifting along the hallway, introducing myself to the Stantnor ancestors, a dozen of whom scowled at me from portraits on the walls. The artists had been selected for their ability to capture their subject's private misery. Every one of those old boys was constipated.

I inventoried three beards, three mustaches, and six clean shaven. The Stantnor blood was strong. They looked like brothers instead of generations going back to the foundation of the Karentine state. Only their uniforms dated them.

All of them were in uniform or armor. Stantnors had been professional soldiers, sailors, Marines—forever. It was a birthright. Or maybe an obligation, like it or not, which might explain the universal dyspepsia.

The last portrait on the left was the General himself, as Commandant of the Corps. He wore a huge, ferocious white mustache and had a faraway look in his eyes, as if he were standing on the poop of a troopship staring at something beyond the horizon. His was the only portrait that hadn't been painted so its subject's eyes followed you when you moved. It was disconcerting, having all those angry old men glaring down. Maybe the portraits were supposed to intimidate upstarts like me.

Opposite the General hung the only portrait of a young man, the General's son, a Marine lieutenant who hadn't developed the family scowl. I didn't recall his name, but did remember him getting killed in the islands while I was in. He'd been the old man's only male offspring. There wouldn't be any more portraits to put up on those dark-paneled walls.

The hall ended in a wall of leaded glass that rose the hallway's two storey height, a mosaic of scenes from myth and legend, all bloodthirstily executed: heroes slaying dragons, felling giants, posturing atop heaps of elvish corpses while awaiting another charge. All stuff of antiquity, when we humans didn't get along with the other races.

The doors through that partition were normal size, also filled with glass artwork from the same school. The butler, or whatever he was, had left them ajar. I took that as an invitation.

The hall beyond could have been swiped from a cathedral. It was as big as a parade ground and four storeys high, all stone, mostly swirly browns from butterscotch to rust folded into cream. The walls were decorated with trophies presumably won by Stantnors in battle. There were enough weapons and banners to outfit a battalion.

The floor was a checkerboard of white marble and green serpentine. In its middle stood a fountain, a hero on a rearing stallion sticking a lance into the heart of a ferocious dragon that looked suspiciously like one of the bigger flying thunder-lizards. Both of them looked like they'd rather be somewhere else. Couldn't say I blamed them. Neither one was going to get out alive. The hero was about one second short of sliding off the horse's behind right into the dragon's claws. The sculptor had said a lot that, undoubtedly, no one understood. I told them, "You two want to scrap over a virgin, you should work a deal."

I headed for the fountain, heels clicking, the walls throwing back echoes. I turned around a few times, taking in the sights. Hallways ran off into the wings. Stairs went up to balconies in front of each of the upper floors. There were lots of polished round brown pillars and legions of echoes. The place couldn't be a home. Only thing I'd ever seen like it was a museum. You had to wonder what went on inside the head of a guy who would want to build a place like that to live.

It was damned near as cold in there as it was outside. I shivered, checked out the fountain up close. It wasn't going, or at least I'd have had its chuckles for company. Seemed a pity. The sound would have improved the atmosphere. Maybe they only turned it on when they were entertaining.

I've always had a soft spot in my heart for the idea of being rich. I guess most people do. But if this was the way the rich had to live, I thought maybe I could settle for less.

My trade has taken me into any number of large homes and every one seemed to have a certain coldness at its heart. The nicest I'd hit belonged to Chodo Contague, TunFaire's emperor of the underworld. He's a grotesque, a real blackheart, but his place at least fakes the life and warmth. And his decorator has his priorities straight. Once when I was there the house was littered with naked lovelies. That's what I call home furnishings! That's a lot more cheerful than a bargeload of instruments of war.

I dropped my duffel bag, put a foot up on the fountain surround, and rested my elbows on my knee. "You boys go ahead with what you're doing. I'll try not to disturb." Hero and dragon were both too preoccupied to notice.

I looked around. Where the hell was everybody? A place that size ought to have a battalion for staff. I'd seen livelier museums at midnight. Well . . .

All was not lost. In fact, things had started to look up.

I'd spotted a face. It was looking at me around a pillar supporting the balconies to my left. The west wing. It was female and gorgeous and too far away to tell much else, but that was all I needed to get my blood moving again. The woman attached was as timid as a dryad. She ducked out of sight an instant after our eyes met.

The part of me that is weak wondered if I'd see more of her. I hoped so. I could get lost in a face like that.

She did a little flit into the nearest hallway. I got just a glimpse but wanted her to come back. She was worth a second look, and maybe a third and a fourth, a long-haired, slim blonde in something white and gauzy, gathered at the waist by a red girdle. Around twenty, give or take a few, and sleek enough to put a big, goofy grin on my face.

I'd keep an eye out for that one.

Unless she was a ghost. She'd gone without making a sound. Whatever, she was going to haunt me till I got a closer look.

Was the place haunted? It was spooky enough, in its cold way . . . I realized it was me. Might not bother someone else. I looked around and heard the clash of steel and the moans of those who had died to furnish all those emblems of Stantnor glory. I was packing my own haunts in and letting the place become a mirror.

I tried to shake a darkening mood. A place like that turns you somber.

The guy from the front door marched in after the girl disappeared, his heels clicking. He came to a perfect military halt six feet away. I gave him the once-over. He stood five-foot-eight, maybe a hundred seventy pounds, in his fifties but looking younger. His hair was wavy black, slicked with some kind of grease that couldn't beat the curl. If he had any gray, he hid it well, and he still had all the hair he'd had when he was twenty. His eyes were cold little beads. You could get ice burns there. He'd kill you and not even wonder if he was making orphans.

"The General will see you now, sir." He turned and marched away.

I followed. I caught myself marching in step, skipped

to get out. In a minute I was back in step. I gave it up. They'd pounded it in good. The flesh remembered and couldn't hear the rebellion in the mind.

"You have a name?" I asked.

"Dellwood, sir."

"What were you before you got out?"

"I was attached to the General's staff, sir."

Which meant absolutely nothing. "Lifer?" Dumb question, Garrett. I could bet the family farm I was the only nonlifer in the place, excepting the girl— maybe. The General wouldn't surround himself with the lesser breeds called civilians.

"Thirty-two years, sir." He asked no questions himself. Not into small talk and chitchat? No. He didn't care. I was one of *them*.

"Maybe I should have come to the tradesman's entrance."

He grunted.

"Tough." The General had my respect for what he'd accomplished, not for who he'd been born.

Dellwood had twenty years on me but I was the guy doing the puffing when we hit the fourth floor. About six wise remarks ran through my alleged brain but I didn't have wind enough to share them. Dellwood gave me an unreadable look, probably veiled contempt for soft civilians. I puffed awhile, then to distract him said, "I saw a woman while I was waiting. Watching me. Timid as a mouse."

"That would be Miss Jennifer, sir. The General's daughter." He looked like he thought he'd made a mistake volunteering that much. He didn't say anything else. One of those guys who wouldn't tell you what he thought you didn't need to know if you burned his toes off. Was the whole staff struck from the same dies? Then why did Peters need me? They could handle anything.

Dellwood marched to an oaken door that spanned half the corridor on the top floor of the west wing. He pushed the door inward, announced, "Mr. Mike Sexton, sir."

A wall of heat smacked me as I pushed past Dellwood.

I'd come with no preconceptions but I was still surprised. General Stantnor preferred spartan surroundings. Other than the room's size, there was nothing to hint that he was hip deep in geld.

There were no carpets, a few straightbacked wooden chairs, the ubiquitous military hardware, two writing desks nose to nose, the bigger one presumably for the General and the other for whoever actually wrote. The place was almost a mausoleum. The heat came off a bonfire raging in a fireplace designed for roasting oxen. Another gink without joints in his spine was tossing in logs from a nearby mountain. He looked at me, looked at the old man behind the big desk. The old man nodded. The fireman marched out, maybe to kill time practicing close order drill with Dellwood.

Having surveyed the setting I zeroed in on its centerpiece.

I could see why Black Pete was suspicious. There wasn't much left of General Stantnor. He didn't look anything like the guy in the picture downstairs. He looked like he might weigh about as much as a mummy, though most of him was buried under comforters. Ten years ago he'd been my height and thirty pounds heavier.

His skin had a yellowish cast and was mildly translucent. His pupils were milky with cataracts. His hair had fallen out in clumps. Only a few patches remained, not just gray or white but with a bluish hue of death. He had liver spots but those had faded, too. His lips had no color left but a poisonous gray-blue.

I don't know how well he could see through those cataracts, but his gaze was strong and steady. He didn't shake.

"Mike Sexton, sir. Sergeant Peters asked me to see you."

"Grab a chair. Pull it up there facing me. I don't like to look up when I talk to someone." There was power in his voice, though I don't know where he found the energy. I'd figured him for a graverobber's whisper. I settled opposite him. He said, "For the moment I'm confident we're not being overheard, Mr. Garrett. Yes. I know who you are. Peters provided me with a full report before I approved bringing you in." He kept staring as though he could overcome those cataracts through sheer will. "But we'll pursue the Mike Sexton fiction in future. Assuming we come to terms now."

I was close enough to smell him, and it wasn't a good smell. I was surprised the whole room didn't reek. They must have brought him in from somewhere else. "Peters didn't say what you needed, sir. He just called in an old marker to get me out here." I glanced at the fireplace. They would be baking bread in here soon.

"It takes a great deal of heat to keep me going, Mr. Garrett. My apologies for your discomfort. I'll try to keep this brief. I'm a little like a thunder-lizard. I generate no heat of my own."

I waited for him to continue. And sweated a lot.

"I have Peters's word that you were a good Marine." No doubt that counted for a lot around here.

"He vouches for your character then. But men change. What have you become?"

"A freelance thug instead of a drafted one, General. Which you need or I wouldn't be here."

He made a noise that might have been laughter. "Ah. I'd heard you have a sharp tongue, Mr. Garrett. I should be the impatient one, not you. I have so little time left. Yes. Peters vouches for you today, as well. And you do get mentioned in some circles as being reliable, though headstrong and inclined to carry out your assignments according to your own lights. They say you have a sentimental streak. That shouldn't trouble us here. They say you have a weakness for women. I think you'll find my daughter more trouble than she's worth. They say you tend to be judgmental of the vices and peccadillos of my class."

I wondered if he knew how often I change my underwear. Why did he need an investigator? Let him use whoever had investigated me.

Again that sorry laugh. "I can guess what you're thinking. Everything I know is public knowledge. Your reputation runs before you." Something that might have been a smile in better times. "You've managed to do a fair amount of good over the years, Mr. Garrett. But you stepped on a lot of toes doing it."

"I'm just a clumsy kid, General. I'll grow out of it."

"I doubt it. You don't seem intimidated by me."

"I'm not." I wasn't. I'd met too many guys who really *were* intimidating. I had calluses on that organ.

"You would have been ten years ago."

"Different circumstances."

"Indeed. Good. I need a man who won't be intimidated. Especially by me. Because I fear that if you do your job right, you may uncover truths I won't want to face. Truths so brutal I may tell you to back off. You won't do that?''

He had me baffled. "I'm confused."

"The normal state of the world, Mr. Garrett. I mean, when I hire you, if I hire you, if you agree to take this job, your commitment will be to follow it through to the end. Disregarding anything I tell you later. I'll see that you're paid up front so you aren't tempted to bend in order to collect your fee."

"I still don't get it."

"I pride myself on my ability to meet the truth head-on. In this case I want to arrange it so I have no choice, however much I squirm and ache. Can you understand that?"

"Yes." Only in the most literal sense. I didn't understand why. We all spend a lot of time fooling ourselves, and his class were masters at that—though he'd always had a reputation for having both feet firmly planted in reality. He'd disobeyed or refused orders more than once because they had originated in wishful thinking by superiors who hadn't come within five hundred miles of the fighting. Each time events had saved him embarrassment by proving him right.

He didn't have a lot of friends.

"Before I make any commitment, I have to know what I'm supposed to do."

"There is a thief in my house, Mr. Garrett."

He stopped because of some kind of spasm. I thought he was having a heart attack. I jumped up and headed for the door.

"Wait," he croaked. "It will pass."

I paused midway between my chair and the door, saw the spasm fade, in a moment he was back to normal. I perched myself on my chair again.

"A thief in my house. Yet there is no one here I haven't known for thirty years, no one I haven't trusted with my life many times."

That had to be a weird feeling, knowing you could trust guys with your life but not with your things.

I got a glimmer of why he needed an outsider. A bad apple amongst old comrades. They might cover up, refuse to see the truth, or . . . Who knows? Marines don't think like people.

"I follow. Go ahead."

"My infirmity came upon me soon after I returned home. It's a progressive consumption, apparently. But slow. I seldom get out of my quarters now. But I've noticed, this past year, that some things, some of which have been in the family for centuries, have disappeared. Never large, flashy things that would be obvious to any eye. Just trinkets, sometimes more valuable as mementoes than intrinsically. Yet the sum should add to a fair amount by now."

"I see." I glanced at the fire. It was time to turn me over so I wouldn't be underdone on one side.

"Bear with me a few minutes more, Mr. Garrett."

"Yes sir. Any strangers in the house recently? Any regular visitors?"

"A handful. People off the Hill. Not the sort who would pilfer."

I didn't say so but in my thinking the worst of all criminals come off the Hill. Our nobility would steal the coppers off dead men's eyes. But the General had a point. They wouldn't steal with their own hands. They'd have somebody do it for them.

"You have an inventory of what's missing?"

"Would that be useful?"

"Maybe. Somebody steals something, they want to sell it to get money. Right? I know some of the retailers whose wholesalers are people with sticky fingers. Do you want the stuff back or do you just want to know who's kyping it?"

"The latter step first, Mr. Garrett. Then we'll consider recovery." Sudden as a lightning bolt he suffered another spasm. I felt helpless, unable to do anything for him. That was not a good sensation.

He came back but this time he was weaker.

"I'll have to close this out quickly, Mr. Garrett. I'll need to rest. Or the next attack may be the last." He smiled. There were teeth missing behind the smile. "Another reason to make sure you get your fee up front. My heirs might not see fit to pay you."

I wanted to say something reassuring, like he'd outlive me, but that seemed too cynically a load of manure. I kept my mouth shut. I can do that sometimes, though usually at the wrong time.

"I'd like to get to know you better, Mr. Garrett, but nature has its own priorities. I'll hire you if you'll have me for a client. Will you find me my thief? On the terms I stated?"

"No punches pulled? No backing off?"

"Exactly."

"Yes sir." I had to force it out. I really was getting lazy. "I'm on it now."

"Good. Good. Dellwood should be outside. Tell him I want Peters."

I got up. "Will do, General." I backed toward the door. Even in his present state the old man retained some of the magnetism that had made him a charismatic commander. I didn't want to pity him. I really wanted to help him. I wanted to find the villain Black Pete said was trying to kill him.

3

The cool in the hallway felt like high winter in the Arctic. For a second I worried about frostbite.

The General was right about Dellwood. He was there, waiting. The way he did it suggested he'd been scrupulous about not getting so close he might overhear anything. Though I doubted explosions could be heard through that door. I decided I could like the guy in spite of the stick up his spine.

"The General says he wants to see Peters."

"Very good, sir. I'd better attend to that. If you'll return to the fountain and wait?"

"Sure. But hold on. What's wrong with him? He had a couple of pretty fierce attacks while I was in there."

That stopped him dead. He looked at me, emotion leaking through for once. He loved that old man and he was worried. "Bad spasms, sir?"

"They looked that way to me. But I'm no doc. He cut the interview short because he was afraid another one would be too much for him."

"I'd better check on him before I do anything else."

"What's wrong with him?" I asked again.

"I don't know, sir. We've tried bringing physicians

in, but he throws them out when he finds out what they are. He has a morbid fear of doctors. From what they've said, I understand that a physician's care might not do any good. They haven't done anything but scratch their heads and say they don't understand it."

"Good to see you can talk, Dellwood."

"I believe the General brought you on board, sir. You're one of the household now."

I liked that attitude. Most people I meet either stay clammed or tell lies. "I'd like to talk to you some more when you get the time."

"Yes sir." He pushed through the General's door.

I found my way to the fountain. Wasn't that hard. But I'd become one of the company scouts after Sexton disappeared. I was a highly trained finder of the way. Peters often reminded me how much the Crown had invested in me.

I'd left my bag leaning against the fountain for lack of desire to lug it around before I decided if I was hired. It had seemed safe enough, still as the place was. I mean, I'd visited livelier ruins.

Someone was digging through it when I reached that temple to overstated militarism.

She had her back to me and a mighty fine backside it was. She was tall and slim and brunette. She wore a simple tan shift in imitation peasant style. It probably set somebody back more money than a peasant saw in five years. Her behind wiggled deliciously as she dug. It looked like she'd only gotten started.

I moved out on scout's tippytoes, stopped four feet behind her, gave her fanny an approving nod, said, "Find anything interesting?"

She whirled.

I started. The face was the same as the one I'd seen

earlier but this time it wasn't timid at all. This face had more lines in it. It was more worldly. That other face had had the placidity, behind timidity, that you see in nuns.

Her eyes flashed. "Who are you?" she demanded, unrepentant. I like my ladies unrepentant about some things, but not about snooping in my stuff.

"Sexton. Who are you? Why are you going through my stuff?"

"How come you're carrying a portable arsenal?"

"I need it in my work. I answered a couple. Your turn."

She looked me up and down, raised an eyebrow, looked like she didn't know if she approved or not. Wound me to the core! Then she snorted and walked away. I'm not the handsomest guy in town but the lovelies don't usually respond that way. Had to be part of a plan.

I watched her go. She moved well. She exaggerated it a little, knowing she had an audience. She disappeared into the shadows under the west balcony.

"Going to be some strange ones here," I muttered. I checked my bag. She'd stirred it up but nothing was missing. I'd arrived in time to keep her out of the little padded box with the bottles inside. I double-checked, though, opening it.

There were three bottles, royal blue, emerald green, ruby red. Each weighed about two ounces. They were plunder from a past case. Their contents had been whipped up by a sorcerer. They could get real handy in tight situations. I hoped I didn't have to use them.

I'd brought along more tight-situation stuff than clothing. Clothing washes.

I prowled the hall while I waited for Dellwood. That was like visiting a museum alone. None of the stuff there meant anything to me. Richly storied, all of it, no doubt, but I've never been a guy to get excited about history for its own sake.

Dellwood took his time. After half an hour I started eyeballing an old bugle, wondering what would happen if I gave it a couple of toots. Then I spotted the blonde again, watching me from about as far away as she could get and still be in that hall with me. I waved. I'm a friendly kind of guy.

She ducked out of sight. A mouse, this one.

Dellwood finally showed. I asked, "The General all right?"

"He's resting, sir. He'll be fine." He didn't sound convinced. "Sergeant Peters will handle the requests you made." Now he sounded puzzled. "I'm curious, sir. What are you doing here?"

"The General sent for me."

He looked at me a moment, said, "If you'll come with me, I'll show you your quarters." After we'd climbed to the fourth floor east wing and he had me puffing again, he tried another tack. "Will you be staying long?"

"I don't know." I hoped not. The place was getting to me already. It was too much a tomb. In the other wing the master was dying and the place seemed to be dying with him. As Dellwood opened a door, I asked, "What will you do after the General passes on?"

"I haven't given that much thought, sir. I don't expect him to go soon. He'll beat this. His ancestors all lived into their eighties and nineties."

Whistling in the dark. He had no future he could see. The world didn't have much room for lifers with their best years used up.

Which made me wonder again why anyone in that

house would want Stantnor to check out early. Black Pete's suspicions were improbable, logically.

But logic doesn't usually come into play when people start thinking about killing other people.

I hadn't looked at the thing yet. I'd keep an open mind till I'd done some poking and prying and just plain listening.

"What's the word on meals, Dellwood? I'm not equipped for formal dining."

"We haven't dressed since the General took ill, sir. Breakfast is at six, lunch at eleven, in the kitchen. Supper is at five in the dining room, but informally. Guests and staff sit down together, if that presents any problems."

"Not to me. I'm an egalitarian kind of guy. I think I'm just as good as you are. I missed lunch, eh?" I wasn't going to be happy here if I had to conform to the native schedule. I see six in the morning only when I haven't gotten to bed yet. The trouble with morning is that it comes so damned early in the morning.

"I'm sure something can be arranged, this once. I'll tell Cook we have a newly arrived guest."

"Thanks. I'll take a minute to settle in, then get down there."

"Very well, sir. If anything is not satisfactory, let me know. I'll see that any problems are corrected."

He would, too. "Sure. Thanks." I watched him step out and close the door.

4

I could not imagine things going awry, considering some scenes I've endured. Dellwood had installed me in a suite bigger than the ground floor of my house. The room where I stood boasted rosewood wainscotting, mahogany ceiling beams, a wall of bookshelves loaded down, and furniture for entertaining a platoon. A dining table with seats for four. A writing table. Various chairs. Leaded and plain glass windows unfortunately facing north. A carpet some old lady had spent the last twenty years of her life weaving, maybe three hundred years ago. Lamps enough to do my whole house. A chandelier overhead loaded with a gaggle of candles, unlighted at the moment.

This was how the other half lived.

Two doors opened off the big room. I made a guess and pushed through one. What a genius. Hit the bedroom first time.

It was of a piece with the rest. I'd never met a bed so big and soft.

I looked around for hiding places, squirreled some of my equipment good, some so it could be found easily and the rest maybe overlooked. I kept the most important stuff on my person. I figured I'd better hit the kitchen while the staff were still understanding. After I stoked the bodily fires I could wander around like an old ghost.

In better times the kitchen probably boasted a staff of a dozen, with full-time specialists like bakers and pastry cooks. When I dropped in, there was only one person present, an ancient-breed woman whose non-human half appeared to be troll. Wrinkled, shrunken, stooped, she was still a foot taller than me and a hundred pounds heavier. Even at her age she could probably break me over her knee—if I stood still and let her lay hands on me.

"You the new one?" she growled when I walked in.

"That's me. Name's Sexton. Mike Sexton."

"Name's mud you don't show on time after this, young'un. Sit." She pointed. I didn't argue. I sat at a table three-quarters buried in used utensils and stoneware. Plunk! She slammed something down in front of me.

"You served with the General, too?"

"Smartass, eh? You want to eat? Eat. Don't try to be a comedian."

"Right. Just making conversation." I looked at my plate. All kinds of chunks of something I didn't recognize mixed up in slimy sauce, piled on rice. I approached it with the trepidation I usually reserve for the stuff they serve at my friend Morley's place, the city's only vegetarian restaurant open to a mixed clientele.

"If I want conversation, I'll ask for it. Look around here. It look like I got time to waste jacking my jaw? Been trying to carry it on my own since they threw

Candy out on his ass. I keep telling the old skinflint, I need another pair of hands. Think he'll listen? Hell, no! All he sees is he's saving a couple marks a week."

I took a bite here, a bite there. There seemed to be mussels and mushrooms and a couple things I couldn't identify, and all damned good. "This is excellent," I said.

"Where you been eating? It's slop. I got no helper, I don't got time to fix anything right." She started tossing pots at a sink, sending sprays of water flying. "Barely got time to get ready for the next feeding. These hogs, you think they know the difference? Feed them hot sawdust mush, they wouldn't know it."

Maybe not. But I'd had old Dean cooking for me for a while and I knew good food when I bit it. "How many do you have to take care of?"

"Eighteen. Counting myself. Bloody army. What do you care, Mr. Nineteen and straw that broke the camel's back?"

"That many? The place is like a haunted house. I've seen the General, Dellwood, and you, and some old boy who was stoking the fireplace in the General's study."

"Kaid."

"And two women. Where are the rest? On maneuvers?"

"Wise ass, eh? Where did you see two women? That ass Harcourt sneaking one of his floozies in here again? Hell. I hope he is. I just hope he is. I'll have the old man put him on KP for a year. Get this cesspool cleaned out. What the hell you doing here, anyway? We ain't had nobody new here for two years. No honest-to-goodness guests in a year and a half, just in and outs from uptown, their noses in the air like they don't squat to shit like everybody else."

Whew! "To tell the truth, Miss . . . ?" She didn't take the hook. "To tell the truth, I'm not quite sure. The General sent for me. Said he wanted to hire me. But he had some kind of attack before . . ."

She melted. The vinegar drained out in two seconds. "How bad is it? Maybe I'd better go see."

"Dellwood's taken care of it. Says he just needs to rest. He got himself overwrought. This fellow Harcourt. He has a habit of bringing girlfriends home?"

"Not since a couple years back. What the hell you asking all the questions for? Ain't none of your damned business what we do or who we do it with."

She had a thought. She stopped dead still, stepped away from the sink, turned, laid a first-class glower on me. "Or is it your business?"

I didn't say. I tried to slide around it by offering her my empty plate. "Wouldn't be a little more of that, would there? Just to fill a couple empty spots?"

"It is your business. The old man has another fantasy. Thinks somebody's out to get him. Or somebody's robbing him." She shook her head. "You're wasting your time. Or maybe not. Long as he's paying you, it don't matter if you find something, does it? Hell. Probably better if you don't. You can rob him yourself, taking money for nothing. Till the fantasy wears off."

I was confused, but covered it. "Somebody's been robbing the General?"

"Nobody's robbing him. The old boy ain't got a pot to pee in, not counting this damned stone barn. And it's too damned big to carry off. Anyway, if somebody *was* robbing him I wouldn't tell you word one. Not no outsider. I don't never say nothing to no outsiders. They're all a bunch of con artists."

"Commendable attitude." I wiggled my plate suggestively.

"I got my hands in dishwater up to my elbows and you don't look like you got no broken legs. Get it yourself."

"Be happy to if I knew where."

She made an exasperated noise, made allowance for the fact that I was new. "On the damned stove. Rice in the steel pot, stew in the iron kettle. I worry about the old boy. These fancies . . . More and more all the time. Must be the sickness. Touching him. Though he always did think somebody was trying to do him out of something."

Wouldn't say a word to an outsider. I was proud of her. "It isn't possible somebody might actually *be* robbing him? Like they say, even paranoids get persecuted."

"Who? You tell me that, Mr. Smartass Snooper. Ain't nobody in this whole damned place wouldn't wrestle thunder-lizards for him. Half of them would take the disease for him if they could."

I didn't make the point, but people work kinky deals with their consciences. I had no trouble imagining a man willing to die for the General being equally willing to steal from him. The very willingness to serve could set off a chain of justifications making theft sound completely reasonable.

She'd figured me out in fifteen minutes. How long would it be before word spread? "You ever have a problem with pixies or brownies?" The countryside suffered periodic infestations, like termites or mice. The little people are fond of baubles and have no respect for property.

"We had any around here, I'd put them to work."

I figured she would. "Dellwood hinted that the General has a prejudice against doctors. In his condition I'd think he'd be ready to try anything."

"You don't know that boy. He's got a stubborn streak a yard wide. He by damned made up his mind when the missus died, he wasn't never going to trust no quack again. And he stuck."

"Uhm?"

She wouldn't talk to no outsider. Not her, no siree! "See, he loved that girl, Miss Tiffany. Such a lovely child she was. Broke all our hearts when it happened. They laughed at him, he was so much older than her. But he was her heart's slave, him that never loved a thing before. Then Miss Jennifer came. She was in labor so long. He couldn't stand to see her in pain. He brought in doctors from the city. After Miss Jennifer finally came, one damned fool gave Miss Tiffany a damned anticoagulant infusion. Thought he was giving her a sleeping potion."

A big mistake and an especially stupid one, sounded like. "She bled to death?"

"She did. Might have anyway. She was a frail, pale thing, but you couldn't never convince him."

Mistakes that cost lives aren't easy to understand or forgive, but they happen. Despite what they want us mortals to believe, doctors are human. And where there are human beings, there's human error. It's inevitable.

When doctors make mistakes, people hurt.

Easy for me to be understanding. I hadn't known and loved the General's wife.

"Changed his whole life, that did. Went off and spent the rest of it in the Cantard, taking out his grief on the Venageti." And when generals make mistakes, lots of people hurt. "You going to hang out here all day, youngster, you better roll up your sleeves and get washing. Round here we don't got no place for drones."

I was tempted. She had plenty to say. Still . . . "Maybe later. If it looks like I'm wasting my time, I might as well wash dishes."

She snorted. "Thought that would get rid of you. Never knowed a man yet with balls enough to wade into a mountain of dirty dishes of his own free will."

"The lunch was great. Thank you, Miss . . . ?"

Didn't work this time, either.

5

That fountain in the great hall was a good hub from which to launch exploratory forays. I perched on the surround, digesting Cook's remarks. I had a premonition. I would get intimate with dishwater before I exhausted that vein of stubborn silence.

I had that creepy feeling you get when you sense somebody watching you. I looked around casually.

There she was. The blonde again, drifting in the shadows, bold enough now to be on the same floor with me. I pretended not to notice. I gave it a minute, got up, stretched. She ducked out of sight. I moved her way pretending I had no idea she was there.

She lit out like a scared pheasant. I bolted after her. "Jennifer!"

I ducked between pillars . . . Where did she go? I didn't see anywhere she could run. But she wasn't there.

Spooky!

"Hey! Mike. What are you doing?"

I jumped about five feet. "Peters. Don't sneak up like that. This place has got me believing in spooks already. Where the hell is everybody?"

Peters looked puzzled. "Everybody? Working."

That made sense. You could lose a lot more than eighteen people in that barn and on those grounds. "You'd think I'd run into somebody once in a while."

"It does get lonely at times." He smiled. That made two times in two days. A record. "Thought you might want a tour."

"I can find my way. I was a scout in the Marines, you know."

His smile vanished. He looked at me like the old Black Pete. Like I wasn't bright enough to tie my own shoes. He jerked his head toward the back of the hall, the north end, which was a wall of leaded glass with fifty furious combats going. There was a door back there.

Hey. Mom Garrett didn't raise many idiots. I got it. "I could use a look at the grounds, though, and somebody to tell me what I'm seeing."

He relaxed some, did a slick about-face and marched. I hup-two-threed behind him. I didn't feel a bit of nostalgia for the bad old days.

Peters didn't say anything till we were out of earshot of the house, clear of the formal garden behind it, away from cover where eavesdroppers might lurk. "You saw the old man. What do you think?"

"He's in bad shape."

"You know any poisons that could do that to him?"

I gave it an honest think. "No. But I'm no expert. I know a guy who is. But he'd have to see the General." Morley Dotes knows whatever there is to know about doing in your fellow man. Or elf, him being a breed with more dark-elfin than human blood.

"I don't think I could swing that. One outsider here has the place in an uproar already."

"Yeah. It's a regular busted-up beehive." Our walk

to isolation hadn't shown me a single body in motion. "It was just a suggestion. You want to know something, you get the answer from somebody who knows."

"I'll give it a shot."

"The business about the thefts. Is it real? The cook thinks it's all in the General's imagination."

"It's not. She'd think that. Back when we first came here he did have a spell when he imagined things. She doesn't get out of the kitchen much and she has a few loose threads herself. Most of the time she doesn't know what year it is."

"She tried to draft me as kitchen help."

"She would. Gods! I remember your cooking."

"I remember what I had to work with. Muskrats and cattail roots. And bugs for garnish."

He grunted, almost smiled again.

"Don't tell me. You can't have fond memories of those days."

"No, Garrett. Even lifers aren't that crazy. I don't miss that part." He shuddered.

"Eh? What?"

"Bad rumor. They may call up the veterans to run Glory Mooncalled down."

I laughed.

"What's so damned funny?"

"Best joke I've heard in weeks. You know how many people that takes in? Every human male in the population over twenty-five. You think *any* of them would go without a fuss? A call-up like that would start a revolution."

"Maybe. You think it *could* be poison?"

"I suppose. Assume it is. Speculate."

"I don't know anything about poisons. How could it be given to him?"

I'm not an expert, but I have a professional interest and keep my ears open when such things are discussed. "It could be in his food or drink. It could be dusted into his bed so it would seep through his skin. It could even be in the air he breathes. Looking for 'how' can be a dead end unless you know 'what.' Better to look at the people. Who has access?"

"Everybody, one way or another."

"Take it a step further. Who'd profit? If somebody's killing him, that somebody has to have a reason. Right?"

He grunted. "Obviously whoever's doing it believes he has. I've been trying to figure that out from the beginning. And I can't come up with one."

I didn't have any trouble. "What's the estate worth? Who does it go to?"

"Doesn't make sense. Jennifer gets half. The other half gets divided amongst the rest of us."

"Give me a value in gold marks. Just a guess. Then ask yourself what some people might do for a share of that."

"Three million for the house?" He shrugged. "A million for the contents. Two or three million for the real estate. He was offered three for the two north sections last year. He was tempted because he's strapped for cash and he wants to set Jennifer up so she's fixed for life, no matter what she does."

"Three million for just part of the property?"

"Somebody wanted the land near the city. But the offer was withdrawn because he dithered. They bought a tract from the Hillmans instead. For less money."

"No bad feelings?"

"Not that I heard."

I did some rough division in my head. I came up

with around a hundred thousand marks each for the minority heirs. I knew guys who'd cut a hundred thousand throats for that kind of money. So there was a motive—assuming somebody was in a hurry to get his share.

"Everybody know they're in the will?"

"Sure. The old man used to make a big deal of it. How if you didn't toe the mark you blew your share."

Ha! "Cook mentioned a Candy . . ."

"Not him. He's long gone. He wouldn't have the balls, either. He wasn't even human. Wasn't in the will, either. Wasn't one of the guys the old man brought home with him. He was one of the crew who managed the place while the General was in the Cantard."

"She mentioned a Harcourt who got in trouble for bringing girlfriends home."

"Harcourt?" He frowned. "I guess he got fed up with what he thought were chickenshit rules. He just took off about six months back. The old man cut him out. He'd know that. So there's nothing for him to gain. Let alone we'd see him around here."

"We may have to back off and go at this from another angle, Sarge."

"Eh?"

"What have I got to go on? Your feelings. But every time I ask you a question you make it sound more like there's nobody who'd want him dead. And nobody who'd profit from it since everybody's getting a cut anyway. We can't hang up a solid motive. And means and opportunity are limited."

"You're sneaking up on something."

"I'm wondering if maybe he isn't just dying of stomach cancer. Wondering if maybe you shouldn't hire a doctor instead of me till you know what's killing him."

He didn't answer for a few minutes. I was talked out. We walked. He brooded and I studied the grounds. Somebody had farmed the fields last summer. There was nobody in them now. I glanced at the sky. They'd thrown on a few more slabs of lead and added icicles to the breeze. Winter was coming back.

"I tried, Garrett. Two months ago. Somebody leaked it to the old man. The doc never got through the front door."

The way he said "somebody" I guessed he knew who. I asked.

He didn't want to say. "Who, Sarge? We can't pick and choose our suspects."

"Jennifer. She was in on the plot but she defected. She's a strange girl. Her big goal in life is to win some gesture of love and approval. And the old man doesn't know how. He's scared of her. She grew up while he was away. It doesn't help that she looks a lot like her mother. Her mother died—"

"Cook told me that story."

"She would. That old hag knows everything and tells anyone who'll listen. You ought to move into the kitchen."

We walked some more, headed south now, circling the house.

Peters said, "Maybe we have a communication problem. The deeper you get in the more you'll think the mess is imaginary. The old man has crazy spells. He *does* think people are out to get him when they're not. That's what makes this diabolical. Unless somebody sticks a knife in him in front of everybody, nobody's going to believe he's in danger."

I grunted. I'd had a friend, Pokey Pigotta, in the same line as me. He's dead now. But once he'd had a case that worked that way. A crazy old woman with a lot of money, always down with imaginary illnesses and besieged by imaginary enemies. Pokey discounted her fears. Her son did her in. Pokey was haunted by that one. "I'll keep an open mind."

"That's all I ask. Stick with it. Don't let it get to you."

"Sure. But we could shortcut everything if we could get a few experts in."

"I said I'd try. Don't hold your breath. It was hard enough selling you."

We continued our circuit of the grounds. At one point we passed near a graveyard. "Family plot?" I asked.

"For three hundred years."

I glanced at the house. It brooded down on us from that point. "It doesn't look that old."

"It isn't. There was an earlier house. Check the outbuildings in back. You can still see some of its foundations. They tore it down for materials to build the outbuildings after the new house went up."

I supposed I'd have to give them the once-over. You have to go through all the motions. You have to leave no stone unturned, though already, intu-itively, I was inclined to think the answer lay inside the big house—if there was an answer.

Peters read my mind. "If I'm fooling myself and we've just got an old man dying, I want to know that, too. Check?"

"Check."

"I've spent more time with you than I should. I'd better get back to work."

"Where do I find you if I need you?"

He chuckled. "I'm like horse apples. I'm everywhere. Catch as catch can. A problem you'll have with everybody, especially during poacher season. Cook's the only one who stays in one place."

We walked toward the house, passing through a small orchard of unidentifiable fruit trees with a white gazebo at its center, climbed a slope, went up the steps to the front door. Peters went inside. I paused to survey the Stantnor domains. The cold wind gnawed my cheeks. The overcast sky left the land colorless and doleful, like old tin. I wondered if it was losing life with its master.

But there would be a spring for the land. I doubted there would be for the old man.

Unless I found me a poisoner.

6

I heard Black Pete's footsteps fading as I stepped into the great hall. The light was dimming there. The place seemed more deserted and gloomy than ever. I went to the fountain, watched our hero work out on his dragon, thought about what to do next. Explore the house? Hell. I was cold already. Why not look at those outbuildings and be done with it?

I felt eyes on me as I moved. Already habituated, I checked the nearest shadows. The blonde wasn't there. Nobody was, anywhere. Then I glanced up.

I caught a flicker on the third floor balcony, east side. Somebody ducking out of sight. Who? One of the majority I hadn't yet met? Why they wouldn't want to be seen was a puzzle. I'd see everyone sooner or later.

I took myself out the back door.

Immediately behind the house lay a formal garden sort of thing that I'd paid no heed before. Peters had wanted to get away where we could talk. I gave it a look now.

There was a lot of fancy stonework, statues, fountains, pools that had been drained because at that time of year water tends to freeze. Ice would break the pool walls. There were hedges, shaped trees, beds for spring and summer plantings. It could be impressive in season. Right then it just seemed abandoned and haunted by old sorrows.

I paused at the hedge bounding the north end of the garden, looked back. The vista seemed a ghost of another time.

At least one someone was watching me from a third floor window in the west wing.

Keep that in mind, Garrett. Whatever you do, wherever you go, somebody is going to be watching.

Twenty feet behind the hedge was a line of poplars. They were there to mask the outbuildings, so the practical side of life wouldn't offend the eyes of those who lived in the house. The rich are that way. They don't want to be reminded that their comfort requires sweaty drudge labor.

There were half a dozen outbuildings of various shapes and sizes. Stone was the main structural material, though it wasn't stone that matched that in the big house. The stable was obvious. Somebody was at work there. I heard a hammer pounding. There was a second structure for livestock, presumably cattle, maybe dairy cattle. It was nearest me and had that smell. The rest of the buildings, including a greenhouse off to my right, had the look of protracted neglect. Way to the left was a long, low building that looked like a barracks. It also looked like nobody had used it for years. I decided to start with the greenhouse.

Not much to see there except that someone had spent a fortune on glass and then hadn't bothered to keep the place up. A few panes were broken. The framework that had been white once needed paint desperately. The door stood open a foot and sagged on its hinges. I had trouble pushing it back enough to get inside.

No one had been in there for a long time. The place had gone to weeds. The only animal life I saw was a scroungy, orange, feral cat. She headed for cover when she saw me.

The building next on the left was small, solid, and very much in use. It turned out to be a wellhouse, which explained why it looked like it handled a lot of traffic. A place this size would consume a lot of water—though I'd have thought they'd pipe it in from a reservoir.

The stable was the next building over. I gave it a skip. I'd talk to whoever was there after I finished snooping. Next over was a smaller building filled with a jungle of tools and farm implements with an air of long neglect. There was another cat in there, a lot of mice, and from the smell, a regiment of bats. There's nothing like the stink of lots of bats.

Next up was the barn and, yes, that's what it was. Bottom level for the animals, dairy and beef. Top level for hay, straw, and feed. Nobody around but the cows and a few more cats. I figured there must be owls, too, because I didn't smell bats. The place needed maintenance. The cows weren't friendly, unfriendly, or even curious.

The day was getting on. The gloom was getting thick. I figured I'd better get on with it and save the detail work for later. Supper would be coming up soon.

The building I'd thought looked like a barracks was probably for seasonal help. It was about eighty yards long, had maybe fifteen doors. The first I looked behind showed me a large, dusty bunkroom.

The next opened on smaller quarters divided into three rooms, a bigger one immediately inside and two half its size behind it. The next several doors opened on identical arrangements. I guessed these were apartments for workers with families. Trouble was, there was a lot of waste space between doors, space unaccounted for.

The far end of the barracks had a kitchen the size of the bunkroom. Its door was on the other side of the building. Glancing along that face, I saw more doors, which explained the missing space. The apartments faced alternate directions. I stepped into the kitchen, a windowless, cheerless place that would have been depressing at the best of times. I left the door propped open for light.

There was little to see but dust and cobwebs and cooking utensils that hadn't been touched in years. Another place nobody had visited in a long time. I was surprised the stuff was still lying around. Tun-Faire and its environs have no shortage of thieves. All this stuff had some market value.

A gold mine that hadn't been discovered?

The door slammed shut.

"Damned wind," I muttered, and edged my way through the darkness, trying to remember what was lying in ambush between it and me.

I heard somebody secure the rusty hasp.

Not the wind. Somebody who didn't want to be my friend.

Not a good situation, Garrett. This place was far from where anybody had any business. The walls were thick stone. I could do a lot of yelling and nobody would hear. The door was the only way out and the only source of light.

I found the door, ran my hands over it, pushed

gently, snorted. I stepped back a few feet and kicked hard.

The hasp ripped out of the dry, ancient wood. I charged through with a ready knife, saw nobody. I roared around the end of the barracks. And still saw nobody.

Damn! I leaned against the building and gave it a think. Something was going on, even if it wasn't what Black Pete thought.

Once I settled down, I went back to the kitchen door and looked for tracks. There were signs that somebody had been around, but the light was so poor, I couldn't do anything with them.

So. Nothing to do about it now. Might as well go to dinner and see who was surprised to see me.

7

I was late. I should have explored the house. I didn't know where we'd eat so I went to the kitchen. I waited there till Cook turned up. She gave me a high-power glower. "What you doing in here?"

"Waiting to find out where we eat?"

"Fool." She loaded up. "Grab an armful and come on."

I did both. She shoved through swinging doors into a big pantry, marched through that and out another swinging door.

The dining room was a dining room. The kind where a guy can entertain three hundred of his closest friends. Most of it was dark. Everybody was seated at one corner table. The decor was standard for the house, armor and edged steel.

"There," Cook said. I presumed she meant the empty place. I settled my load on an unused part of the table, sat.

Wasn't much of a crowd. Dellwood and Peters and the brunette I'd caught rifling my duffel bag, plus three guys I hadn't met. And Cook, who planted herself across from me. The General couldn't make it, apparently. There weren't any other places set.

The girl and guys I hadn't met looked me over. The men looked like retired Marines. Surprise, surprise. The girl looked good. She'd changed into her vamping clothes.

Garrett, you dog . . . The thought fled. This one gave off something sour. She was radiating the come-and-get-it and my reaction was to back off. Here was trouble on the hoof. What was it Morley said? Don't never fool around with a woman who's crazier than you are?

Maybe I was growing up.

Sure. And tomorrow morning pigs would be swooping around like swallows.

I didn't plan to outgrow *that* for about another six hundred years.

Peters said, "This is Mike Sexton. He was with me in the islands about ten years back. Mike, Cook." He indicated the troll-breed woman.

"We've met."

"Miss Jennifer, the General's daughter."

"We've also met." I rose and reached across, offering my hand. "Didn't get the chance before. You had both of yours in my duffel bag."

Cook chuckled. Jennifer looked at me like she wondered if I'd taste better roasted or fried.

"You've met Dellwood. Next to him is Cutter Hawkes."

Hawkes was too far off to shake. I nodded. He nodded. He was a lean rail of a character with hard gray eyes and a lantern jaw, middle fifties, tough. He looked more like a fire-and-brimstone prophet than an old soldier. Like a guy with the sense of humor of a rock.

"Art Chain." The next guy nodded. He had a monster black mustache going gray, not much hair on top, and was thirty pounds over his best weight. His eyes were beads of obsidian. Another character who was allergic to laughter. He didn't bother to nod. He was so happy to see me he could just shit.

"Freidel Kaid." Kaid was older than the General, maybe into his seventies. Lean, slow, one glass eye and the other one that didn't work too good. His stare was disconcerting because the glass eye didn't track. But he didn't look like a man who had spent his whole life trying not to smile. In fact, he put one on for me when Peters said his name. He was the guy I'd seen stoking the fire in the General's quarters.

"Pleased to meet you, Mr. Sexton."

"Likewise, Mr. Kaid." See? I can be a gentleman. Rumors to the contrary are sour grapes and envy.

Jennifer didn't give me a chance to start eating. "What are you doing here?"

"The General sent for me." Everybody was interested in me. Nice to be the center of attention sometimes. I have to set the Dead Man on fire just to get him to listen.

"Why?"

"Ask him. If he wants you to know, he'll tell you."

Her mouth pruned up. Her eyes shot sparks. They were interesting eyes, hungry eyes, but eyes that had been brushed by a darkness. I couldn't tell if they were green or not. The light wasn't good enough. An odd one. Maybe unique. A one in a million beauty and not the least attractive.

"What sort of work do you do, Mr. Sexton?" old Kaid asked.

"You could call me a diplomat."

"A diplomat?" Surprised.

"Sure. I straighten things out. I get people to

change their minds. Kind of like the Corps, only on a small scale. Personal service."

Peters shot me a warning look.

I said, "I enjoy good conversation as much as the next guy. But I'm hungry. And you folks got a jump on me. How about you let me catch up?"

They all looked at me oddly. Cook more so than the others. She was wondering if maybe she'd missed the mark with her earlier guess.

I stoked the fires some, then asked, "Where's everybody else, Sarge?"

Peters frowned. "We're all here. Except Tyler and Wayne. They have the night off."

Kaid said, "Snake."

"Oh. Right. Snake Bradon. But he never comes in the house. Hell. He may not be around anymore. I haven't seen him lately. Anybody seen Snake?"

Heads shook.

Cook said, "He come for supplies day before yesterday."

I didn't want to ask too many questions too soon so I let Snake Bradon slide. I'd get Black Pete alone sometime and get a rundown on everybody. I said, "That doesn't add up. I heard there were eighteen in the house besides me."

Everybody looked puzzled except Cook. Chain said, "Ain't been that many people around here in years. You got us guys, Cook, Tyler, Wayne, and Snake trying to keep this barn from falling apart."

I ate some. I don't know what it was. As good as lunch but less identifiable. Cook was fond of stuff she could do in a pot.

After a while the silence got to me. I had a feeling it wasn't just for my benefit. These people wouldn't talk much more without me there. "What about the blonde girl? Who's she?"

That got them looking perplexed. Peters asked, "What blonde?"

I looked at him for about ten seconds. Maybe he wasn't yanking my leg. "About twenty, gorgeous. As tall as Jennifer, even slimmer, hair almost white that hangs to her waist. Blue eyes, I think. Timid as a mouse. Dressed in white. I caught her watching me several times today." A recollection. "Dellwood. I saw her when you were there. You told me she was Jennifer."

Dellwood made a face. "Yes sir. But I didn't see her. I assumed it was Miss Jennifer."

"I didn't wear white today," Jennifer said. "What kind of dress was it?"

I tried my best, which isn't bad. The Dead Man's big accomplishment is that he's taught me to observe and recollect.

Jennifer said, "I don't have anything like that," trying to sound bored and failing. They all exchanged glances. I took it none of them knew who I was talking about.

I asked, "Who's taking care of the General? If you're all here?"

"He's sleeping, sir," Dellwood said. "Cook and I will wake him for supper after we're finished."

"Nobody with him?"

"He doesn't want to be coddled, sir."

"You sure as hell ask a lot of question," Chain said.

"A habit I've got. I'm working on it. There any beer around the place? I could use some dessert."

Dellwood explained. "The General doesn't approve of drink, sir. He doesn't permit it on the property."

No wonder they were such a cheerful bunch. I looked at Peters hard. "You didn't mention that." If he'd done his homework, he would have known I liked my beer. He smiled and winked. The son of a bitch.

"Not a bad meal, Cook. Whatever it was. You need a hand clearing away?"

The others looked at me like I was crazy. She said, "You ask for trouble, you get it. Grab a load and follow me."

I did. And by the time I got back for a second load, the rats had scattered.

I was going to have to ask Peters about the disparity between Cook's head count and everyone else's.

8

After supper I wandered up to my quarters. As I approached the door, digging for the key Dellwood had left in the primitive lock, I noticed the door was a quarter inch ajar. So.

I wasn't surprised. Not after Jennifer's bold peek into my duffel bag and the trick at the old workers' barracks.

I paused. Go ahead like the cavalry? Or exercise a little caution? Caution didn't go with the image I wanted to project. But it did contribute to an extended life. And nobody was looking.

I dropped to my knees by the doorframe, examined the lock. There were a few fine scratches on the old brass plate surrounding the keyhole. As I said, a primitive piece of hardware, pickable by anyone with patience. I leaned forward to see what I could glim through the keyhole.

Nothing. It was dark in there. I'd left a lamp burning. Trap?

If so, a dumb one. Especially not getting the door all the way shut. These old boys weren't pros but I didn't see them making that basic a mistake. And if not a trap, but just a search, I doubted they'd snuff the lamp. That was a dead giveaway.

The word *disinformation* trotted through my mind. From the spy game. Provide not just false information but more information than necessary, most of it untrustworthy, so that all information received came under the shadow of doubt.

I backed off, leaned against a wall, nodded to myself. Yeah. That felt like a good intuition. I was going to be allowed to find out all kinds of things, most of which were untrue, useless, or misleading. Hard to put a puzzle together when you've got three times too many pieces.

Which still left me faced with a decision what to do right now. It was still possible there was some clumsy idiot hiding in the dark waiting to whack me.

So why not play the game right back?

The hall was a good twelve feet wide, oversize like everything else in that house, and cluttered up with the usual hardware. Not twenty feet from me was a suit of armor. I got it and lugged it over in front of the door, pushed it up close, backed off, snuffed the nearest hall lamps so whoever was inside wouldn't see anything but a silhouette. Then I got behind the tin suit, gave the door a nudge, walked the armor ahead a couple of feet, stopped like I was startled.

Nothing happened. I backed out and got one of the hall lamps and took it inside.

Nobody there but me and my decoy. I checked the closets and bedroom and dressing room. Nobody there and nothing obviously disturbed. If the place had been tossed, it had been done by an expert so good he'd noticed and replaced the little giveaways I'd rigged.

So what did we have here? Somebody had gone to the trouble of picking the lock just to snuff a lamp?

I closed the door, patted the armor's shoulder.

"Somebody's playing games, old buddy. I think I'll let you stick around."

I lugged it over and shoved it into a cloak closet just big enough to contain it, lighted my lamps, took the hall lamp back, lighted the lamps there, went inside, locked up, sat down at the writing table to let my dinner digest.

Didn't work too well. I need a beer or two to get the most out of those occasions. I had to do something about the shortage. In fact, it might be a good idea to vanish for a while and consult some experts.

There was ink and paper and whatnot in the drawer under the table. I got it out and started making notes. I put down the names of everyone I'd met and hadn't, and a mystery woman to the side. Peters, Dellwood, the General, Cook, Jennifer. Hawkes, Chain, and Kaid. Tyler and Wayne, who had the night off, and somebody named Snake Bradon, who was antisocial and wouldn't come in the house. Somebody named Candy who, theoretically, didn't count because he'd been fired long ago. And Harcourt, who used to sneak his girlfriends in, but who had left six months ago.

Eighteen people here, according to Cook. By my count, eleven, plus the mystery blonde. We had us what the Marines call a manpower shortfall.

Someone tapped on the door. "Yeah?"

"Peters, Mike."

I let him in. "What's up?"

"I brought you a list of the missing stuff. Can't guarantee it's complete. Not the kind of stuff you see every day and notice is gone right away." He handed me a wad of papers. I sat down and looked it over.

"This is a lot of stuff." And all small. Each item had a guessed value noted. Stuff like gold medals, old jewelry belonging to Stantnor women long dead, silver serviceware disdained by rough, tough ex-Marines, decorative weapons.

"If you want, I can go through the house room by room and get a better count. Trouble is, it's hard to tell what's gone because there isn't anybody who knows what all belongs."

"Doesn't seem worth the trouble. Unless you could find out about something that could be traced." Little on the list fit that description. The thief had shown restraint.

Even so, he'd gotten enough so the bottom line made my eyes bug. "Twenty-two thousand marks?"

"Based on my best guess at the intrinsic value of metal and gems. I assume there'd be a big knockdown at a fence."

"There would be, partly offset by artistic value. A lot of this don't look like the junk that gets melted down."

"Maybe."

"Are we committed to finding the thief?" I was, that being the commission I'd accepted from the General. I was fishing for Black Pete's feelings.

"Yes. The old man may not have long. I don't want him going off burdened by knowing somebody got away with betraying him."

"Right. Then what I'll do is subcontract a search for the fence. Sometimes it helps to come back at a thief from the other end. Work me up a description of four or five outstanding items and I'll have somebody try to find them."

"You'll have to pay for that?"

"Yes. You going to squeeze the General's coppers?"

He smiled. "I shouldn't. But I'm not used to not having to watch every one. Anything you need?"

"I need to know more about the people here." I looked at my list. "Counting three guys I haven't met and not counting my ghost lady, I come up with eleven names. Cook tells me eighteen. Where're the the other seven?"

"I told you she has some loose threads. She's been here since they built the first place—literally—and she never quite knows what year it is. When we first came here from the Cantard there were eighteen people, counting her and Jennifer. More before the old man finished dismissing the old staff. Now eleven is right."

"Where did the others go?"

"Sam and Tark just up and died on us. Wollack got on the wrong end of a bull when we were breeding cows and got himself gored and trampled. The others just drifted away. They got fed up, I guess, hung around less and less, then just didn't come back."

I leaned forward, got a fresh sheet of paper, divided five million by two and gave two and a half mil to Jennifer, then divided two and a half by sixteen and came up with a hundred fifty-six thousand marks and change.

Not bad. And I never knew anybody who would walk on a hundred fifty thousand, gold or silver.

I did some more math. Nine into two and a half million came out two hundred seventy-seven thousand and change. Damned near double your money.

Was there something else going on here?

I didn't mention it. It was something to keep in mind, though.

"You onto something?" Peters asked.

"I doubt it."

Time for some footwork. "Having a little trouble

making sense of things. There any way we can find out where those four men are now? Also, I'm going to need to know more about the General's bequeathal arrangements."

He frowned. "Why?"

"It's a large estate. You said he used his bequests as a hammer. Maybe he ran those guys off. Maybe one of them might be trying to get even, either by doing the stealing or slipping him poison."

"You've got me there." He looked it.

"Two things, then. A copy of the will. And find out if there was a clash between the General and any of those four."

"You don't really think they'd be sneaking back?"

I didn't, no. I thought they were dead. With my confidence in human decency aroused, I was sure somebody was playing a game of last one left—and doing such a damned good job, nobody else was suspicious. But . . . If somebody was, then that somebody was innocent of trying to murder the old man. That somebody would want to keep the General healthy while the field was narrowed. That somebody might even bring in an outside specialist . . . presuming he had a genuine cause for concern.

"Anyone have a spare key or master key for my room?"

That caught him from the blind side. "Dellwood. Why?"

"Somebody picked the lock and got in between the time I left for supper and the time I came back here."

"Why would . . . ?"

"Hey. That's a petty one compared to why would somebody want to kill the General. If that somebody exists he might be real nervous about me. What did you all do when you split up after supper?" I was going to play logical puzzle. Eliminate me and Cook because I didn't do it and she was with me. Take Dellwood off the hook because he didn't need to pick locks. Peters because he knew about me already. Eliminate anybody who was with them the whole time. . . .

"Dellwood would have gone to get the General up and ready for dinner. I assume Jennifer went with him. She usually does. She stays till Cook brings his food and helps him eat if he can't manage himself. I was in my quarters writing up the list from notes."

"Uhm." I thought a minute. "I do have one problem with this, Sarge. And that's a reason for being here. I need to ask questions. I need to find loose strings I can pull on. Kind of hard to do that when I don't have a good excuse. Cook's already told me I'm too nosy."

"I suppose. I had hopes but I didn't really think you could manage without giving yourself away."

"How many people know about the missing trinkets? As opposed to how many know you think somebody's trying to kill the General? Why not tell the truth? Say the old man hired me to find out who's stealing from him. They might even find it amusing if they think he's imagining it. And the would-be assassin should relax. The others might open up after I convince them somebody *is* stealing from the old man. Right?"

"I suppose." He didn't like it, though.

"Figure out a way to let it get out. So everybody knows but it seems like I don't know they know. Maybe joke about the General having another fantasy."

"All right. Anything else?"

"No. I'm going to turn in. I'm going to roll out

early and make a run into the city to put somebody on the track of the stolen goodies."

"Is that a hint?"

It was. "I didn't think of it that way. But I guess it is."

"I'll see you in the morning, then." He went out.

I locked the door behind him, returned to the writing table.

Seemed to me there might·be three puzzles here: who was stealing from the General, who was trying to kill him, and who was eliminating his heirs. It seemed reasonable to suppose that each thing—if any were fact—would be going on independent of the others, since the thefts were petty compared to murder and killing the General wouldn't be in the interest of whoever was trying to enlarge his share of the estate.

I could be up to my neck in villains.

I did hit the sack right away. I doubt Peters believed I would, because he knew the hours I keep. But I did need sleep and I had plans for the wee hours of the morning.

9

At home I usually control my internal clock. Go to sleep when I want, wake up when I want, give or take ten minutes. I didn't leave the clock behind. I woke right on time.

And was aware of a presence before I opened my eyes. I don't know how. Some sound so soft I didn't catch it consciously. Some subtle scent. Maybe just a sixth sense. Whatever, I knew somebody was there.

I was on my left side, facing the wall opposite the door, sunk so deep in eiderdown, I couldn't move fast if you branded me. I tried sneaky, faking a slow rollover in my sleep.

I didn't fool, anybody. All I saw was the tail end of the blonde sliding out the bedroom door. "Hey! Hang on. I want to talk to you."

She bolted.

I climbed up out of that bed, tangled myself in the covers, fell on my face, said colorful things. That's Garrett. Light on his feet. A real gymnast. Has moves like a cat. When I hit the sitting room she was gone and there wasn't a sign she'd been there. The door was locked.

I lighted a few lamps and surveyed the big room.

I hadn't heard the door. I hadn't heard a key in the lock. I didn't like that.

Damned spooky old house was the kind that might come equipped with secret passages and hidden panels and all that stuff, maybe with secret dungeons below the root cellar and bones buried behind false foundations.

I was going to have a nice time here, I was, I was. All I needed to make it a real vacation were ghosts and monsters. I went to the window. The sky was clear. A nail paring of moon was headed west.

"Come on. You're not trying. We need some rain and lightning. Or at least some fog on the moor and something howling in the night."

Back for a circuit of the room. I didn't find any secret entrances.

I'd deal with that later, when there was time to measure walls and whatnot. Right now I had to prowl, while at least some of the denizens of the place weren't keeping track.

I dragged my tin suit friend out of the closet, into the bedroom. I detached him from the support that held him upright, put him in bed. Better than using pillows to make it look like somebody was home. Looked perfect once I pulled a sheet over his helmet. "Rest easy, buddy."

I didn't like the way things were going. Somebody here might be less than friendly. I collected my favorite head-knocker, an oak nightstick with a pound of lead in the business end, then slipped into the hall. I was alone out there. One lamp burned. Presumably Dellwood had been around to snuff the others to save oil. He was the only guy I'd seen working, other than Cook.

I'd have to find out what everybody did. Should've asked Peters while I had him.

I went to the east end of the hall where a small window looked out on the grounds. Nothing out there but darkness and stars. The werewolves and vampires were taking the night off. I retreated to the first door on the left.

I seemed to be the only inhabitant of that floor in the wing so I didn't try for quiet. I picked the lock and marched in, lamp in front in my left hand, head-knocker in my right. I needn't have bothered. The room was a warehouse for cobwebs. Nobody had been in there in a decade.

I did a cursory inspection, went to the room across the hall. Same story.

Every suite on the floor was the same, except the last, which showed signs that someone had visited recently. In that room I noted circles on the mantel where the dust was thinner. Like something had been removed. Candlesticks or small doodads. I tried to get something from the marks left by the visitor's feet. There's always hope you'll find something unique, like maybe feet the size of pumpernickels or only two toes if they run barefoot. It didn't pay off this time. The intruder had shuffled, probably not intentionally. Not the sort of thing your average thief thinks of.

The search was taking longer than I'd expected. I decided to take a quick tour and leave detail work for later. At least I'd know my way around.

There was a partial floor above mine, reached via an enclosed stair. I went up. That floor was one vast dark room over the great hall. It was stuffed with junk, mostly as dusty as the rooms below. But there was a path beaten from the stairhead across to a stair down to the fourth floor of the west wing. A shortcut.

The alternative was to descend to the second floor and cut across on a narrow balcony above the back door, placed there so somebody could address a crowd.

Might as well go across, work my way down the west wing, come back on the ground floor, and work my way up.

The west wing was inhabited. I didn't enter any rooms. Maybe tomorrow night. Maybe while I was in town I could have a locksmith check my key to see if he could create a skeleton key for its type of lock.

Fourth-floor hall and a stroll on the balcony there. Nothing. Likewise the third floor and its balcony. The design differed from my wing. The halls were shorter, ending at the doors of the suites of the masters of the estate. Two doors on the third floor showed light underneath. Either somebody was up late or somebody was scared of the dark.

Second floor had only five large suites, probably for honored guests like dukes and counts, firelords and stormwardens, and others a ranking commander might entertain.

The ground floor boasted rooms meant for other purposes. The west wing was where, in times past, the businesses of the estate and its masters had been conducted. The doors to several rooms were open. I invited myself in. I didn't find anything.

From the west wing I walked across to the east, where I knew I'd be into the kitchen, pantries, dining hall, and whatnot. I'd been through some of that but hadn't had a chance to pry.

As I passed the brave champion still stubbornly skewering his dragon, I got that creepy sensation. I looked around, saw no one. My blonde admirer? I was beginning to think she was a spook.

Not literally. The place was creepy at high noon. It had fallen from a ghost story, but I didn't entertain the notion that it was haunted. The world is filled with the strange, the magical, the supernatural, but I didn't figure I'd need haunts to explain anything here. Any schemes here had been set in motion by the root of all evil amongst the living.

A closer examination of the dining room proved it to be what I'd figured, big, with decorations fitting the theme of the house. I wondered how many battles the Stantnors had fought.

The room had a high ceiling, which suggested that part of the second floor east didn't exist. True. I found out when I explored the pantry.

A door there opened on stairs. One set went up, another down. It was as dark as a vampire's heart in there. I went up. The way led to storerooms filled with housekeeping goodies, some of which looked like they'd been laid in before the turn of the century. Some dead Stantnor had saved by buying wholesale.

Nobody swept or dusted but the place was orderly. It was inhabited by moths who found my lamp irresistible.

Why so much room for storage?

I came on stacks of four-inch-thick oak things, bound in iron, each with a number chalked onto the black iron. Curious, I looked closer.

They were covers for the windows, to seal them if the house was besieged. They had to be as old as the house itself. Had they ever been used? Not in the past century, I was sure.

I found a strong room in the southeast corner. The door was latched but not locked. It was an armory. Inside were weapons enough for a company—as though there weren't enough around the house already. Everything steel was covered with grease, everything wood coated with paraffin. Might be interesting to find out what the climate was like when the house was built. Troubled times, apparently.

I spent too much time there. When I descended it was too late. Cook was banging around in the kitchen. I slipped out before she tripped over me.

As I hit the fourth floor I caught a glimpse of white across the way. My lovely mystery lady. I blew her a kiss.

10

I'd had another visitor. This one had left in a hurry. He'd left a key in the lock with the door standing open. I saw why when I went into the bedroom.

My visitor had murdered the suit of armor. He'd walked in, wound up with an antique battle-ax, and had let the poor boy have it. The ax was still there.

I laughed. Bet he drizzled down his leg, thinking he'd walked into a trap.

I sobered quickly. That was twice. Next time more care might go into the attempt. I was way out on a limb here. I had to take steps.

I locked up, pocketed the key—which wasn't identical to mine, so might be a skeleton key. I got the tin man out of bed and the ax out of him. "Sorry about that. But we'll get our revenge." I used the ax to rig a booby trap. Anybody who walked through the bedroom door was in for a rude welcome.

Then I took an hour nap.

I was early for breakfast, first to arrive. Cook was up to her ears in work setting platters ready. "Need a hand?"

"I need ten. I don't know what you're up to, boy,

sucking up to me, but you better believe I'll use you. Get over to the oven and see how them rolls are coming."

I did. "Maybe a minute more."

"What you know about baking?"

I explained the arrangement at my house, where old Dean handles the drudgery and cooking. He's a good cook. He taught me. I can put together a decent meal when I want. Like when I give him time off because I want him out while I entertain.

"Don't know if you're lying or not. Probably are. I never seen a man yet who could cook."

I didn't tell her Dean thought the only good cooks were men. "I should get you together. To watch the sparks fly."

"Huh. Time's up. Get them rolls out. Drag that pot of butter over."

I glanced at the butter. "Fresh?"

"Snake just brung it in."

"He going to join us?"

She laughed. "Not Snake. He don't have nothing to do with nobody. Just grabbed him some food and lit out. Not sociable, Snake."

"What's his problem?"

"Head got scrambled in the Cantard. He was down there twenty years, never got a scratch. On the outside." She shook her head, started piling sausages and bacon on a platter. "Sad. I knew him when he was a pup. Cute kid, he was. Too delicate and sensitive for a Marine. But he thought he had to try. So here he is, an old man with his head in knots. Used to draw the prettiest pictures, that boy. Coulda been a great painter. Had him a magic eye. Could see right inside things and drawed what he saw. Any damn fool can draw the outside of things, the way they want we should see them. Takes a genius to see the truth. That boy saw. You going to stand there jawing till lunchtime? Or you going to eat?"

I fixed myself a plate without mentioning the fact that I couldn't get a word in edgewise because I couldn't get a word in edgewise. She rolled right along. "I told the General then—he was just commissioned—it was a raging shame to waste the boy down there. And I told him again when he come back. And the General, he told me, 'You were right, Cook. It was a sin against humanity, taking him.' But, you know, he couldn't have stopped the boy if he'd wanted. Had that damnfool stubborn streak and thought it was his duty to go with the lord to war."

The rush came while she chattered. There were two new faces, presumably Tyler and Wayne. They looked like they hadn't slept. The whole crowd took their platters to the dining room.

I asked Cook, "That Tyler and Wayne?"

"How'd you guess?"

"Lucky stab. Anybody else I haven't met?"

"Who else could there be?"

"I don't know. Yesterday you said there were eighteen people here. I've seen ten, plus this Snake that's shy and a blonde that only I can see. Comes up short of eighteen."

"Ain't eighteen."

"You said eighteen."

"Boy, I'm four hundred years old. 'Less I concentrate, I don't remember where I am in time. I just cook and set table and wash and don't pay no attention to nothing else. Just sort of drift. Don't see nothing, don't say nothing. Last time I looked up they was eighteen, counting me. Must've been a while.

Hell. Maybe that's why there's so many leftovers. Been cooking too much."

"I didn't notice too many places set at the table."

She paused. "You're right. Part of me must keep track."

"Been with the Stantnors a long time?"

"Came to them with my momma when I was a kit. Long time back, when the humans hereabouts still had emperors. 'Fore they ever moved out here and built the first house. This one's only maybe two hundred. Was a sight when she was new, she was."

"You must've seen some sights in your time."

"Seen some," she agreed. "Served every king and stormwarden and firelord right there in that dining room." She headed that way. That ended our conversation.

I stuck my head in. Nobody showed any special disappointment. Nobody turned handsprings, either. They were a depressing bunch.

These guys had spent their whole lives together. You'd think they could make conversation—unless they'd said everything there was to say. I feel that way with some people, sometimes before anything gets said at all.

Tyler and Wayne were cut from Marine lifer cloth. Whatever the physical differences between men, they gain a certain uniformity in service. Tyler was a lean, narrow-faced character with hard brown eyes, salt-and-pepper hair, and a thin, speckled beard trimmed within a half-inch of his skin. Wayne was my size, maybe twenty pounds heavier, not fat. He looked like he could throw cows around if the passion took him. He was six inches taller than Tyler and blond, with icy blue eyes, yet you felt the sameness in them.

You even felt the identity with Chain, who had gone to seed.

I'd spent five years in the company of men like them. Any one of them would be capable of murder if he took a mind. Human life wasn't anything special to them. They'd seen too much death.

Which did present one puzzle.

Marines are straightforward kinds of guys. If one wanted the General dead, chances were he'd just do it. Unless there was some overpowering motive to make it a lingering death.

Like, say, hanging onto a share of the old man's estate?

Worrying about it was pointless. You can't force these things. They have to unfold.

I helped Cook clear away, then put on my traveling shoes.

11

I hadn't been to Morley's place in months. It wasn't that we'd had a falling out or anything; I just hadn't had a need, nor any urge to graze on the cattle food that comes out of his kitchen. I arrived about nine. He's closed to business then. He's open from eleven to six in the morning, catering to every sentient species there is, all so warped they try to subsist on vegetables.

It takes all kinds. Some of my best friends eat there. I've done so myself. Without enthusiasm.

So. Nine o'clock. The place was locked up. I went to the backdoor and gave the secret knock, which means I hammered and howled till Morley's man Wedge brought a four-foot piece of lead pipe and offered to move my face to my belly button region.

"This's business, Wedge."

"I didn't figure you was in heat for some bean curd. You don't come around unless you want something."

"I pay for what I get."

He snorted. He didn't think it was right, me using Morley just because Morley had taken advantage of me, at deadly risk and without my consent, to get out of some heavy gambling debts.

"Cash money, Wedge. And he don't have to get off his butt. He just needs to have somebody do some legwork."

That didn't cheer him up. He's one of the guys who does Morley's legwork. But he didn't slam the door.

"Come." He eased me in and barred the door, led me through kitchens where cooks were butchering cabbages and broccoli, parked me at the serving bar, drew me a mug of apple juice. "Wait." He went upstairs.

The public room was naked and forlorn, almost painfully quiet. The way it ought to be all the time, instead of overcrowded.

Morley Dotes is a headhunter. A kneebreaker and a lifetaker. Most of the guys who work for him help. Morley is a deadly symbiote feeding on society's dark underside. He's the best at what he does, barring maybe a couple of guys who work for Chodo Contague.

Adding up the account, Morley Dotes is everything I don't like. He's the kind of guy I wanted to take down when I decided to put on my good-guy hat. But I like him.

Sometimes you can't help yourself.

Wedge came down shaking his head. "What's up?" I asked.

"He's taking this health stuff too far."

"You're telling me? He's like born again, trying to save everybody else." The world's only vegetarian lifetaker. Wants to save the world from the perils of red meat—before he cuts its throat. I don't know.

Maybe there's no conflict but it sounds like one to me. "He's added to the list?"

"Been a few months, right?"

"Last time I was here he'd sworn off gambling and was making it stick. He tried women but couldn't hold out."

"He forgot that crock. Say that for him. The thing now is early to bed, early to rise. He's up. Now. Up and dressed and fed and doing his morning workout. A year ago you wouldn't have caught him dead out of bed this time of day."

You could have if there was enough money in it. "Wonders never cease, do they?"

"He said come up. You want a refill?"

"Why not? Fruit juice is the only thing here I can handle."

He winked. He wasn't one of Morley's converts. He topped off my mug. I took it up to Morley's office, which is the barbican to his personal quarters. I'm about as close to a friend as he has, but I've never been past the office. My hair is too short and I don't wear enough makeup.

Dotes was doing sit-ups, chunking them out like a machine. My stomach hurt just watching.

"You're in pretty good shape for a guy your age," I told him. I wasn't sure what that was. It could be substantial. He's part dark-elf. Elves can last a long time.

"I take it you're working again." He said it while popping up and down. Like there was no strain to what he was doing.

I told myself I had to start doing a few exercises. At my age, when you lose it, it's hard to get back. "Why do you assume—"

"You don't come down here unless you want something."

"Not true. I used to bring Maya in all the time." That was before she and I had gone our own ways.

"You lost a gem there, Garrett." He rolled over, started doing push-ups.

His dark-elf blood doesn't scream out. He looks like a short, slim, dark-haired man in good shape. He's quick on his feet. There's an air of the dangerous about him, but not one of menace. Maybe that's why women find him irresistible.

"Maybe. I do miss her, some. She was a good kid."

"Pretty, too. So you going on with Tinnie?"

My friend Tinnie Tate, professional high-tempered redhead. Ours is an unpredictable relationship. "I see her. When she doesn't think I deserve to be punished by not seeing her."

"Only smart thing you've done since I've known you is not tell her about Maya." He completed fifty fast ones, jumped up. He wasn't sweating. I felt like kicking his behind. "What's up?"

"You heard of General Stantnor?"

"Used to be Marine Commandant?"

"The same."

"What about him?"

"A guy who works for him, my old company sergeant, called in a debt. He got me to do a job for the old boy."

"Don't you ever work just to be working? I never saw anyone like you."

"I know. I'm a dog. You never see a dog do anything when he's not hungry. If I'm not hungry, why work?"

"What about the General? I do work when I'm not hungry. And I've got plenty of that here."

"The old boy is trying to die. My old sergeant thinks somebody is trying to kill him. Slowly, so it looks like a wasting disease."

"Is somebody?"

"I don't know. He's been doing it a long time. You know a way to do that?"

"What's his color like?"

"His color?"

"Sure. There are poisons you could use in cumulative dosages. The color is the giveaway."

"He's kind of a sickly yellow. His hair is falling out in clumps. And his skin has a translucent quality."

Morley frowned. "Not blue or gray?"

"Yellow. Like pale butterscotch."

He shook his head. "Can't tell you based on that."

"He has seizures, too."

"Crazies?"

"Like heart tremors, or something."

"Doesn't sound familiar. Maybe if I saw him."

"I'd like that. I don't know if I can arrange it. They're all paranoid about strangers." I gave him a rundown on the players.

"Sounds like a bughouse."

"Could be. All of them, except Jennifer and Cook, spent at least thirty years in the Marines, mostly in the Cantard."

He grinned. "I'm not going to say it."

"Good for you. We all make the world a little holier when we resist temptation. One more thing. The old man thinks he hired me to find out who's stealing the silver and his old war trophies." I produced the list. Morley started reading. "I'll pay legwork fees for somebody to make the rounds and see if any of that is moving through the usual channels."

"Saucerhead needs work."

Saucerhead Tharpe is a friend, of sorts, in a line somewhere between Morley's and mine. He has more scruples than Dotes and more ambition than me, but he's as big as a house and looks half as smart. People can't take him serious. He never gets the best jobs.

"All right. I'll pay his standard rate. Bonus if he recovers any of the articles. Bonus if he gets a description of the thief."

"On the cuff?" That was a hint.

I gave him advance money. He said, "I thank you and Saucerhead thanks you. I know you're doing an old buddy a favor but it seems damned tame. Especially if the old guy is just dying."

"There's something going on. Somebody tried to off me." I told him.

He laughed. "I wish I could have seen the guy's face when he swung that ax and you bonged like a bell. You've still got the luck."

"Maybe."

"Why are they after you?"

"I don't know. Money? That's the one angle that makes this interesting. The old boy is worth about five million marks. His son is dead. His wife died twenty years ago. His daughter, Jennifer, gets half the estate and the other half goes to his Marine cronies. Three years ago he had seventeen heirs. Since then two died supposedly natural deaths, one got killed by a mad bull, and four disappeared. A little basic math shows that nearly doubles the take for the survivors."

Morley sat down behind his desk, put his feet up, cleaned his pearly white teeth with a six-inch steel toothpick. I didn't interrupt his thoughts.

"There's potential for foul play in that setup, Garrett."

"Human nature being what it is."

"If I was a betting man I'd give odds that somebody is fattening his share."

"Human nature being what it is."

"Nobody walks out on that kind of money. Not you, not me, not a saint. So maybe you have something interesting after all."

"Maybe. Thing is, I don't see any way to tie it up in a package. If I find out who's stealing—which makes no sense considering the payoff down the road—I'm not likely to find out who's killing the old man. That doesn't make sense for whoever is cutting down the number of heirs. He'd want the old man to hang on."

"What happens if the daughter checks out before he does?"

"Damn!" A critical point and it hadn't occurred to me. If everything went to the boys she'd really be on the spot. "The odd thing is, none of them act like they know what's going on. They seem to get along. They don't watch each other over their shoulders. I did, and I was only there one night."

"A marvelous aspect of your species is that most of you see only what you want."

"What's that mean?"

"Maybe those guys are old buddies and only one of them realizes that throat-cutting can be profitable. Maybe nobody is suspicious because they all know their old buddies wouldn't do something like that after all they've been through together."

Could be. I'd kind of had that problem myself. I couldn't picture me turning on anybody I'd been running with that long. "And the whole thing could be what they say it is. Three dead by explainable cause and four who couldn't handle the lifestyle and walked because money didn't mean anything."

"And the moon could be mouse bait."

"You have a dark outlook."

"Supported every day in the street. The other night a thirty-six-year-old man knifed his mom and dad because they wouldn't give him money for a bottle of wine. That's the real world, Garrett. We're our own worst nightmares." He chuckled. "You're lucky this time. You don't have anything weird. No vampires, no werewolves, no witches, no sorcerers, no dead gods trying to come back to life. None of the stuff you usually stumble into."

I snorted. Those things aren't on every street corner, but they're part of the world. Everybody brushes against them eventually. They didn't impress me, though I was happy not to deal with them.

I said, "I could have seen a ghost."

"A what?"

"A ghost. I keep seeing a woman that nobody admits is there. That nobody else sees. Unless they're pulling my leg. Which they probably are."

"Or you're crazy. She's a gorgeous blonde, right?"

"A blonde. Not bad."

"You're daydreaming out loud in your eyes. Your wishful thinking has gotten to you."

"Maybe. I'll know before I'm done. There was something else I wanted but it escapes me now."

"Must not have been important."

"Probably not. I'd better get back out there."

"You take some equipment? Hate to think of you up to your ears in killers with nothing but your teeth and toenails."

"I've got a trick or two."

He grunted. "You always do. Don't turn your back on anybody."

"I won't."

As I started to close the door, he asked, "What's the daughter look like?"

"Early twenties. A looker but not a talker. Spoiled rotten, probably."

He looked thoughtful, then shrugged, got up, dropped down and started doing more push-ups. I shut the door. I can't stand seeing a man abuse himself.

12

I headed south feeling smug. I knew my Morley Dotes. Curiosity would get him. He'd push his end beyond what I'd hired him to do. He'd go fishing amongst his contacts. If there was something going on involving the Stantnors, he'd find out.

The smugness disappeared after I walked out South Gate.

That's when the drizzle started. That's when I started cussing myself for my distrust of horses. Hell, if I couldn't ride, I could hire a coach. I had a client. I could charge it to expenses. Expenses are wonderfully flexible—especially if the client fails the attitude test.

I got some wet before I reached my destination.

Odd. Most of those big country places have names. The Maples. Windward. Sometimes something that doesn't make any sense, like Brittany Stone. But this one could have been a squatter's hut. The Stantnor place. Ancient family seat and museum but not enough of a home for anybody to give it a name.

I was still a quarter mile off when Jennifer Stantnor flew out the front door, headed toward me. She hadn't put a wrap on. Peters came after her, gaining but not looking like he was trying to catch her.

They reached me at the same time. Jennifer looked irked that Peters had come. Peters looked exasperated at her. I did my best to look puzzled, which isn't hard. That's where I am most of the time. I raised an eyebrow way up. It's one of my best tricks. Jennifer just stood there, panting. Peters, less winded despite being almost three times her age, said, "There's been a hunting accident."

I kept a straight face. "Oh?"

"Let's get in out of the rain."

I looked at the girl. I think she wanted to talk. Grimly, she said, "I don't think it was an accident."

It probably wasn't, if someone had gotten killed. But I didn't say that. I just grunted.

Peters talked while we walked. "We've had trouble with poachers. There are deer on the grounds. A fair herd."

Jennifer interjected, "We put out feed. We don't take many."

"Three all last year," Peters said. "Peasants . . . The animals make easy targets. They're not so wary here. The past month we've had six intrusions. That we know of."

Jennifer said, "Dad gets more upset about the trespassing than the poaching. He has a thing about boundaries. Like they're lines of steel."

"After the last incident," Peters said, as we climbed the steps to the house, "the General ordered regular patrols. He wanted someone caught and an example made. Today Kaid, Hawkes, Tyler, and Snake had the duty. Hawkes apparently caught somebody in the act. He sounded his hunting horn."

Jennifer said, "When the others got there, he was on the ground with an arrow in him. A gutted deer was hanging in a tree fifty feet away."

"Interesting. And sad. But why tell me? Sounds like something you people can handle."

Jennifer looked puzzled. Peters said, "This is going to sound silly. You're the only scout around here. All these lifers and none of them can follow a trail."

"Oh." Maybe. "It's been years. And I wasn't that good." I recalled my stumbling around during a few recent cases.

"Mediocre is better than what the rest of us are." Peters looked at Chain, who was headed our way. "How is he?"

"I don't think he'll make it. He needs a surgeon."

"You know the old man. No doctors in the house."

"We can't move him without killing him."

Jennifer snapped, "Get a doctor! My father doesn't have to know. He never comes out of his room."

"Dellwood will tell him."

"I'll handle Dellwood."

"Go," Peters told Chain, and Chain got his carcass moving.

I said, "I take it Hawkes is still alive."

"He's fighting."

"Can I talk to him?"

"He's out. Way out. Not much chance he'll come around unless Chain gets a cutter in time."

"Show me where it happened before the rain wipes out the sign."

I got to ride. Lucky me. The horse was hospitable all the way out, but I knew it had heard of me through the grapevine those monsters have. It grinned when it heard my name. It was waiting for a chance.

It was a good ride out. The Stantnors had a lot of land. We didn't talk much. I took in the countryside, getting the lay, the landmarks. I might need to know them.

I'd developed the habit young. It was my apparent knack for knowing my way around that got me volunteered as a scout when the real Sexton vanished.

"Looks like Snake came back out," Peters said as we crossed a rise and came to the scene.

I saw a man under an oak near a hanging animal carcass. "Sarge, I never knew any of these guys when I was in. Did any of them know Sexton?"

He looked at me funny. "I don't think so."

I dismounted, tied the reins to an oak sapling. My mount got a forlorn look. "Thought I'd just drop them and you'd scurry when I turned my back, didn't you?"

"What?" Peters asked.

"Talking to the horse. I talk to horses. They make more sense than people."

"Snake, this is Mike Sexton. Scouted for me in the islands. You probably heard he's here."

Snake grunted. He looked me over. I returned the favor.

If Chain had gone to seed, this one had gone a step beyond. His hair hadn't been cut since he'd gotten out. His beard was a bramble patch. He didn't change clothes or bathe very often. His pants were covered with curious colored stains. He said, "I heard."

"You found anything?"

Snake grunted. It sounded negative.

I looked at the carcass. Wasn't much to it. "Kind of puny, isn't it?"

"Fawn," Snake said. "Just lost its spots."

Yes. A little rusty, Garrett. Why would a poacher take a fawn? If he was after the meat and the herd wasn't spooky, he'd go for a bigger kill. I gave the carcass a closer look.

It was ten years since I'd done my own butchering, but this job looked amateurish. Like it had been done by someone who'd seen animals butchered but who hadn't ever done it himself.

"This patrol this morning. Was there a set plan? Specific assignments?"

Peters said, "We had a routine, if that's what you mean. Routes we'd figured so four men could cover everything."

Not exactly what I wanted to know. I couldn't be more specific without giving away more than I wanted. "Where was Hawke when he was hit?"

"Up here."

I followed Peters. The spot was obvious once you got there. Hawkes had thrashed around after he'd fallen. He'd lost enough blood to draw flies too stupid to go for the bonanza in the tree. The spot was fifty feet from the deer. A blind archer could have made the shot.

I picked out what I thought was Hawkes' back trail. I followed it, found a place where he'd stopped. "I'd guess this is where he sounded the horn. Then he went down and stopped again there."

"And the poacher let him have it."

Somebody did. "What time did it happen?"

"About nine."

"Uhm." That fawn had been dead a lot longer than that.

I walked back down. Snake still stood staring at the carcass. I asked, "You look around some?"

He grunted. "Why'd anybody want to do that to

a little fawn?" An old buddy getting an arrow through the brisket didn't bother him. The fawn did.

I took another look at the carcass. I couldn't find its death wound. "Was there an arrow in it?"

"No."

Snake wasn't going to be much good for anything.

The tree where the fawn hung was a loner ten yards from the edge of a wood that followed a creek. That wood was only a hundred yards across. I headed downhill, swinging back and forth, looking for the poacher's trail.

I found it. Somebody in a big hurry had charged straight through the underbrush. Understandable, if you've just plinked some guy and you know he has friends coming.

Peters followed me. I asked, "Was there a set pattern to who rode where on these patrols?"

No way to keep him from wondering why I asked. He frowned. "No. We mixed it up so we wouldn't see the same ground every time."

Then the sniper hadn't been after somebody in particular, just somebody. Assuming the arrow hadn't come from the bow of a panicky poacher but someone who had laid a trap.

I was sure that when Hawkes stopped the second time, he'd seen whoever let him have it. That he'd been startled into halting. Otherwise, he'd have kept moving.

How much of that was Peters figuring out? The man wasn't stupid.

"How do you get along with your neighbors?"

"We ignore them. They ignore us. Most of them are scared of us."

I'd be scared if I had neighbors like them.

The sniper had become less panicky after fifty yards of flight. He'd turned onto an old game trail. There were too many leaves down for the ground to take good tracks but I could tell which way he had gone by the way they were disturbed. "Got any dogs? Or know where we could get some?"

"To track with? No."

The game trail went down to the creek, split. One fork crossed over, the other ran along the bank My quarry had taken the latter.

A hundred fifty yards along, that path dipped into a wide, shallow, sandy-bottomed section of creek. And didn't come out the other side. I looked around. "I've lost it."

"God damn it, look again."

I looked, satisfied that he hadn't noticed the horse apples in the shallow water. Whoever had come down here had ridden away, down the streambed. No big deal, since the water was never more than a foot deep.

How many peasants forced to poach deer could afford to keep a horse?

"Sorry. There's nothing."

"Then I'll find some damned dogs."

As we walked back uphill I asked, "Who takes care of the stables here?"

"Mostly Snake, with help from Hawkes and Tyler. I don't get Snake. Takes care of the animals. Likes to. But you can't get him on a horse to save his life."

That made sense to me, though it was a little extreme.

I asked questions that got me curious looks but no answers. Unless they were liars and fast to boot—or in cahoots—none of the men on patrol could have dropped Hawkes. And Hawkes didn't do it to himself. That narrowed the field of suspects, but not enough. I wanted rid of Snake and Peters so I could prowl down that creek to wherever the sniper had left it.

"Shit!" Black Pete exploded. "We've got our heads up our asses."

"What?"

"What did we do every time we hit the Venageti on the damned island? What did I pound into you guys every damned day we were there?"

He'd gotten it. "Yeah. You don't leave tracks on water." Before a raid we'd always made sure we had an escape route crossed by a lot of water.

"The bastard walked down the creek. That's why you couldn't find anything."

"Yeah."

"Let's go."

"I'll check it out. No need you taking any more time off."

He looked at me hard, checked to see where Snake was. "What're you thinking, Garrett? I've seen you like this before. I haven't forgotten the stuff you pulled."

"I'm doing my job the best way I know. Nothing personal, but everybody's a suspect till I prove otherwise. No matter how well I think I know them."

He started getting angry.

"Can it. You wanted me to find out who's killing the old man, right? Which one of you guys would do that? None of you. Right? But one of you is. Till I nail it down you get treated like everybody else. If only because I'm supposedly looking for a thief. Get me?"

"You want to play a lone hand. You're the professional. I'll put up with it. For a while."

"Good. You don't have a choice, anyway. And that's nothing to get mad about."

He got mad anyway. They always do. They all think they ought to be the exception to the rule.

He rode off in a huff.

I didn't care, so long as he rode off.

13

My horse looked forlorn. I got it and led it down along the edge of the wood, looking for tracks. If I didn't find anything before I reached the property line, I'd work my way back up the far side of the woods.

Our villain had cunning in limited amounts. The stunt would have been sufficient if there'd been no cause for suspicion. But there was.

I found where a horseman had come out of the wood barely far enough away to be out of sight of the place where Hawkes had gotten it. The spacing of hoofmarks said he'd been in no real hurry once he'd gotten away from the woods. Meaning he hadn't been worried about explaining his presence.

That put Tyler and Chain back on the suspect list. They wouldn't have been questioned because they belonged out here.

I'd have to question the survivors, find out who said and did what before they set out. Might be some subtle indicator there.

Whoever the killer was, he'd been bold. He'd ridden around behind the rise you crossed to reach the ambush, then had headed home. At least, I presumed that was what he'd done while the poacher-hunters were fussing over Hawkes. I lost the trail.

I circled and circled, quartered this way and that, and couldn't find it again. The drizzle and the chill breeze overcame my devotion to my craft. I headed for the house.

I was stomping through that museum of a central hall, headed for a change of clothes, when Jennifer fluttered out of nowhere. She looked more feminine and frail and vulnerable than she had. She was flustered and frightened. I waited, though I had no urge to see her.

"Sergeant Hawkes died," she blurted. "Right there in front of me. He just shook all over and made this funny sound and he wasn't alive anymore."

"When?"

"Just a few minutes ago. I was looking for Dellwood when I saw you. I need somebody to tell me what to do."

If she was looking for comfort she'd come to the wrong man. I didn't feel like comforting anybody. Not even a gorgeous brunette who had all the right stuff in all the right places, put together to make a dead bishop howl. My late night and early morning had me feeling like I was carrying an extra fifty pounds. Worse, I'd missed lunch.

I'd already determined that Cook was immune to my golden tongue. She didn't even know what was happening. It went right past her. "Dellwood would be the best man to tell you. And speak of the devil."

Here he came, moving without the usual sedate deliberation. "Miss Jennifer, you were supposed to stay with Hawkes."

"He doesn't need me anymore."

Dellwood's eyes got big. "He . . . He . . ."

"Yes. What do we do now?"

I said, "Dellwood, I need to see the General. At his earliest convenience. I'll be in my quarters."

I was going to take a nap. I expected I'd have another long night. I'd better rest while I could.

I glanced back at Jennifer and Dellwood. Maybe they were good actors. Maybe they were genuinely frazzled and upset. Whatever, they had exaggerated just that little bit that told me they wanted me to see them in a favorable light.

I didn't care if they cried or danced with joy. As far as I was concerned there was only one good guy in the house and his name was Garrett.

14

I woke up in time for dinner. I didn't feel rested. The floor of my dressing room wasn't that comfy. But it was safer than the bed. That tin man's wounds proved that.

I decided I'd set up camp in one of the vacant suites. Make them hunt for me to murder me in my sleep.

Had Hawkes died because of me? I'd fallen asleep wondering. Had my presence nudged somebody into pushing his murder schedule? Things like that, that I can't control, nag me.

I walked to the end of the hall, surveyed the central chamber. Jennifer was seated by the fountain, leaning against one of the dragon's wings. Chain and Kaid walked past without acknowledging her. They were headed for dinner.

As I started moving I spotted the blonde on the third floor balcony opposite, in shadow, looking down. "There goes a theory shot to hell." She glanced up. I waved.

Black Pete stepped out of the hall across the way. He caught my wave, frowned, returned it. I pointed down. He leaned over the rail.

Too late. She'd caught my gesture and drifted into deeper shadow.

I descended the stairs beginning to consider, if only half-seriously, the notion of a resident haunt.

I'd thought the blonde was Jennifer in a wig, making quick clothing changes. Their builds were similar, their faces much alike. My romantic streak made the blonde prettier, barely. I'd never seen them both at once. All I'd needed was some screwy motive on Jennifer's part to tie the knot.

Sometimes you guess right and sometimes you don't. I don't a lot more than I do.

When I hit the ground floor, I'd convinced myself I should've known better. The blonde really was prettier. Moreover, she had a lonely, ethereal quality Jennifer couldn't mimic.

Not that I knew much about Jennifer. I'd been on the job a day and hadn't gotten close to anybody but Cook, and her not close enough. Chances were I wasn't going to get close to anybody. These weren't the kind of people who would let you.

The case looked stranger by the minute. At least it was more low-key than the bloody whirlwinds that had swept me up lately.

Peters met me at the foot of the stair. "You wanted something?"

"The wave? I wasn't waving at you. The blonde was on the balcony under you. She ducked out when I pointed."

He looked at me like he wondered if he'd brought in the wrong man. I figured I'd better distract him. "I have a question for you. Completely hypothetical. If you were to kill somebody here and wanted to get rid of the body, where would be the best place on the property?"

His look got stranger. "Garrett . . . You're getting weird. Or maybe you got weird since you left the Marines. What do you want to know something like that for?"

"Just tell me. Asking questions is what I do. They don't have to make sense to you. Hell, they don't always make sense to me. But they're the tools I use."

"Can you give me a hint? If I was going to bury somebody . . ." A little light went on inside. He thought I was looking for a place somebody might cache the General's goodies. "It would depend on the circumstances. How much time I had. How good a job I wanted to do. Hell, if I had time, I'd put the body ten feet down where nobody would have any reason to dig. If I was in a big hurry I wouldn't do it here at all. I'd take it up the road to the marsh, tie it to a couple of rocks, and throw it in."

"What marsh?"

"On down the road, the other side of the rise out front. Look out the front door, past the cemetery. You can see the tops of the trees. It's about a hundred-acre swamp. There's been talk about draining it because of the smell. Old Melchior, who owns the land, won't hear of it. Take a look sometime. It'll bring back memories."

"I will. Let's feed our faces before Cook forgets us."

She was delivering the final load when Peters and I arrived. She looked at me like I'd betrayed her by not showing up to help. Some people. Whatever you do, they expect you to do it forever.

It was a meal like last night's. No conversation except grumbles about how they might find the poacher and what they could do with him afterward. Nobody seemed suspicious of the circumstances.

Could that be? Somebody was picking them off and they didn't realize it?

Maybe it was their background, all those years in the war zone. When my company went in, there were two hundred of us, officers, sergeants, and men, who had trained together and been hammered into a single unit. Two years later there were eighteen originals left. Guys went down. After a while you accepted that. After a while you accepted the fact that your turn was coming. You went on and stayed alive as long as you could. You become completely fatalistic.

I asked, "Who took care of the stables today?"

They all looked at me like they'd just noticed me.

Peters said, "Nobody. Snake was on patrol." He wanted to ask why I wanted to know. So did the others. But they just looked at me.

My glance crossed Jennifer's. She was thawing. She smiled faintly. With promise.

Dellwood said, "I spoke to the General. He'll see you after we eat."

"Good. Thanks. I was wondering if you'd remembered."

All those eyes turned on me again. They wondered what business I had with the old man. I wondered what their theories were about my presence. It was obvious Peters hadn't spread the word.

I asked, "What do you guys do for entertainment? This place is pretty bleak." I'd forgotten to smuggle in some beer. Maybe tomorrow.

Chain growled, "Got no time for entertainment. Too much work to do. And the General won't hire anybody on. Which reminds me, troops. We got to cover for Hawkes. Which means we have to let something else go to hell."

Wayne said, "The whole place is falling apart. Even with us hopping like the one-legged whore the day the fleet pulled in. Dellwood, you got to try to get through to him."

"I'll try." Dellwood didn't sound optimistic.

They went on, now the ball was rolling. I learned more than I wanted to know about how and where the place was falling apart, what had been allowed to slide too long and what had to be done right now to stave off disaster.

Tyler said, "I say we worry about that damned poacher in our spare time. And say the hell with trying to catch the others. The General don't come out no more. How's he going to know we're not wasting time looking for them? They want a few deer, I say let them have them. We need to keep this place from falling apart."

That debate raged a while.

Jennifer contributed not a word. She seemed more interested in me. My fatal charm. My curse. Or maybe she just wondered how I'd gotten those old boys so animated.

15

I helped Cook clear away. Dellwood helped me help. He didn't seem inclined to let me out of his sight. Cook was as tight-lipped as she claimed with a third party present.

Dellwood wanted to talk. He started as soon as we left the kitchen. "I hope you have some progress to report. It would be a good time to give the General an emotional lift."

"How come?"

"He had a good day today. He's been alert. His mind has had a keen edge. He managed to eat his lunch without help. Your presence seems to have motivated him. It would be nice if you could give him something to keep him feeling positive."

"I don't know." What I had to tell the General wasn't positive. "I'll try not to bring him down."

We were watched going up. This time I wasn't wrong about it being Jennifer. A strange woman. Pity. She was gorgeous.

I didn't get it. When was the last time a woman like that left me cold? I couldn't recall. Female is my favorite sport. Wasn't anything obviously wrong with her, either. Maybe it was bad chemistry. The opposite of lust at first sight.

"Who raised Jennifer?"

"Cook, mostly. And the staff."

"Oh. What became of them?"

"The General released them to make room for us. We should've been able to manage the place, putting the cropland out for rent. Hasn't worked out, though."

"He kept Cook. Why her?"

"She's a fixture. Been here forever. Raised him, too. And his father before him, and his father, too. He has his sentimental streak."

"That's nice." He hadn't been sentimental when he'd been my supreme commander. Of course, I hadn't gotten to know him.

"He takes care of his own." Dellwood opened the General's door, seated me in the room where I'd met the old man before. Old Kaid was stoking the fire. "Wait here. I'll have him out in a few minutes." The temperature was obscene.

"Sure. Thanks."

It was more than a few minutes but the old man was worth seeing when he came out. He had a smile on. His cheeks had gained some color. He waited till Dellwood and Kaid departed. "Good evening, Mr. Garrett. I take it you've made progress?"

"Progress, General, but I don't have any good news." Had his health improved because the poisoner had backed off with me around?

"Good news, bad news, better get on with it."

"I went into the city this morning. I put some acquaintances to work tracing the missing items through those people who deal in articles that stray from home. They're competent. If the thief disposed of anything through those channels, they'll find out and get a description of the seller. I do need instructions. Should they recover the articles? If they've been sold, you could be at the mercy of the new owners."

"Very good, sir. Very good. Yes. By all means. I want to recover whatever I can. I expect you'll have problems getting them back from someone who's taken a fancy to them." He smiled.

"You seem in good spirits, sir."

"I am. I am indeed. I haven't felt this well in months. Maybe years. Not your doing but it did start after your arrival. You're good luck. If I keep improving at this rate, I'll be dancing within the month."

"I hope so, sir. Sir, that brings me to the bad news. But first a confession. I didn't come out here just to unmask a thief."

"Ah?" There was a sparkle in his eye.

"Yes sir. Sergeant Peters believes someone is poisoning you slowly. He wanted me to find out who. If it's being done at all."

"And? You've found something?" He seemed troubled now.

"No sir. Nothing like that."

That pleased him.

"On the other hand, there's no negative evidence. And one has to wonder about your recovery. It pleases me but I'm suspicious by nature."

"And this is your bad news?"

"No sir. That's nastier. More pervasive, if you will."

"Go on. I'm not one to slay the bearer of ill tidings or to ignore them because they aren't what I want to hear."

"Let me preface this by saying I'd like to read your will."

He frowned. "Peters asked for a copy. Was that your doing?"

"Yes."

"Go on."

"I'm afraid it may be written so as to encourage villainy." I was starting to sound pompous. But it was hard to be one of the boys with General Stantnor. "If the number of heirs decreases, does the take for the survivors increase?"

He gave me the fish-eye.

"I gather half goes to Jennifer and the rest to everyone else. Sixteen people originally. After this morning, only eight. Meaning the take for survivors has doubled."

He looked at me hard. I thought he might throw me out, earlier protests to the contrary. "Support your suspicions, Mr. Garrett."

"I don't think the four men who left you could have. One, maybe. Two at the most. But people aren't built to walk away from so much money. Four?"

"I can see that. Maybe. What else?"

"Whoever put the arrow into Hawkes set it up ahead of time. The deer was too long dead to be a fresh kill. The sniper rode away on a horse. Would a peasant who has to poach have a horse? And the horseman headed this way after the ambuscade. Though that's circumstantial. I lost the trail partway here."

He was quiet for a long time. His color deserted him. I pitied him then.

"On a more personal level, two attempts have been made on my life since I've been here. I don't know by who."

He looked at me but didn't say anything.

"Unearthing that wasn't part of my brief. But I

thought you should know what I think is happening. Should I pursue it?"

"Yes!" He paused. "It doesn't add up. Theft that's almost petty. Someone possibly trying to poison me. Someone trying to kill everyone else."

"That's true. I can't make it add up."

"I don't want to believe you, Mr. Garrett. I know those men better than that . . . Two attempts on your life?"

I told him about them.

He nodded. "I don't suppose you . . . No. I believe you. Get Dellwood."

I rose. "A question first. General?"

"Go ahead."

"Could an outsider be responsible? Do you have enemies vicious enough to try to set your house against itself?"

"I have enemies. A man my age, who's been what I've been? Of course I have enemies. But I don't think any of them would try for the pain in something like this. . . . There'd still have to be an inside man, wouldn't there?"

I nodded, opened the door. Dellwood was in the hall a decorous distance away. "The boss wants you."

16

I'll say this for that old man: He took the bull by the horns. I didn't think he was doing the smart thing, but it was his house, his life, his sanity, and his choice to take the risk.

He had Dellwood bring everybody in and get them seated. He had me stand beside him, facing them. They looked at him and me and wondered while Peters and Chain looked for Snake. Kaid tossed logs on the bonfire. I sweated.

Nobody said a word.

Then Jennifer tried. She barely got her mouth open. The General said, "Wait." One word, softly, that stung like a whip's bite.

Snake ambled in with Chain and Peters. He'd tried to clean himself up. He hadn't done a great job but passed inspection well enough to be given a seat. Stantnor said, "Close the door, Peters. Lock it. Thank you. Hand me the key, please."

Peters did so. The others watched with varying expressions, mostly in the frown range.

"Thank you for coming." As if they'd had any choice. "We have a problem." He reached out. I put his will in his hand. He'd let me read it while we waited. It was an invitation to mayhem, incredibly naive.

"My will. You know the details. I've hit you over the head with them often enough. They seem to have created the problem. Therefore."

A candle sat on the table before him. He shoved the end of the will into the flame, held it till it caught, laid it on the table, and let it burn.

I watched them watch it. They were shocked. They may have been disappointed or outraged. But they didn't move, didn't protest, didn't fall down and confess.

"That instrument has been a murder weapon, sure as any blade. But I won't make a speech. There's the fact. Motive has been eliminated. The will has been abrogated. I'll write a new one in a few days."

He looked them in the eye, one by one. Nobody shied away. Everybody looked baffled and dismayed.

Dellwood said, "Sir, I don't understand."

"I certainly hope you don't. Those of you who don't, be patient, it will become clear. First, though, I want to introduce the man next to me. His name is Garrett. Mr. Garrett is an investigative specialist, amongst other talents. I employed Mr. Garret to find out who's been stealing from me. His efforts have been quite to my satisfaction so far."

The old boy was a chess player.

"Mr. Garrett found evidence of more heinous crimes. He's convinced me that some of you have been killing your comrades to gain a larger share of my legacy."

"Sir!" Dellwood protested. The others stirred, looked at each other.

"Mr. Garrett *was* a scout during his service, Dellwood. He tracked today's poacher back to our stable."

He wasn't maundering or speaking imprecisely. He wanted them to think I'd done just that, not lost the trail in the fields. He wanted somebody to feel pressed.

"Mr. Garrett has an excellent reputation for handling these things. I've asked him to find the killer. He's agreed. I have every confidence in his ability. I tell you all this by way of letting you know where you stand. If you're innocent, I want you to cooperate with him. The sooner it's wrapped up the better. If you're guilty, maybe you ought to put on your running shoes. Be advised that I shall hunt you as implacably as the hounds of hell. You've betrayed my trust. You have done me a hurt I can't forgive. I'm going to have your head and heart when I find you."

I didn't look at him, though it was hard not to. The old devil had gone farther than I'd expected.

By burning the will he'd eliminated the threat to the innocent. Nobody stood to gain now. If he died intestate, the estate could go to the Crown, which meant everyone lost. Even the poisoner ought to want to keep him alive till he wrote a new will.

A clever man, General Stantnor. But he'd left me swinging in the breeze.

"You understand your positions," he said. "Mr. Garrett. Ask what questions you like."

Chain said, "Sir—"

"No, Sergeant Chain. Mr. Garrett will ask. You're not to speak unless spoken to. We'll stay here till Mr. Garrett is satisfied."

I said, "Mr. Garrett doesn't think he can stay awake that long."

I'm not the kind of guy who can pull all the suspects together and expose a villain by weaving a web of clever questions. My style is bull in the china shop. It's jump in the pond and thrash till the frogs start jumping. I wished I had the Dead Man handy. One of his more useful talents is an ability to read minds. He could settle this in minutes.

I still entertained the possibility of an outside force with motives unfathomable. The arguments against these people being involved had to be answered before I could discard that possibility.

They looked at me, waiting. The General turned his gaze on me as though to say, *Show us the old Garrett razzle-dazzle, boy.*

"Anybody want to confess? Save us time and let us get to bed?"

Nobody volunteered. Surprise, surprise. "I was afraid you'd be that way."

Chain cracked, "I swiped a piece of rock candy from my sister when I was nine."

"There's a start. A criminal mastermind in the budding. I don't think we need to go back quite that far, though. Let's confine ourselves to this morning. What did you do today, Sergeant Chain? Account for your time and movements. Tell us who you saw doing what, and who saw you doing what you were doing." This would get tedious before we finished nine stories. But it might do the job. Each story would add a color to the portrait of the morning. Every tale told true would leave our villain less room to hide.

Chain got pissed. But before he could do more than grumble, Stantnor said, "I demand cooperation, Chain. Do exactly as Mr. Garrett says. Answer his questions without reservation. Or get off the estate.

Followed by the knowledge that you've made yourself the prime suspect."

Chain swallowed his protests. He didn't look at me like a guy who wanted to become my drinking buddy.

I said, "Try to attach times to the major events of your day."

"I don't pay no attention to what time it is. I'm too busy doing what I got to do. I mean, I do as much as I can. Ain't possible to get done everything that needs doing."

"Thanks to our killer, who keeps taking away pairs of hands. Estimates will do. Once we've heard from everybody, it should be pretty clear who did what where and when. Go ahead. Just ramble along. Take all the time you need. You can't go into too much detail."

Clever, clever Garrett sets himself up for an excruciating night. It took Chain forty-five minutes to tell me he hadn't done anything interesting and that, between breakfast and lunch, he'd seen only five other members of the household. Excepting Dellwood and Peters, those had been on the patrol.

"Anybody disagree?" I asked. "Anybody want to call him a liar?"

Nobody volunteered.

"All right. Snake. You're uncomfortable here. How about we get you off the hook? Go ahead."

Snake's story wasn't any more interesting than Chain's. He'd seen nobody in anything but innocent circumstances. Dellwood before they'd ridden out. The other hunters during the hunt. Peters when he'd come out with me. Then he'd gone back to his stables to get away. "I don't like people that much anymore," he confessed. "I ain't comfortable around them. Can I go now, General?"

The old man had begun to doze, apparently. But he was alert enough. "You aren't concerned about what somebody might say if you're not here?"

"No sir. I ain't got nothing to hide. And I'm getting awful uncomfortable." He looked like he was about to suffer a panic attack.

The General looked at me. I shrugged.

Stantnor handed me the key. "Up to you."

I unlocked the door, held it for Snake. "Good night."

As he passed me he whispered, "You come out when you're done. Maybe I can guess who done Hawkes."

It didn't seem a good time to get hardassed. I just added him to a lengthening list of things to do while everybody slept. I closed the door, turned, glanced around, wondered if anyone had overheard. Their faces revealed nothing. But it had been a loud whisper.

I took Wayne next. He was a bust. Cook would've talked all night and next day if I hadn't gotten her to edit some. She'd seen everybody and they'd seen her.

Four down. Three hours gone. Five to go. A pattern had begun to develop. A trivial one, but a pattern. Dellwood had been seen too often to have had time for a ride in the country.

I hadn't thought him much likelier than Cook, anyway.

I had Peters go next. He resented having to be a suspect but he did what he had to do. The General seemed to be dozing again, but that meant nothing.

Peters didn't tell me anything I didn't already know.

He'd barely finished when Jennifer came to life. "Mr. Garrett. If that isn't a false name, too. How about me next? This's really wearing me down."

"Welcome to the club. Go ahead."

She hadn't done a damned thing all morning. She'd sat in her room knitting. Dellwood could attest to that. He'd found her there when he'd brought the news about Hawkes.

Fine.

"Can I go? I'm tired and I have a splitting headache."

I could empathize. I was developing one myself. It was part of an oncoming cold that seemed to be a legacy of the weather. "Not yet. Bear with me. I'll try to hurry it along. Anyone want to go next?"

No volunteers. I picked Tyler. He didn't bother to conceal his resentment as he described the events of his morning. They were dull. They dovetailed. They didn't point a finger. He added another Dellwood sighting to the list.

"Kaid?" I said. "How about you?"

Another dull tale, mostly to do with the patrol.

The idea wasn't working out. Only Dellwood and Cook—ninety percent—were out of the noose. "Dellwood, it's probably a waste of time but go ahead."

His report was only slightly less detailed than Cook's. He didn't put me on anybody's trail. Most everyone had had time to go do it to Hawkes.

Well, you can't leave the stones unturned.

"Thank you all for your patience and cooperation. I'll talk to you again, for as long as it takes. No killer is invulnerable. If you think of anything, let me know. I'll hold your name in confidence. You can go."

They headed for the door in a pack, forgetting that I had the key. Jennifer remembered first. She hollered for it, as ladylike as a wolverine in a bad temper. I tossed it to her. "One thing, folks. I've seen another woman around the house." I described her. "I want to know who she is. Secret or not."

Mostly they gave me baffled looks. A couple looked like they wondered about my sanity. They all went out except for Dellwood, who brought the key to the writing table. "I'll put the General to bed now, sir. If you don't mind."

"I don't if he doesn't."

"Go, Garrett," the old man said, proving he hadn't been asleep. "I'm not alert enough to continue. See me after breakfast."

"Yes sir." I got up and went out.

It was after midnight. I was tired. Should I grab a few hours? Sleeping would be a real problem now the old man had made me a target.

No. Snake first. The way things were going, he probably didn't have anything I could use. On the other hand, he might. If he did I might not have to worry about getting the ax in my sleep anymore.

I headed down the hall. And got distracted immediately.

I spotted that woman again. She was on the balcony across from the head of the General's hall. My balcony. I froze, watched her just sort of drift along in a daydream. She didn't notice me. I darted to the stair leading to the fifth floor, stole to the east wing, crept down to the balcony below.

All for nothing. She was gone.

I'd have to trap her if I wanted to talk to her.

I wanted to.

The mind plays games. She was getting a grip on that part of me inexplicably immune to Jennifer's fetching charms.

17

As long as my room was just down the hall, I figured it would be wise to stop for some extra equipment. A sap and a sheath knife might not be enough if tonight's party got somebody excited.

The bit of paper between the door and the doorframe was the way I'd left it. But it was a decoy, meant to flutter down and catch the eye. The real telltale was a hair I'd left leaning against the door two inches in from the handle-side frame. It couldn't be replaced by somebody who stayed inside.

The hair was out of place.

Go on in? Or just walk away? I presumed somebody was waiting. There hadn't been time for a comprehensive search since the adjournment.

I considered getting comfortable and waiting them out. But every minute I wasted was a minute longer before I heard from Snake.

How about we just surprise the surprise party?

I got a shield off the wall, a mace, dug my key out, turned it in the lock, kicked the door in hard enough to mash anybody waiting behind it, went in with the shield up to take the blow of somebody against the wall on the other side.

Nobody. And it was dark in there. Someone had snuffed the lamp again.

I backed into the hall fast, not wanting to stand there in silhouette. A man with a crossbow could fix me up good.

Someone came toward the doorway, just far enough to be seen. "It's me." Morley Dotes.

I glanced along the hall. Nobody. I went inside. "What the hell are you doing here?" I shucked the shield and felt around for a lamp.

"Curiosity. Thought I'd see what was happening."

I got the lamp going and the door shut. "You just walked in?"

"Anybody could. They don't lock the doors."

"How'd you find my suite?"

He tapped his nose. "Followed my honker. We elves have a good sense of smell. Your suite is so heavy with the stink of meat eater, it's easy to pick out."

He was putting me on. "You're here. What do I do with you?"

"Any developments?"

"Yeah. There's another dead one. While I was in town this morning. So tonight the old man calls a meeting, tells everybody who I am and says I'm going to nail hides to the wall. Meantime, he burns his will. Anything from town?"

"Saucerhead made some rounds. Didn't find much. Some of those medals, you know how many they handed out? Every hock shop in town has a bucket full. The only ones worth anything are the silver ones. People on the Hill are worried about their silver supply."

The Hill is TunFaire's heart. All the biggies live there, including a gaggle of witches and wizards and whatnot who have to have their silver if they want to stay in business. Silver is to sorcery as wood is to fire. Since Glory Mooncalled whipped up on everybody in the Cantard, prices have soared.

But that was of no concern now. "What about the candlesticks and stuff?"

"He found a couple of things. Maybe. The people who had them didn't remember where they got them. Literally. You know Saucerhead. He can be convincing."

Like a landslide. You didn't talk when he said talk, chances were you would real quick. "Great. There's a dead end."

"He's going to try again tomorrow. Pity your thief didn't take something special so somebody would remember him."

"Thoughtless of him. Look. I've got an appointment with a man who says he knows the killer. Maybe. I'd like to see him before he changes his mind about talking."

"Lead on, noble knight." Morley rags me about being romantic and sentimental. He has his moments himself—like turning up here. He'd never admit he was concerned about me swimming in a school of sharks. He'd just claim he was curious.

"This is a real haunted house," he muttered as we stole downstairs. "How can they stand it?"

"Maybe they're right when they say there's no place like home. Maybe you don't notice after a while."

"Who's the brunette I spotted when everybody charged out of the hall across the way?"

"That's the daughter, Jennifer. A dead loss, near as I can tell."

"Maybe you don't have what it takes."

"Maybe not. But I think it's bad chemistry." We hit the bottom of the stairs. Nobody was around. We headed for the back door. There was a sliver of moon out, just enough to keep me from stumbling over things. Morley had no trouble. His kind can see inside a coffin.

"At least it's straightforward. No dead gods. No vampires. No killer ogres. Just greedy people."

I thought about the woman in white and hoped she wasn't supernatural. I didn't know how to deal with spooks.

Morley grabbed me. "Somebody moving over there."

I didn't see anything.

Somebody tripped over something.

"Heard us." Morley said. He took off.

I went to the stable, called, "Snake? Where you at? It's Garrett."

No answer. I stuck my head inside. I didn't see anything. The horses were restless, muttering in their sleep. I decided to circle around outside before I risked the inside.

Wavering light spilled between boards on the north end, near the west corner. It was feeble, like the light of a single guttering candle. There was a narrow door. I'd found Snake's hideout. "Snake? You there? It's Garrett."

Snake didn't answer.

I opened the door.

Snake wouldn't be answering anybody in this world again. Somebody had stuck a knife in him.

It wasn't a good job. The thrust had gone in on the wrong side of his breastbone, piercing a lung. The tip of the dagger had lodged in his spine.

Morley materialized. "Lost him." He looked at

Snake. "Amateur work." Always a student, Morley. And always a critic.

"Pros make mistakes if they're in a hurry with somebody tough. This guy was a commando, way I hear. Be hard to take him clean."

"Maybe." Dotes dropped to his haunches, toyed with a cord twisted around Snake's neck. The killer had finished it the hard way. "Interesting."

I'd started looking for physical evidence. A killer in a hurry could have dropped something. "What's that?"

"This is a Kef sidhe strangler's cord."

"A what?" I squatted beside him.

"Kef sidhe. They have strict religious injunctions against spilling blood. They think if you spill blood, the murdered man's spirit can't pass on till he's been avenged. So they kill without spilling blood because murder is part of their religion, too. Using a cord is an art with them."

I looked at the cord. It wasn't a piece of rope.

Morley said, "The master assassin makes his own cords. Making your own cord is the final rite of passage to master status. Look. The knot is like a hangman's knot, except the noose is round so it can be drawn with the hands pulling apart. These knots in the cord aren't really knots, they're braided over cork cones. They work like barbs on an arrowhead. The cord can be pulled through the knot in only one direction."

It only took a second to see how that worked—with an example right there. I felt one of the tapered bulges in the cord. Morley said, "The cork crushes down going through the knot, expanding again on the other side."

"How do you get your cord off?"

"They don't. They use it only once, then it's tainted. I've only ever seen one before. Cut off his own throat by a man I knew years ago. Excepting you, he was the luckiest guy I've ever known."

I looked around, less interested in Snake than he was. If our killer wasn't good he was lucky. There wasn't a spot of physical evidence. "Kind of sad," I said.

"Death usually is." Which was a surprise, considering the source. But Morley has been full of surprises as long as I've known him.

"I mean the way he lived." I gestured at our surroundings. He'd lived like his horses. He'd slept on straw. His only piece of furniture was a paint-stained table. "This was a professional soldier. Twenty years in, mostly spent in the Cantard. Combat pay. Prize money. A man careful enough to stay alive that long would be careful about his money. But he lived in a barn, like an animal. Didn't even have a change of clothes."

Morley grunted. "Happens. Want to bet he came out of the worst slum? Or off a dirt farm where they never saw two coppers the same month?"

"No bet." I'd seen it. Raised poor, they can get pathological about squirreling it away for a rainy day—and death comes before the deluge. Sad way to live. I touched Snake's shoulder. His muscles were still knotted. He hadn't relaxed when he'd died. Curious.

I recalled what Cook had told me about him. "Put it on his tombstone, he was a good Marine." I rolled him over in case there was something under him. There wasn't, that I could see.

"Morley. It takes awhile to strangle. Maybe whoever killed him tried that first, then stuck him. Instead of the other way around."

He glanced at the damage, which wasn't all that obvious, considering the state of the place. "Could be."

"You ever try to strangle somebody?"

He gave me a look. He didn't answer questions like that.

"Sorry. I have. I was supposed to take out this sentry during a raid. I practiced before we went in."

"That doesn't sound like you."

"That was me then. I don't like killing and I didn't like it then, but I figured if I had to do it and wanted to get out, I'd better do it right."

He grunted again. He was giving Snake's former downside the once-over.

"I did it by the book. The guy was half-asleep when I got him. But I blew it. He threw me around like a ragdoll. He beat the shit out of me. And all the time I was hanging onto that damned rope. Only good I did was keep him from yelling till somebody could stick a knife in him."

"The point?"

"If you don't snap a guy's neck, he's going to fight you. And if he breaks loose, even with that Kef sidhe thing around his neck, he sees you and you got to make sure of him any way you can."

"What you're sneaking up on is this Snake guy was stronger than whoever hit him. Like that Venageti soldier."

I hadn't said the Venageti was stronger than me, but it was true. "Yes."

"Somebody in the house probably has bumps and bruises. If someone from the house did this."

"Maybe. Damn! Why couldn't I have had some luck this once?"

"What do you mean?" He thinks my luck is outrageously good.

"Why couldn't the killer leave something? A scrap of cloth. A tuft of hair. Anything."

"Why not just wish for a confession?" Morley shook his head. "You're so slick, you slide right past yourself. He left you a dagger and a Kef sidhe strangler's cord. How exotic do you want to get? I told you how rare the cord is. How many daggers have you seen like this one?"

It had a fourteen-inch polished steel blade, which was unusual, but the hilt made it especially interesting. It was black jade, plain except for being jade. But at its widest point, where the middle finger of the hand would rest, there was a small silver medallion struck with a two-headed Venageti military eagle.

"A war souvenir?" Morley suggested.

"An unusual one. Venageti. Nobody lower than a light Colonel would carry it. A battalion commander in their elite forces or a regimental commander or his second in the regulars."

"Couldn't be a lot of those around, could there?"

"True." It was a lead. Tenuous, but a lead. I looked down at Snake. "Man, why didn't you blurt it out when you had the chance?"

"Garrett."

I knew that tone. Morley's special cautionary tone he saves for when he suspects I'm getting involved. Getting unprofessional, he'd call it. Getting bullheaded and careless, too.

"I have it under control. I just feel for the guy. I

know what his life was like. It shouldn't have ended like this."

"It's time to go, Garrett."

"Yes."

It was time. Before I got more involved emotionally.

I walked away thinking the old saw, *There but for the grace of the gods . . .* Over and over.

18

Morley wanted a crack at tracking whomever we'd heard fleeing. I gave him his head. He didn't accomplish anything.

"It's not right, Garrett."

"What?"

"I'm getting a bad feeling. Not quite an intuition. Something beyond that. Like an unfounded conviction that things are going to turn real bad."

Just so I couldn't ever call him a liar, somebody screamed inside the house. It wasn't a scream of pain and not quite one of fear, though there was fear in it. It sent those dread chills stampeding around my back. It sounded like a woman, but I couldn't be sure. I'd heard men scream like that in the islands.

"Stay out of sight," I told Morley, and took off.

The screams went on and on. I blew inside. They came from the west-side, third-floor balcony. I hit the stairs running. Two flights up I slowed down. I didn't want to charge into something.

The stair steps were spotted with water drops and green stuff in bits and gobs. Under one lamp lay what looked like a dead slug. I poked it. It wiggled and I recognized it. It was a leech. I'd become closely acquainted with its relatives on that one swampy island.

There was an awful smell in the air. I knew it from that island, too.

What the hell?

There was all kinds of racket up there now. Men yelled. Peters shouted, "Get one of those spears and shove it back down."

Dellwood, with a squeak higher than the screaming, asked, "What the hell is it?"

I moved upward carefully. I saw men against the head of the stairs, a couple with spears jabbing at something heaving on the stairs. There wasn't enough light to show it clearly.

I had a suspicion.

Draug.

I got a lamp.

I didn't want to see what I saw. That thing on the stair was something nobody ever wants to see, and whoever made it least of all.

It was a corpse. One that had been immersed in a swamp. What folklore called a draug, a murdered man who could not rest in death while his killer went unpunished. There are a million stories about draugs' vengeance but I'd never expected to be a player in such a tale. They're apochryphal, not concrete. Nobody ever *really* saw one.

Funny how the mind works. The thoughts you'd expect didn't come to me. All I could think was: Why me? This shot hell out of my simple case.

Peters yelled, "What do we do, Garrett?"

Besides puke? "I don't know." You can't kill a draug. It's dead already. It would just keep coming till it wore them out. "Try to cut it up."

Dellwood did upchuck. Chain shoved him aside,

flailed away with the ax part of a halberd. A couple of fingers came wriggling down where I stood. They didn't lose their animation.

"Hold it there. I'll come around the long way." I backed down to the balcony.

As I retreated to the stairs to the first floor, I spied the woman in white watching from the top balcony east, from a spot where she wouldn't be seen by the bunch above me. She looked more interested and animated than usual. Like she was enjoying herself. I tried to sneak up on her but she wasn't there when I got there.

I wasn't surprised.

I crossed through the loft, went down. The guys were hard at work, poking and hacking and stumbling over each other. Peters said, "This is getting old, Garrett."

"I'll buy that. Who's it after?"

"How the hell should I know?"

"Who did the screaming?"

"Jennifer. She ran into it down there somewhere. It followed her up here."

"Where is she now?"

"In her suite."

"Hang in there. You're doing a great job." I started down the hall. Then came back. Kaid and Chain cursed me. I asked, "Who was it when it was alive?"

Peters bellowed, "How the hell should I know?" He needed to work on his vocabulary. He was in a rut.

"Catch you in a minute." I headed for Jennifer's suite, which was identical to her father's, apparently, one floor below. I tried the door at the end of the hall. Locked and barred. I pounded. "Jennifer. It's Garrett."

I heard vague movement sounds. They stopped. She didn't open up.

I wondered if I'd have the nerve, considering all the tricks the stories say draugs and haunts try.

I tried again. She wasn't receiving callers. I rejoined the boys. They were hanging in there. Chunks of corrupt, stinking flesh were everywhere. And the draug kept coming. Stubborn cuss. I found a spot from which I could kibbitz. "Figure out who it was yet, Peters?"

"Yeah. Spencer Quick. Disappeared two months ago. The clothes. Nobody dressed like Quick. Lots of black leather. Thought it made the women swoon. You bastard. You just going to stand there?"

I rounded up a five-foot broadsword, the kind they'd used in knighthood days to bash each other into scrap metal. I tested its edge. Not bad, considering. I took up position out of the way, behind where the thing would emerge onto the balcony. "Let it come."

"You're crazy," Kaid told me.

Maybe. "Go ahead. Back off."

"Do it," Peters said, trusting me way too much.

They skipped away.

The dead man came in a cloud of stench, dragging what was left of him, lurching into the wall. "What're you waiting for?" Wayne shrieked at me.

I was waiting for the draug to jump its murderer, that's what. But it didn't.

Of course.

They all panicked, grabbed axes and swords, and started swinging. Six of them in a crowd like that, it was a miracle they didn't kill each other.

I stood back and watched to see if anybody took advantage of the confusion to eliminate another heir.

Now that they had room, they carved the draug into little frisky pieces. Didn't take them long, either. They were motivated. Wayne, Tyler, and Dellwood kept hacking away long after that was necessary.

They backed off finally, panting. Everybody looked at me like they thought I ought to be next. I got the impression they weren't satisfied with my level of participation.

"Well, then. That takes care of that. Be smart to collect up the pieces and burn them. Peters, you want to fill me in on this Quick? Who was he and how did he happen to go away without anybody thinking that was strange?"

Chain exploded. Before he could get out a coherent sentence, I said, "Chain, I want you to come with me and Peters and Tyler. We're going to backtrack that thing."

"Say what?" Chain gulped air. "Backtrack it?"

"Yes. I want to see where it came from. Might tell us something useful."

"Shit," he said, and started shaking. "I want to tell you, I'm scared. I don't mind admitting it. All my years in the Cantard I wasn't scared like I am now."

"You never ran into anything like this. Not to worry. It's done."

Peters said, "We have some other men missing, Garrett. Suppose more of those things turn up?"

"Doesn't seem likely. Draugs don't run in packs. Usually." I recalled a couple of stories. There was the Wild Hunt, a whole band of dead riders who hunted the living. "You saw how slow it was. Stay alert. You can outmaneuver them. The thing to remember is, don't get excited. We might have wrapped this mess up if we'd let the draug go after whoever killed it."

"Shit!" Chain swore. "It didn't care. It just wanted to get somebody. Anybody."

"Maybe. So let's hit the trail." I tried to sound perky. "Another glorious night in the Corps." I didn't feel perky, not even a little. I was scared stiff. "Arm up if that makes you feel better. And get lanterns."

Peters grumbled, "I hope you know what you're doing, Garrett."

I didn't have the faintest. I was just rattling around, hoping something would shake loose.

19

"Tyler, move out to the left about ten yards. Chain, you go to the right. I don't see much of a trail. Keep an eye out." I disposed myself and Peters between them so we spanned thirty yards. We started from the base of the front steps. "Let's go."

Peters said, "It was walking when it came. Wouldn't leave much of a trail."

"Probably not. You going to tell me who Quick was before we carved him up?"

"We?" Chain bellowed. "Will you listen to that shit?"

"Calm down," Peters told him. "I know what he was doing. He was right. You should have told us, Garrett."

"And warn the villain?"

"He's pretty well warned now."

"Safe, too. Oh. Add a name to the victim list. Somebody did it to Snake."

Peters stopped, held his lantern overhead, glared at me. "You aren't kidding. Snake? Why the hell Snake?"

I tried to recall who'd been sitting where when I'd let Snake out that door. Hell. Anybody with good ears could have heard. He'd used a stage whisper. Maybe he'd wanted the killer to know. Maybe he'd had something planned and it had turned in his hand. I wouldn't let a known killer get close enough to put a noose around my neck.

"Here," Chain said. We moved over. A strip of rotten leather hung on a bush. We redeployed.

I said, "You going to tell me about Quick?"

"I can't," Peters said. "I didn't know him. He was almost as spooky as Snake. Stayed to himself, mostly. You had to use a pry bar to get three words out of him. He did fancy himself a lover. You want to find out about him, talk to the gals at the Black Shark. All I can tell you is he was somebody the General knew and thought he owed. Like all of us."

I'd passed the Black Shark on the way to the Stantnor place. It was an evil-looking dive. I'd been considering taste-testing the house brew. Now I had business reasons to visit.

"Chain. You know anything about him?"

"Not me. Hell, sour as he was, I wasn't surprised when he walked. Him and the old man feuded all the time. He never gave a shit about the money, far as I know. He just didn't have nowhere else to go."

"Tyler?"

"I didn't know him, except he played a big role at the Black Shark. Guy was a werewolf, the way he changed personality when a woman was in sight. I figured he found somewhere he wanted to be more than he wanted to stay here."

Great. The live ones were weird and the dead ones weirder.

We were spread out just enough. We kept finding another trace just before we lost the trail. We adjusted and kept on. It was slow going.

"Who do you think is doing it, Garrett?" Peters asked.

"I don't have a clue."

Chain said, "He'll pass the word when there's only one of us left."

"That would work," I admitted.

Tyler kicked in, "I'd have put money on Snake. He was kill-crazy in the islands. He'd go hunting alone if he went too long without action."

I'd known a few like that, guys who got hooked on the killing. They hadn't made it through. Death has a way of devouring its acolytes.

"Here," Peters said. He'd found a place in tall grass where the draug had stopped. The trail was easy now. The grass was trampled down.

The trail pointed toward the swamp Peters had mentioned.

I asked, "You ever heard of Kef sidhe?"

"Kef she? What?"

"Sidhe. As in the race sidhe. Kef sidhe are professional killers. Religious assassins."

"No. Hell. The nearest sidhe are a couple thousand miles from here. I've never seen one."

Neither had I. "They're something like elves."

"What about them?"

"Snake was strangled with a Kef sidhe strangler's cord. Not exactly a common item in these parts."

Peters just looked baffled, near as I could tell by lantern light. Damn, he was ugly.

"How about a Venageti colonel's dress dagger? Were there any souvenirs around?"

"Black-handled thing with a silver medallion? Long blade?"

"Yes."

"Can I ask why?"

"You can. I won't tell you till I know more about the knife."

"Snake had one he took off a Venageti colonel that he snuffed during one of his private excursions," Chain said.

"Damn!"

"What's the matter?"

"Somebody stuck it in him when the strangler's cord didn't work fast enough." Wouldn't you know it? Stuck with his own sticker. Hell, next thing I knew I'd find out he committed suicide.

Our villain was probably more lucky than clever, full of tricks that were working out by accident.

Chain said, "Holy shit," in a soft voice. "We got trouble."

"What?" Peters demanded.

"Look at this."

We joined him. He held his lantern as high as he could.

Now there were two trails through the grass, one a yard to the side of the other. Peters and I exchanged glances, then looked at Chain. "Tyler! Get over here."

Tyler hadn't come. His lantern hung about two feet off the ground as he knelt to study something. "Wait a second."

I asked, "What have you got?"

"Looks like . . ."

Dark movement behind him. "Look out!"

The draug grabbed Tyler by the throat and hoisted him into the air. His neck snapped. He made a sound like a rabbit's scream; his lantern fell and broke. Fire splashed the draug's feet. It lifted Tyler overhead, heaved him into the darkness, turned on the rest of us.

"Spread out," I said.

"You damn well better do more than watch this time," Chain told me.

The fire blazed till the lantern's fuel was gone. The grass didn't catch. Neither did the draug. Both were too wet.

"We'll cut it up," I said. "Like the other one."

Chain said, "Let's don't talk, let's do."

I didn't want to. But this draug wasn't particular about whom it stalked. It hated life. If it had been after Tyler specifically, it would have fallen down, done, revenge complete. But it wanted the rest of us, too.

It didn't have much chance against three of us. We were faster and armed. But it kept coming. And coming. And coming. It's hard to cut a body up when it's chasing you.

The horror and fear subsided after a few minutes. I got my head working. "Either one of you know who this was?"

"Crumpet," Chain said. He concentrated like a clockmaker, making every move and stroke count.

"Crumpet? What kind of name is that?"

"Nickname," Peters said. "Real name was Simon Riverway. He didn't like it. Crumpet was all right. The ladies hung it on him in Full Harbor. Said he was a sweet bun."

Weird. I unleashed a roundhouse cut at the draug's neck. It got a hand in the way. My stroke sheered halfway through its wrist, one bone's worth. The thing kept turning toward me while I was off balance, grabbing with its other hand.

It grabbed hold of my sleeve. I thought I was a goner. Chain came in with a two-handed, overhead stroke, all his weight behind it. It hit the thing's shoulder hard enough to shake its hold. "I owe you one, Chain." I danced back a few yards, decided I'd follow Chain's example, and set my lantern down.

The draug kept after me—which was fine with Peters and Chain. Peters jumped in behind and took a wild cut at its right Achilles tendon, hamstrung it on his backstroke.

And it kept coming, though not as fast as it had.

It seemed to take forever, but we wore it down. It fell and couldn't get up. We carved it up good to make sure, spending a lot of fear energy. Once we were finished, I recovered my lantern, said, "I think we'd better hole up till dawn. If there were two of them there might be more. We can explore later."

"You said they don't run in packs," Peters said.

"Maybe I was wrong. I don't want to find out the hard way. Let's get out of here."

"First smart thing I've heard you say," Chain said. He examined Tyler. "Dead as a wedge. You think he's the one that killed them?"

"I don't know. I wouldn't bet on it. That one didn't care who it killed. It just wanted to kill somebody."

"Like the old joke about the hungry buzzard? Let's go. Before Tyler gets up and comes after us, too. I couldn't take that."

I didn't argue. Draugs are supposed to be dead a few months before they get up, but I wasn't ready to field test the folklore.

20

As soon as we reached the house I went to check on Dellwood, Kaid, and Wayne. They were out back. They'd gotten a roaring bonfire going and were feeding it pieces of the first draug. I told them, "Throw it all in and get inside."

"Sir?" Dellwood asked. He had his color back.

"There may be more of them out. We ran into one who used to be called Crumpet. It killed Tyler. Let's not find out what else is waiting in the dark."

They didn't fool around. They didn't ask questions. They pitched the draug in the fire and headed for the house. I glanced around as I followed, wondering what had become of Morley.

The survivors gathered at the fountain. They were chattering about Snake and Tyler when I joined them. Wayne and Kaid held the opinion that the second draug had gotten the right man.

I told them, "I'm not so sure. It just wanted to kill. It wasn't satisfied with Tyler. Dellwood, check the doors. Peters, are there other ways to get in?"

"Several."

"Take Chain and Kaid and check them out. We stay in threes till the sun comes up."

"How come?" Chain asked.

"I think the killer is working alone. If we're stuck with him, we'll outnumber him two to one."

"Oh."

Peters said, "Ask these guys about that sidhe thing."

Right. "Dellwood. Wayne. Kaid. You know anything about Kef sidhe? Especially a Kef sidhe strangler's cord?"

They frowned. Dellwood, puffing from his hasty trip to the doors, asked, "What's that?"

I described the thing I'd found around Snake's neck.

"The General had something like that in his study."

Peters brightened. "Yes! I remember it. It was with a whole bunch of junk, whips and stuff, in the corner by the fireplace."

I recalled the whips. I hadn't paid much attention. "Dellwood, next time you're up there, see if it's gone. Ask the General where it came from. And where it went if it's not there."

Dellwood nodded. I hated to turn loose but I couldn't keep him on my suspect list. He just didn't seem capable. If I discounted Peters, who'd have to be crazy to hire me if he was guilty, I didn't have many suspects left.

The others were thinking the same way. Chain, Kaid, and Wayne started giving each other plenty of room.

Peters started to go.

"Wait," I said. "There's one question I should've asked before. I've been too busy with murder to worry about theft. Does anybody have a drug habit?

Or gamble? Or keep a woman on the outside?" All of those might explain the thievery.

Everybody shook their heads.

"Not even Hawkes or Snake or Tyler?" Three in one day. The old man wasn't going to be happy about the job I was doing, though he hadn't exactly hired me to keep people alive.

"No," Peters said. "You don't stay alive in the Cantard if you're the slave of your vices."

True. Though vice had been rampant in places like Full Harbor, where we'd taken our rare leaves and liberties. A hellhole for a kid, Full Harbor. But you learned what life was like there. You had no illusions when you left.

Karenta hadn't yet evacuated Full Harbor, though Glory Mooncalled said they had to go. His deadline had passed. Something would happen down there soon. A really big explosion. And Glory Mooncalled wouldn't have his usual advantages. You can't outrun, outmaneuver, or even sneak up on a fortified city waiting for you. I doubted he had friends inside the walls. His enemies there would include Karenta's top sorcerers, against whom he had no defense.

I didn't think he could take Full Harbor. But he had to try. He'd shot off his mouth one time too many. He was committed.

The fate of Full Harbor meant nothing now, of course. We had our own siege here, a siege of horror.

Peters's group split to make sure the house hadn't been penetrated. The rest of us stayed at the fountain, in reserve. After a while, I asked, "Dellwood, what do you figure on doing after the General passes?"

He looked at me funny. "I never really thought about it, Mr. Garrett."

That was hard to believe. I said so.

Wayne chuckled. "Believe it, Garrett. This guy isn't real. He ain't here for the money. He's here to take care of the old man."

"Really? And why are you here?"

"Three things. The money. I got nowhere else to go. And Jennifer."

I lifted an eyebrow. I hadn't gotten much chance to show off my favorite trick lately. "The General's daughter?"

"The same. I want her."

Pretty blunt, this one. "What's the General think?"

"I don't know. I never brought it up. I don't intend to before he goes."

"What do you plan to do with your share of the money?"

"Nothing. Let it sit. I won't need it if I have Jenny, will I?"

No, he wouldn't.

"Which is why I ain't your killer, Mister. I don't have to skrag anybody to get half the estate."

A point. "What's Jennifer think about this?" She hadn't shown any interest in Wayne.

"Straight? She ain't exactly swept away. But she ain't got no other offers and she ain't likely to get none. When the time comes, she'll come around."

What an attitude. He sounded like a guy who could work his way up a hit list fast.

"What do you think about that, Dellwood?"

"Not much, sir. But Miss Jennifer will need somebody."

"How about you?"

"No sir. I haven't the force of personality to deal with her. Not to mention the fact that she isn't a very pleasant person."

"Really?" I was about to probe that when Wayne jumped up and pointed.

There was a vague shape at the back door, not clearly visible through the glass. It rattled the door. I figured it was Morley. I walked toward the door slowly. Make him wait.

Halfway there a face pressed against the glass. I was able to make out decomposed features. I stopped.

"Another one. Don't panic. I don't think it can get in. If it does, stay out of its way." I returned to the fountain, settled, disturbed but not afraid. The draugs weren't particularly dangerous when you were ready for them.

One in a night was unpleasant enough, but not that unreasonable—except for the assault on reason. In this world almost anything can happen and it does, but I'd never seen the dead get up and walk before. I'd never known anybody who'd seen it— unless you counted vampires. But they're a whole different story. They're victims of a disease. And they never really die, they just slip into a kind of limbo between life and death.

Once was unpleasant, twice was doubly unpleasant, but three times was just too much to have been animated by hatred and hunger for revenge alone. Not all in the same night.

Mass risings of the dead, in story and legend, were initiated from outside, by necromancers. By sorcerers.

"Hey, uh, Dellwood. Anybody around here a trained sorcerer? Or even an amateur?"

"No sir." He frowned. "Why?"

I lied. "I thought we could use a little help laying some restless spirits."

"Snake," Wayne said. "He could do some spooky stuff. Picked it up from a necromancer. He was her chief bodyguard for a while. He painted her picture and she taught him some tricks." He snickered. Must have been a variety of tricks. "He wasn't much good at it."

"And he's dead."

"Yeah. That's how you get off the hook around here."

But . . . "Suppose he could think like a sorcerer?"

"What do you mean?"

"What I . . . ? Let me reach. I was supposed to meet him. He was going to tell me who the killer was. He seemed sure he knew. He'd be wary. But somebody got to him despite his training and precautions. Suppose he knew that might happen? Suppose that, if he had a mind to, he could turn himself into a booby trap."

"Somebody's a booby."

"Flatterer. Look, it's in stories all the time. The curse that gets you after you kill a sorcerer. Suppose he fixed it so that, if he got killed, everybody else the killer killed would get up and go after him?"

Wayne grunted. "Maybe. Knowing that spooky, paranoid bastard, he'd rig it so they'd get up and go after everybody."

That fit, too. Sometimes I'm so brilliant I blind myself.

So what? Suppose that was true? It explained the draugs but didn't settle anything. There was a killer on the loose—if that hadn't been Tyler. No way to know unless he struck again.

If he had an ounce of brains, he'd retire while he had the chance to get out free.

I have such confidence in human nature. "Gents, I'm bone tired. I'm going to bed."

"Sir!" Dellwood protested.

"That thing isn't going to get in." It was still trying. And getting nowhere. "Our killer, if he's still alive, has got a great out now. He can let Tyler take the rap."

What you call planting a seed for the slow of wit.

I was so tired, my eyes wouldn't stay open. I needed to set myself up with some safe time. "Good night, all."

21

Morley was in my sitting room when I arrived. He had his feet up on my writing table. "You're getting old, Garrett. You can't take one long night anymore."

"Huh?" I was right on top of things. We investigator types have minds like steel traps. We're always ready with a snappy comeback.

"Heard your speech to the troops, shucking them so you can make with the snores."

"My second long night in a row. How'd you get in? Thought we had the place buttoned up."

"You might. Trick is, walk in before the buttoning starts. You went off chasing the walking dead. I just strolled around front and let myself in. Poked around the house some, came up here when the troll woman started rattling pots and pans."

"Oh." I got the feeling my repartee lacked something tonight. Or this morning. The first ghost light of dawn tickled the windows.

"I looked through the kitchen. The things you people eat. The sacrifices I make."

I didn't ask. Cook favored basic country cooking, heavy stuff, meat and gravy and biscuits. Lots of grease. Though Morley might have liked what she'd had for lunch my first meal here.

He was saying he planned to stay around. He went a little farther. "I figure you can use a ghost to balance off theirs."

"Huh?" I wasn't making a comeback.

"I'll haunt the place. Roam around where they're not looking, doing things you'd do if you weren't busy keeping them calmed down."

That made sense. I had a list of a hundred things I wanted to do, like look for hidden passageways and sneak into people's rooms to snoop. I hadn't had time for them and probably wouldn't because somebody would be in my pocket constantly.

"Thanks, Morley. I owe you one."

"Not yet. Not quite. But we're getting up close to even."

He meant for a couple of tricks he'd pulled on me back when. The worst was having me help carry a coffin with a vampire in it he'd given a guy he didn't like. He hadn't warned me for the good reason that, if I'd known, I wouldn't have helped. I hadn't known till the vampire jumped up.

I'd been a little put out.

He'd been paying me back with little favors ever since.

He said, "Fill me in so I won't go reinventing the wheel."

I got myself a handkerchief first. "This cold feels like it'll turn bad. My head's starting to feel like the proverbial wool pack."

"Diet," he told me. "You eat right, you don't get colds. Look at me. Never had a cold in my life."

"Maybe." Elves don't get colds. I gave him the full

account as I would've given it to the Dead Man. I kept an eye on him, watching for giveaways. He finds ways to profit when he weasels his way in to help me. I'd watched him enough to recognize that moment when he grabs onto something.

The obvious way here would be to recruit a gang to loot the place. That would be easy. Not so easy would be eluding an excited and bloodthirsty upper class afterward. Not that that would intimidate him much.

They might not have much use for General Stantnor, but as a class they couldn't tolerate the precedent. Every stormwarden, firelord, sorcerer, necromancer, whatnot would join in to pass out the exemplary torments.

"We have three separate things going, then," Morley said. "Thievery. Slow murder, maybe. Mass murder. You have the wheels turning on the thievery. So forget that. The General . . . The thing to do is let me and a doctor look at him. On the other killer, the only thing you can do is keep talking to people. Eliminating suspects."

"Go teach grandma to suck eggs, Morley. This is my business."

"I know. Don't be so touchy. I'm just thinking out loud."

"You agree Dellwood and Peters look unlikely?"

"Sure. They all do. The old man is bedridden and probably couldn't be fixed up with a motive anyway."

I hadn't considered the General.

"The Kaid character is too old for the pace and not strong enough to shove these other guys around."

"Maybe. Sneakiness is the killer's trademark, though. An old man would be sneaky."

"Sure. Then there's the Wayne character, who plans

to marry money. So who does that leave if everybody else is honest?"

"Chain." Obnoxious, argumentive, overweight Chain, to whom I'd taken an instant dislike.

"And the daughter. And the outside possibility. Not to mention maybe somebody who went away but didn't disappear because he'd been murdered."

"Wait. Wait. Wait. What's that?"

"You have four men who rode off into the sunset, right? Snake Bradon's presumptive necromancy recalled three. Where's the other one? Which one was he? What were the will provisions regarding those men?"

I didn't recall. One had gotten cut out, I'd heard that. But if somebody was good for a share even if he wasn't around, and everybody thought he was gone, or dead now, he'd be in great shape to do dirty deeds, then turn up for the reading of the will.

"Whoever got Hawkes headed for the house here."

"You lost the trail."

True. "If it was somebody who isn't on the inside, he wouldn't know about the General burning the will."

"Yes. He might keep on keeping on."

True again. "Somebody tried giving me the ax."

"There's that. But it could be related to your other problems."

"Morley, trying to puzzle it out will drive me crazy. I don't want to bother."

He gave me a look something short of a sneer. "Good thinking. You're goofy enough now."

I said, "Look, at this point what I do is just bull around and try to make things happen. When the bad boys get nervous, they do something to give themselves away."

Morley chuckled. "You have style, Garrett. Like a water buffalo. What good will bulling around do if your villain was Tyler?"

"Not much," I admitted.

"What about the cook? If she's been around four hundred years, she might think the family owes her a fatter chunk than the old man was going to give her."

I'd considered that in light of the fact that the non-human races don't think like us and trolls are pretty basic. Somebody gets in a troll's way, the troll flattens him.

"Cook's time is accounted for when Hawkes got it. Not to mention, if she was on a horse and her weight didn't kill it, it would leave tracks a foot deep."

"It was an idea. How's she look for poisoning the old man?"

I shrugged. "She's got means and opportunity but I come up short on motive. She raised him from a pup. I'd think there'd be some love of a sort."

He snorted. "You're right. We're not going to reason it out. Sleep on it. I'll go haunt."

"Don't walk into the bedroom," I warned him. "I have an ax rigged to carve sneaky visitors." I'd decided to go back to the featherbed. The floor in the dressing room was too hard. Maybe I'd move later, like I'd been thinking.

Morley nodded. Then he flashed a grin. "Wish there was your usual compliment of honeys in this one. That would make it a lot more interesting."

I couldn't argue with that.

22

It seemed I'd just drifted off when somebody started pounding on the door—though the light through the window said otherwise. I cursed whomever and rolled over. I'm not at my best when wakened prematurely.

In the process of rolling I cracked my eyes. What I saw didn't register. It was impossible. I wriggled into the down, the old hound searching for perfect comfort.

I sat up like I'd gotten a pin in the sitter.

The blonde smiled faintly as she drifted out my bedroom door. I didn't even yell, I just gaped.

She'd been sitting on the edge of the bed looking at me. She'd gotten in without getting carved up. I checked the booby trap. It sat there looking back, loaded and ready to splash blood over half a county if some villain should cooperate and trip it. Just sitting here waiting, boss.

And the door was open.

It hadn't worked.

That gave me the spine chills. Suppose it hadn't been my lovely midnight admirer? Suppose it had been somebody with a special gift? I imagined being stuck to the bed like a bug with a pin through him.

By the time I got through the supposes and lumbered out of the bedroom, the blonde was gone. Without having used the hall door, where some obnoxious fellow was pounding away, trying to get my attention. He'd gotten my goat already.

I collected my head-knocker and went to see who wanted me up at such an unreasonable hour— whatever hour it was.

"Dellwood. What's happened now?"

"Sir? Oh. Nothing's happened. You were supposed to see the General this morning, sir."

"Yeah. Sorry. I was too busy snoring to remember. Missed breakfast, didn't I? Hell. I needed to diet anyway. Give me ten minutes to get presentable."

He looked at me like he thought it might take me a year longer than that. "Yes sir. I'll meet you there, sir."

"Great."

I'm getting old. It took more than ten minutes. It was twenty before I started hoofing it across the loft to the old man's wing. I wondered about the blonde. I wondered about Morley. I wondered why I didn't just go home. These people were nuts. Whatever I did, I wasn't going to strike any blow for truth and justice. Ought to fade away and come back in a year, see how things stood then.

I was in a great mood.

Dellwood was waiting in the hallway outside the General's door. He let me in. The preliminaries followed routine. Dellwood went out. Kaid followed after making sure the fire was the size and heat of the one that's going to end the world. I sweated. The General suggested, "Sit down."

I sat. "Did Dellwood bring you up to date?"

"The events of the night? He did. Do you have any idea what happened? Or why?"

"Yes. Surprisingly." I told him about Snake's whisper, our date, how I'd found him. "Dellwood suggested the cord might have come from this room."

"Kef sidhe? Yes. I have one. Inherited from my grandfather. He collided with the cult around the turn of the century, when he was a young lieutenant sent to battle the crime rings on the waterfront. They were bad back then. One of the nonhuman crime lords had imported some sidhe killers. The cord should be there with the whips and such."

I checked. "Not here now." I wasn't racked with amazement. Neither was he. "Who could have gotten it?"

"Anyone. Anytime. I haven't paid attention to it in years."

"Who knew what it was?"

"Everybody's heard me maunder on about my grandfather's adventures. And about the adventures of every other Stantnor who ever was. Since my son's death there's been no future to look to. So I relive the glories of the past."

"I understand, sir. He was a good officer."

He brightened. "You served under him?"

Careful, Garrett. Or you'll spend your stay having the old boy bend your ear. "No sir. But I knew men who did. They spoke well of him. That says plenty." Considering how enlisted men discuss their officers.

"Indeed." He knew. He drifted off to another time, when everyone was happier—or at least he remembered them being happier. The mind is a great instrument for redesigning history.

He came back suddenly. Apparently the past wasn't

all roses either. "A disastrous night. Talk to me about those dead men."

I gave him my theory about Snake having raised them.

"Possible," he said. "Entirely possible. Invisible Black was the sort of bitch who'd think it an amusing practical joke to arm an untutored Marine with the weapons to accomplish something like that."

The name meant nothing to me except that another sorceress had adopted a ridiculous handle. Her real name was probably Henrietta Sledge.

"Have you nothing positive to report, Mr. Garrett?"

"Not yet."

"Any suspects?"

"No sir. Everybody. I'm having trouble making sense of the situation. I don't know the people well enough yet."

He looked at me like he was thinking I should be living up to one of those Corps mottos like "The difficult we do immediately; the impossible takes a minute longer." "What will you do now?"

"Poke around. Talk to people till I get hold of something. Shake it. I had one thought during the night. The man who's been picking the rest off could be one who apparently left you—if he thought he could turn up for the reading of your will."

"No sir. Each man executed an agreement when he joined me in retirement. To remain eligible he'd have to remain here."

I lost some respect for him there. He'd bribed them and indentured them so he wouldn't be alone. He was no philanthropist. His motives were completely selfish.

General Stantnor was a mask. Behind it was someone who wasn't very nice.

I wouldn't call it an epiphany but it was an intuition that felt true. This was a mean-spirited old man in a carefully crafted disguise.

I examined him more closely. His color wasn't good this morning. His respite was over. He was on the road to hell again.

I reminded myself it wasn't my place to judge.

Then I reminded myself that when I remind myself, what I'm doing is looking for justification.

Someone knocked. That saved me confusion and stole the General's opportunity to get righteous.

I'd sensed that coming.

"Enter."

Dellwood opened the door. "There's a Mr. Tharpe to see Mr. Garrett."

The General looked at me. I told him. "That's the man I had trying to trace certain items."

"Bring him up, Dellwood."

Dellwood closed the door. I asked, "Here?"

"Is he likely to report something you don't want me to hear?"

"No. It just seemed an inconvenience to you."

"Not at all."

Hell. He was fishing for entertainment again. He didn't care what Saucerhead had to tell me, much. He just didn't want to be alone.

"Mr. Garrett, could I impose on you to build the fire a little?"

Damn. I was hoping he wouldn't notice it was down to a volcanic level. I wondered if Kaid had a full-time job just hauling in fuel.

Saucerhead arrived lugging a bag. In his paw it

seemed small. He hulks like a cave bear. Dellwood seemed a little intimidated. The old man was impressed. He cracked, "Cook sees him, she'll fall in love." That was the first I'd heard him try for humor. "That'll be all, Dellwood." Dellwood got out.

Saucerhead wiped his brow and said, "Why don't you open a goddamned window? Who's the old prune, Garrett?"

"The principal. Be nice."

"Right."

"What's up?" I was surprised he'd make a trip out, considering what he was getting paid.

"I maybe found some of the stuff." He dumped the sack on the writing table. Silver candlesticks. They wouldn't have been remarkable if silver hadn't become important lately.

"General?" I asked. "This your stuff?"

"Look on their bases. If they belong to the family, there'll be a seahorse chop beside the smith's."

I looked. Little sea critters. "We have a lead, looks like. What's the story, Saucerhead?"

Saucerhead has a kind of pipsqueak voice when he's just making conversation. Doesn't go with his size at all. He said, "I was jawing with some guys at Morley's last night, bitching about the job. Looked like it wasn't going anywhere. Talking about this and that, you know how it is. Then this one guy asks did I think there might be a reward for the stuff. I didn't know, you never told Morley if there was or not, so I said maybe and did he know something?"

"To make a long story short?"

"He knew some fences I didn't. Outside guys. So this morning I go to check them. First one I hit, he has the sticks. We talk a little, I threaten a little, he blusters a little, I make mention of how I know he don't have a connection with the kingpin and I happen to know Chodo personal, would he like me to arrange an introduction? All of a sudden he's eager to help. He loans me the sticks. I promise to bring them back."

Which meant he would and, if the General tried to grab them, Saucerhead would walk through him and the rest of the house. He keeps his promises.

"Got you. Can the fence finger the thief?"

"He don't know squat. Bought the stuff wholesale from somebody out in the country. He'll sell the wholesaler's name."

"Did you follow that, General?"

"I believe so. This dealer in stolen goods bought the candlesticks from another dealer closer to home, here. For a price he'll sell the man out."

"That's it."

"Go beat it out of him."

"It doesn't work that way, General. He offered a straight deal. We should follow through on those terms."

"Deal with criminals as though they were honorable men?"

"You have all your life, with those bandits off the Hill. But let's not argue. We have a lead. We could settle the theft problem today. Saucerhead. How much does he want?"

I was thinking long-term now. An unconnected fence? He'd need friends. He could be nurtured and stroked on the head and maybe become a good source someday. If he stayed alive. People aren't scared of fences the way they're scared of Morley Dotes or Chodo Contague.

Saucerhead named a price that was pleasantly low.

"It's a bargain, General. Go with it. How much more are you willing to lose to avoid spending a few marks?"

"Collect from Dellwood. He handles the household monies."

That sounded like a cue for me to get away from a place where I was uncomfortable. "I'll take care of this, sir."

Maybe Stantnor sensed my discomfort. He didn't protest. But there was a glimmer of hurt in his eyes.

I'd never seen it in an old person before, but I'm not around them much. I'd seen it in children, the pain when an adult doesn't have time to be bothered with them.

That hit me in the spot where I think of myself as one of the good guys. Guilt. Its lack is something I envy Morley. Morley never feels guilty. Morley does what he wants or has to do and is puzzled by the behavior of those of us who had mothers. Where does it come from, that niggling little nasty?

23

Saucerhead said, "That old boy didn't look good, Garrett. What's he got?"

"I don't know. You're going to help me find out."

"Say what?"

"Dellwood, the General said give my friend enough to cover some upcoming expenses. How much do you need, Saucerhead?" Hand him a chance to make his trip worth the trouble.

He didn't bite. Not very big. "Twenty. The guy tries to jack me up, I'll pull his ears off." He would. And wrap them with a bow.

"Get the name, then get the guy. Right? But find a doctor somewhere and bring him out here, too."

"A doctor? You lost me somewhere, Garrett. What you want a doctor for?"

"To look at the old man. He's got a thing about croakers. Only way to get one close is fool him. So you do that. All right?"

"You're paying the freight."

"Hurry all you can."

"Right." He was supposed to be too simple for sarcasm but I smelled a load there.

Dellwood gave him twenty marks. He left. I went

to the front door, watched him head out in a buggy he'd probably rented from Sweetheart, a mutual friend. I grumbled about his expenses. The old man had given me a nice advance but I hadn't counted on quite so many expenses.

Dellwood joined me. "May I ask what that was all about, sir?"

"You can ask. Don't mean I'll tell you. Part of the job. You going to tell the General I'm sneaking a doctor in on him?"

He gave it a think. "No sir. It's appropriate. Except for yesterday he's been sinking fast. He's pretending to bear up today, but last night is gnawing at him, too. If there's a way . . . Let me know if I can aid in the deception."

"I will. I have a lot to do today." Like what? Not that much specific. "I'll let you know before Tharpe gets back."

"Very well, sir."

We parted. I went upstairs to see if Morley was in the suite. He'd have a part to play. As I reached the top balcony I spied my friend in white across the way. I waved. She surprised me by waving back.

Morley wasn't there. Just like him, not to be handy when I needed him. Thoughtless of him. I grabbed my coat and headed out.

The blonde was still there. She wasn't watching for me. I decided to take one more crack at sneaking up on her. Slipped up to the loft, across, went down.

Ha! Still there!

Only . . . My imagination had run away with me. This wasn't my blonde. This was Jennifer wearing white and not the same white the blonde wore. She smiled kind of sadly as I approached her. "What's the matter?" I asked.

"Life." She leaned her elbows on the rail. I joined her, leaving a few feet between us. Below, our hero remained locked in mortal combat with the dragon. Chain passed without giving them a glance. I knew how the knight felt. Us heroes like to be applauded for our efforts.

I answered Jennifer with one of those "Uhm?" noises that mean you'll listen if your companion wants to share her troubles.

"Am I ugly, Garrett?"

I glanced at her. No. She wasn't. "Not hardly." I've known several equally gorgeous women who were more insecure about their looks than your less-than-average-looking ladies. "The guy who didn't notice would have to be dead."

"Thanks." Trace of a smile, trace of warmth. She moved maybe three inches closer. "That helps." Half a minute. "But nobody does notice. Even that I'm female."

How do you tell a woman it isn't her looks, it's her inside? That, nice as she looks, she feels like a black widow spider?

You don't. You fib a little to avoid the cruelty and hate.

Even standing close, with her radiating a need to be wanted, I couldn't find any interest inside me.

I began to worry about me.

"You don't notice me."

"I notice you plenty." Only somebody with very skewed standards, like maybe a ratman, would call her hard on the eyes. "But I'm taken." That's always an out.

"Oh." That infinite sorrow again. That's what it was. Sorrow. Sorrow that stretched back to the dawn of her days. An abyss that could gobble the world. "What's her name?"

"Tinnie. Tinnie Tate."

"Is she attractive?"

"Yes." The redhead is in the same class as Jennifer. That is, the howl-at-the-moon class. But we have our problems, one of which is that we aren't going anywhere. Sort of a can't-live-with-and-can't-live-without arrangement, neither of us with enough confidence to risk commitment.

I might have, with Maya . . . Or maybe she just said she was going to marry me so often that I accepted the possibility. I wondered what she was doing. Wondered if I was supposed to track her down. Wondered if she'd ever be back.

"You're awful thoughtful, Garrett."

"Tinnie does that to me. And this place . . . This house . . ."

"Don't be apologetic. I live here. I know. It's a sad place. A ghost town all by itself, haunted by might-have-beens. Some of us live in the past and the rest live for a future that'll never come. And Cook, who lives in another world, is the rock that holds us together."

She wasn't so much talking to me as putting feelings into words.

"There's a road down front, Garrett. Less than half a mile away. Its other end is TunFaire, Karenta, the world. I haven't been past the front gate since I was fourteen."

"How old are you now?"

"Twenty-two."

"Who's holding you here?"

"Nobody but me. I'm afraid. Everything I imagine I want is out there. And I'm afraid to go see it. When I was fourteen, Cook took me to the city for the summer fair. I wanted so badly to go. It's the only time I've ever been off the estate. It terrified me."

Odd. Most beautiful women don't have much trouble coping because they've had attention all their lives.

"I know my future. And it frightens me, too."

I looked at her, thinking she meant Wayne. I'd be disturbed, too, if I were the object of such plans.

"I'll stay here, in the heart of my fortress, and turn into a crazy old woman while the house crumbles around me and Cook. I'll never find nerve enough to hire the workmen to put it right. Strangers scare me."

"It doesn't have to be that way."

"It has to. My destiny was laid down the week I was born. If my mother had survived . . . But she probably wouldn't have changed things. She was a strange woman herself, from what I hear. Daughter of a firelord and a stormwarden, raised in an environment almost as cold as mine, betrothed to my father by arrangement between his parents and hers. They never met before their wedding day. My father loved her, though. What happened really hurt him. He never mentions her. He won't talk about her. But he has her picture in his bedroom. Sometimes he just lies there and stares at it for hours."

What do you say when somebody tells you something like that? You can't kiss it and make it better. Not much you can do. Or say. I said, "I'm going to take a walk. Why don't you get a wrap and come along?"

"How cold is it?"

"Not too bad." Winter was just blustering and

fussing, bluffing, too cowardly to jump in there and bully the world. Which was fine with me. Winter isn't my favorite season.

"All right." She pushed away from the rail and walked to the stairs, down, headed for her own suite. I tagged along, which was fine till we neared her door. Then she got nervous. She didn't want me inside.

Fine. For now her fortress would remain inviolate. I retreated halfway down the hall.

If I'd had doubts about her lack of social skills, they disappeared when she returned in less than a minute. I've never known a woman who didn't spend half an hour changing her shoes. She'd done that and had donned a very sensible, military-type winter coat that, surprisingly, was flattering because it centered attention on her face. And that face made me wince because such beauty was shut up here, wasted. Such beauty, like a great painting, should be out for all to appreciate.

We went downstairs and through that hall between the Stantnor forebears, all of whom noted our passing with grave disapproval. So did Wayne, who maybe thought I was trying to beat his time.

It wasn't as mild as I'd promised. The wind had picked up since Saucerhead's departure. It had a good bite but Jennifer didn't notice. We descended the steps. I set course along the path that Chain, Peters, Tyler, and I had taken last night.

I asked, "Would you like to see the city? If you could do it without too much discomfort?" I had in mind turning Saucerhead loose on her. He has a knack for making women comfortable—though his taste runs to gals about five feet short.

"It's too late. If you're trying to save me."

I didn't say anything to that. My attention was on last night's trail.

"I saw something strange today," Jennifer said, shifting subject radically. "A man I don't know. I went up where you found me looking for him, but he wasn't there anymore."

Morley. Had to be. "Maybe my blonde's boyfriend."

She glanced at me sharply, the first time she'd looked up since we'd left the house. "Are you making fun of me?"

"No. Of a situation, maybe. I see a woman, over and over. Nobody else sees her. At least, nobody admits she's there. But now you're seeing ghosts, too."

"I saw him, Garrett."

"I didn't say you didn't."

"But you don't believe me."

"I don't believe or disbelieve. The first rule of my business is keep an open mind." The second is remember that everybody lies to you.

That seemed to satisfy her. She didn't speak again for a while.

We came to the place where Tyler died. Tyler wasn't there. Neither was the draug. I walked around trying to discover what had happened. I couldn't. I hoped Peters and the others had collected them. I'd have to find out.

The wind was biting, the grass was brown, the sky was gray, and the brooding Stantnor place loomed like a thunderhead of despair. I glanced at the orchard, all those bare arms reaching for the sky. Spring would come for the trees but not for the Stantnors.

"Do you dance?" I asked. Maybe we could force gaiety into the place at swords' points.

She managed a joke. "I don't know. I've never tried."

"Hey! We're making headway. Next thing you'll be smiling."

She didn't respond for half a minute, then bushwhacked me again. "I'm a virgin, Garrett."

Not exactly a surprise. It figured. But why tell me?

"The other day when you caught me in your stuff, I thought you were the man who would change that. But you aren't, are you?"

"I don't think so."

"Peters warned me—"

"That I have a reputation? Maybe. But the way this is, it wouldn't be right. It has to be right, Jennifer." Carefully, carefully, Garrett. Hell hath no fury, and all that. "You shouldn't want to do it just because you don't want to be a virgin. You should do it because that's what you want to do. Because you're with someone special and you want to share something special."

"I can get preached at by Cook."

"Sorry. Just trying to tell you how I think. You're a lovely woman. One of the most beautiful I've ever met. The kind men like me only dream about. I'd take you up on it in a second, if I was a guy who could just use a woman and discard her like a gnawed bone, and not care how much she hurts."

That seemed to help.

Believe me, all that analysis and nimble-footing had me real nervous, prancing around a lot of mixed feelings.

"I think I understand. It's actually kind of nice."

"That's me. Mr. Nice Guy. Talk myself out of the winner's circle every time."

She gave me a look.

"Sorry. You're not used to my brand of wit."

I was following the backtrails of the draugs slowly now, climbing a gentle slope toward the family cemetery. Jennifer seemed too preoccupied to notice. After we'd walked another fifty yards, she stopped. "Would you do one thing for me?"

"Sure. Even what we were talking about, if it ever becomes right."

Strained little smile. "Touch me."

"Huh?" I was back into my trick bag of brilliant repartee.

"Touch me."

What the hell? I reached out, touched her shoulder. She raised her hand, grabbed mine, moved it to her cheek. I rested my fingers there gently. She had the silkiest skin I'd ever touched.

She started shaking. I mean shaking bad. Tears filled her eyes. She turned away, embarrassed or frightened. After a while she turned back and we started walking again. As we reached the low rail fence around the cemetery, she said, "That was almost as much."

"What?"

"Nobody ever touched me before. Ever. Not since I was old enough to remember. Cook did, I guess, when I had to be changed and burped and all those things you do with babies."

I stopped dead, faced that grim old mansion. No wonder it was so goddamned bleak. I faced her. "Come here."

"What?"

"Just come here." When she stepped closer, I pulled her into a hug. She went as rigid as an iron post. I held her a moment, then turned loose. "Maybe it's not too late to start. Everybody's got to touch sometime. You're not human if you don't." I understand what she wanted when she wanted to stop being a virgin. Sex had nothing to do with it. She might not realize it consciously but she thought sex was the price she had to pay for what she needed.

How many times has Morley told me I'm a sucker for cripples and strays? More than I like to remember. And he's right—if you call wanting to ease pain being a sucker.

I stepped over the cemetery fence, held her hand as she followed. She caught the hem of her dress, which wasn't exactly designed for a stroll in the country. She cursed softly. I helped her keep her balance while she worked it loose, looking around as she did so. My gaze fell on a tombstone less aged than most, as simple a marker as there was there. Just a small slab of granite with a name: Eleanor Stantnor. Not even a date.

Jennifer stepped over to it. "My mother."

That was all? That was the resting place of the woman whose death had warped so many lives and turned the Stantnor place into the house of graydom? I would've thought he'd built her a temple . . . Of course. The house had become her mausoleum, her memorial. The house of broken dreams.

Jennifer shuddered and moved closer. I put my arm around her. We had a biting cold wind, a gray day, and a graveyard. I needed to be close to somebody, too.

I said, "I've reconsidered. Somewhat. Spend the night with me tonight." I didn't explain. I didn't say anything more. She didn't say anything, either, neither in protest, shock, or accusation. She stiffened just the slightest, the only sign she'd heard me.

It was an impulse, almost, kicked up by that part of me that hates to see people hurting.

Maybe there's such a thing as karma. Our good deeds get their reward. A small thing, but if I'd overcome that impulse, I'd probably be dead.

24

We stood looking at the tombstone. I asked, "Do you know much about your mother?"

"Only what I told you, which is all Cook ever told me. Father won't say anything. He fired everybody after she died, except Cook. There wasn't anyone else to tell me."

"What about your grandparents?"

"I don't know anything about them. My grandfather Stantnor died when I was a baby. My grandmother Stantnor went when my father was a boy. I don't know who they were on my mother's side except that they were a stormwarden and a firelord. Cook won't tell me who they were. I think something bad happened to them and she doesn't want me to know."

Ting! A little bell rang inside my head.

A favorite pastime of our ruling class is plotting to snatch the throne. Though we haven't lately, sometimes we go through periods when we change kings like underwear. We had three in one year, once.

There'd been a big brouhaha when I was eight, maybe seven. About the time Jennifer had been born. An assassination attempt had gone awry and had been so blackhearted at its core that the would-be victim had gotten so righteously pissed off, he'd made a clean sweep. Not a bit of forgive-and-forget. Necks got stretched. Heads and bodies went their separate ways. Arms and legs got hauled around the kingdom and buried individually beneath crossroads. Great estates got confiscated. It hadn't been a good time to be related to the conspirators, however remotely.

From my neighborhood it had been great fun, watching the ruling class chase its tail and get it caught in a door. Or some such mixed metaphor. When those things come up, everybody on the outside hopes that crowd will wipe themselves out. But they never do. They just select out the least competent schemers.

Shouldn't be hard to find out who her grandparents had been. "Would you want to know?" I asked. "Is it important to you?"

"It's not important. It wouldn't change my life. I don't know if I care anymore." After some silence, "I used to dream about them when I was little. They were going to come take me home to their palace. I was really a princess. They'd sent me and my mother here to hide us from their enemies, only something happened. Maybe they'd forgotten where they'd hidden us. I don't know. I never figured out why they never came. I just pretended that they would, someday."

A common childhood mind game. But, "It could be true, Jennifer. Things were unsettled politically in those days. It's possible the marriage was arranged to put your mother out of harm's way. With your grandparents dead, your father might have been the only one left who knew who your mother was."

"You're kidding."

"No. I was young but I remember those days. Some people tried to kill the King. They blew it. He went crazy. A lot of people died, including some who had nothing to do with the plot." Sometimes you tell the white lie. Wouldn't hurt to leave her the option of believing her grandparents had been innocents caught in the storm.

She laughed without humor. "Wouldn't that be something? If my kid's daydreams were true?"

"Do you still not care?" I could find out about her grandparents without doing much but poke through some old records. Worth the effort if it would brighten her life.

"I think I do care."

"I'll find out, then." I started moving again. She followed, caught up in her thoughts, paying no attention, while I got back onto the trail of the draugs. We were almost to the road before she realized we were still headed away from the house. She might not have noticed then if we hadn't gotten into some cockleburs.

"Where are you going?" She sounded almost panicky. There was a touch of wildness in her eyes. She looked around like she'd suddenly wakened in enemy territory. Only the peaks of the house were visible above the hummock where the cemetery lay. Once we reached the road, those would be out of sight.

"I'm backtracking the thing that came to the house last night." I was backtracking all three, really. There were three trails smashed through the weeds. But there were no return trails. That left me a little uneasy. We'd only disposed of two. "I think it came from the swamp that's supposed to be up ahead there."

"No. I want to go back." She looked around like she expected something to jump out at us. And maybe something could. Those draugs hadn't behaved like story draugs. Who was to say they weren't immune to daylight? And I wasn't equipped to handle them. It hadn't occurred to me to bring any heavy weaponry.

Still, I wasn't particularly nervous. Without the dark to mask them, they couldn't sneak up on us.

"Nothing to worry about. We'll be all right."

"I'm going back. If you want to go out there . . ." She said "out there" like I was headed for another world. "If you want, you go ahead."

"You win. You seen one swamp, you've seen them all. And I got a plenty good look in the islands."

She'd already started walking. I had to trot to catch up. She looked relieved. "It's almost lunchtime, anyway."

It was. And I still had to find Morley and rehearse him for Saucerhead's return. "I should thank you. I've missed so many meals, I'm light-headed."

We went straight to the kitchen. We ate. The others eyed us curiously. Everyone knew we'd gone for a walk. Each invested that with his own special significance. Nobody mentioned it, though Wayne looked like he had a few words he wanted to say.

As Peters was about to leave I asked, "Where can I catch you later?"

"The stable. I'm trying to catch up for Snake." He didn't look pleased. That kind of work wouldn't thrill me, either.

"I'll be out. Need to ask you something."

He nodded and went his way. I ingratiated myself by helping Cook for a while. She didn't say much with Jennifer there, fumbling around. Cook never said much with a third party present. Made me wonder.

I hoped Jennifer wasn't going to attach herself permanently. But it did seem that way.

I'd just been kind to a stray. But pups run to where the kindness is. My own fault. A sucker, as Morley says.

I had to see him soon or adjust my scheme for the afternoon. I told Cook I'd be back to help later, then headed upstairs, hoping Morley would be in my suite. Jennifer tagged along till it was obvious where I was headed. Then she chickened out. Afraid of a guy with my reputation.

I said good-bye and kept a straight face till I'd let myself in.

No Morley. No sign of Morley. Curious.

It made me uneasy. Morley is an odd bird but he'd make an effort to stay in touch.

I had a bad moment imagining him dead in some hidden place, ambushed. Not a pleasant thought, a friend getting offed for helping with something that wasn't his concern. But Morley was too much a pro to get taken that way. The mistakes he makes aren't those kind. When he buys it, it will be because an irate husband appears unexpectedly while he's in no position to react.

I took a quick guess at how long it would be till Saucerhead returned, decided I'd have to manage without Morley. Black Pete would have to carry the load.

I shrugged into my coat and headed for the stable, making sure my telltales were in position.

I kept an eye out for my blonde sweetheart, but the only person I saw was Kaid on the fourth-floor balcony west scoping out how to haunt the place after his own death.

Kaid was close to the old man. I ought to spend some time with him. He might give me a lead on who might want the General out.

25

I shoved my head into the stables, didn't spot Peters. A couple of horses grinned at me like they thought their hour had come. "Think what you want," I told them. "Plot and plan and scheme. I've got an arrangement. The General can pay me in horseflesh. Horses that aggravate me are going to end up at the tannery."

I don't know why I said that. Pure bull, of course. They wouldn't believe it, anyway. Wish I understood why horses bring out the silliness in me.

"Peters? You here?" Not seeing him right away worried me. I'd had enough guys turn up dead.

"Here." From the far end.

It was dark in there. I moved warily, even assuming Peters wasn't one of the villains.

I found him at the nether end, all right, hard at it with a pitchfork. He grumbled, "That damned Snake must have been playing with his paint set all the time. He hadn't cleaned out in months. Look at this mess."

I looked. I wrinkled my nose. Peters was tossing manure and soiled straw into a spreader wagon. "I'm no expert but isn't this the wrong time of year to spread manure?"

"You got me. All I know is, it's got to be cleaned out and this's the wagon you haul it in." He mumbled some rakledly rikkenfratzes and colorful commentary on Snake Bradon's ancestors, then added, "I have enough to do without this. What's up, Garrett? And why don't you grab a fork and help while you're resting?"

I grabbed a fork but I wasn't much help. I was always lucky, even in the Marines, and never had to learn the practical side of keeping horses. "What's up is, I've found the fence who bought the stolen stuff. One of my associates will bring him out this afternoon."

He stopped pitching. He stared long enough to start me wondering if maybe he wasn't less than thrilled. He said, "So you are doing something after all. I was starting to think you were a drone. That the only effort you were putting out was trying to get Jennifer to put out."

"Nope. Not interested. Not my type." I guess there was an edge to my voice. He dropped it.

"You just wanted to give me the news?"

"No. I need your help. My associate is bringing a doctor, too."

"And you want me to distract the old man while this croaker gets a look at him?"

"I want you to go down the road and meet them, explain to the doc so he don't get himself booted before he gets a look. Not that I have any hopes he can tell much without laying hands on."

Peters grunted and started throwing horse hockey. "When are they coming?"

I tried guessing an optimum turnaround time. With Saucerhead there wouldn't be many delays. He'd just grab them by the collar and drag them.

"I'd think two more hours. If we can, I'd like to get the fence in without anybody seeing him. So we can spring him on whoever."

He grunted again. "You're slacking." We tossed. He said, "I'll manage. I'll have to see the old man first. Always something around here."

I told him, "I have hopes for this."

"Yeah?"

"Maybe it'll start things unraveling. If it goes right, we could get it tied up by tonight."

"You always were too optimistic."

"You don't think so?"

"I don't. You're not dealing with your average idiots. These guys aren't going to rattle. They aren't going to panic. Watch your back."

"I intend to."

He put his fork down. "You go ahead. I'm going to go clean up."

I watched him walk toward the open doorway, grinned. Those ears stuck out like the handles of jugs.

I tossed about three more forksful and quit. Mama Garrett didn't raise her boy to be a stable hand.

I'd gone a dozen steps toward the house when I had a thought. I turned back and invited myself into Snake Bradon's den. I fiddled around for five minutes getting a lamp going. Snake wasn't there anymore. I wondered what they'd done with him. Nobody had done any digging in the cemetery.

Damn! I'd meant to ask Peters about Tyler and the draug!

I missed the Dead Man's nagging. I just wasn't alert enough. Getting too turned inward or something. Not paying close enough attention. I didn't do that when I had the Dead Man to tell me what to do. I went down the list, by the numbers.

All right. I would. I'd failed to meet Snake in time. That didn't mean Bradon couldn't still tell me something, as the Dead Man would remind me. They could all tell me things, want to or not, if I concentrated. So let's start here, now, Garrett.

I did the things I'd done when we'd found Snake. I didn't learn anything this time, either. But I did pay attention to the paint-splashed worktable. I hadn't before. I hadn't considered that side of Snake at all.

Cook said he'd had tremendous artistic talent. Someone else said he might have painted the sorceress Invisible Black. Here, there, there'd been remarks to the effect that he remained an active artist. That side of the man didn't fit the rest of the Bradon image, to my mind. Artists sponge off the lords of the Hill. However good they are, they can't make a living doing what they do. I hadn't considered Bradon an artist because he hadn't fallen into the groove.

That table was evidence he'd worked plenty. But where were the results? The table wasn't his product.

I started a thorough search, working outward from the center of Snake Bradon's life. I found nothing interesting in his room except squirreled stuff for making paints. I recalled that he'd been messy when we were checking what had happened to Hawkes. He'd been working on something recently.

There was a fifteen-by-twenty tack room next to Snake's hole. The place had been torn apart.

I just stood there, surprised. Somebody was worried about Snake after he was gone? My, my. And Garrett hadn't been smart enough to get to it first.

If the searcher found something, he did a fine job of getting rid of it. There was nothing there now but a scatter of brushes, some broken underfoot. I wondered if Bradon's hobby had been a secret. One of those kind everybody knows but nobody mentions. Painting pictures wasn't a manly, Marine sort of thing to do. He might not have shared with the others.

I was having a little trouble making sense of these people. Again. Still.

I paused to wonder where I'd have hidden something if I'd been Snake. As the searcher probably had, knowing him better.

Brilliant thinker that I am, I came up with a big nothing.

Nothing for it, then. A general search. Every nook and cranny. Whoever had gone before me wouldn't have had a lot of time. He'd have to be seen places when he was supposed to be. Hell. Maybe he'd done his hunting before Morley and I came along last night. Or maybe while he was supposed to be loading manure?

Whatever, there was a chance he hadn't found anything.

If anything existed.

I did a quick tour of the ground level. Nothing caught my eye. I felt the imminence of the confrontation with the thief and kept getting more hurried, somehow hoping to have an extra dart when the showdown came.

I climbed into the hayloft, perched on a bale and muttered, "What the hell am I looking for, anyway?" Paintings? He'd painted, obviously. And the product wasn't in evidence. But what could paintings tell me if I found them?

I shrugged, got up, looked around. Snake had gotten a damned good hay supply in, considering. All neatly bailed, too. From what I recalled the country boys saying back when, that wasn't common. Ordinary folks filled their lofts with loose hay.

"Ha!" A story recalled. A guy in the outfit, Tulsa something, hell of an archer, did our sniping. Farm kid. Poor background. Died on that island. But he used to laugh about games he'd played with the daughters of the lord of a nearby manor. They'd done it in a secret room they'd built in the hayloft of the lord's main barn.

I raised my lamp high and stared at all that hay, too much for the state of the place. Might that pile be hollow? I muttered, "That has to be it."

I poked around the outside, trying to guess how Bradon would have gotten inside. Elimination left me three good spots to find entrances. I set the lamp on a beam and went to work.

I moved maybe ten bales before I decided I'd tried the wrong place first. I went to the next spot, moved another ten bales and felt foolish. Looked like I'd outfoxed myself again.

My activities drew the attention of the natives. Three ugly cats joined me, including an evil old calico. Me moving the bales got the mice stirring. The cats were snacking. They worked as a team, not something cats usually do, as far as I know. When I'd turn a bale, one would jump into the vacated spot to scare mice toward the others. At one point the calico had one mouse under each forepaw and another in her mouth.

"See?" I told them. "I'm not all bad."

One more try.

Third time was the charm, as they say. I tipped a

few bales. Cats flew around. And, behold! A three-foot-high, eighteen-inch-wide hollow, black as a priest's heart, ran back into the pile. I got the lamp. I asked the cats, "One of you want to run in there and let me know what's up? No? I didn't think so."

I got down on hands and knees and crawled.

26

It smelled in there. Not too bad a smell, but a strong one of moldy hay. It didn't do my cold any good. My nose ran like a fountain.

There was a room inside the hay, larger than I'd expected. Snake had spanned it with planks to support the bales on top. It was maybe six feet wide and ten feet long. His paintings were there, along with other treasures, mostly what we'd consider trivial or trash. Junk from the war, mostly. And medals. Snake had accumulated him a potful of medals, proudly displayed on a tattered Karentine banner against the narrow end wall.

I couldn't help feeling for the guy. A hero had come to this. A life for his country, for this.

And our rulers wonder why Glory Mooncalled is a folk hero.

Both side walls were lined with paintings, none of them framed, all just leaning there, stacked three and four deep. They were every bit as good as Cook said they could be. Better, maybe. I'm no expert but they looked like the product of a driven genius.

They weren't cheerful paintings. They were the spawn of darkness, visions of hell. One caught my eye immediately and hit me like a blow in the gut. It was a swamp. Maybe not the swamp that became my home away from home during my stint, but a place just as horrible. And that painting was no simple, brooding landscape faintly touched with the dark side. Swamp things swarmed there the way they seemed after they'd driven you mad for months. Mosquitos the size of hornets, eyes that watched from the dark, stagnant water. Human bones.

In the foreground was a hanged man. The scavengers had been at him. A dark bird perched on his shoulder, pecked his face. Something about the way he hung left you certain he'd hanged himself rather than go on.

A couple of guys in the company *had* killed themselves when they couldn't take it anymore.

Gods. I felt like I could fall into that painting and tumble right back through time.

I turned it around. It got to me that much.

Shaking, I went down the row on that side, then up the other. No other piece had the personal impact that one did but the same genius drove them. They'd have as much power for the right viewer.

"He was crazy," I murmured.

I couldn't hear anything well but it seemed the horses below were restless.

I went around again, checking the paintings behind the ones displayed.

Most seemed less maniacal, more illustrative, yet there was no doubt they portrayed places beheld by the same eye that had interpreted the war in the others. One I recognized as a view of Full Harbor contorted into a hellish dreamscape, more proof that Snake had put his memories or haunts onto his canvases.

Snake hadn't been just a painter of places. The first portrait I encountered was of Jennifer, I'd guess, at the time the General had come home. She was indefinably younger and maybe more beautiful—yet interpreted by mad eyes.

I studied it hard but couldn't figure it out. Yet Snake had done something with Jennifer that gave me the creeps.

There were portraits of the others, too. Kaid looked old and tired and worn out and you got the feeling that death was watching over his shoulder. The General had some of the creepiness that illuminated Jennifer and something of the fox about him. Chain looked plain mean. Wayne looked like a greedy burgher. I got it! Part of it. Part of the interpretation was how Bradon had clothed them. That was the crude statement. But there were the faces, too, painted like the man had been able to read the bones and souls beneath.

There was a later portrait of Jennifer, crueler than the first but with the lady more beautiful. Then a couple of guys I hadn't met, presumably among the missing. Then one of Dellwood that reminded me of a basset hound. I guess Snake saying he was a faithful old dog without a soul or mind of his own. Then one of Peters, either a failure for the artist or observer. I couldn't read anything into it. Then one of Cook that must have been romantic excess because she came off like a saint, like a mother to the world. Then still another of Jennifer, almost repulsive in its portrayal of the dualities, beauty and horror.

Once I got over being startled, I examined it more closely. Part of the effect came at a subconscious level, almost. I don't know how he did it but he'd painted two faces, one over the other, the outer one of blinding beauty and the other the skull face of death. You didn't see that one without staring long and hard.

The horses were excited downstairs. I wondered why but was preoccupied with the magic—yeah, the *sorcery*—of Snake Bradon's artistry.

If it was a sin that Jennifer's beauty should be hidden, it was the crime of the century that Bradon's paintings should go unseen, certain to fall victim to mold and moisture.

Before I left Jennifer, I vowed I'd find some way to bring the paintings out. Snake Bradon wouldn't go unremembered.

Had he been in love with Jennifer? She was the only subject he'd painted more than once, excepting a scene that looked like a before and after of a nonhuman holy place that had had the misfortune to stumble into the middle of a human battle. The later painting reeked of defilement by the corpses and ravens and bones. It felt like a parable of the world.

I blew my nose, hit the motherlode. Before it watered up again, I caught a whiff of a new odor. What? I shrugged and went on.

"Damn! Ah, damn my eyes!" That was no curse, friends. That was a squeal of triumph.

Snake had painted my lady in white. He had caught her as the incarnation of beauty—yet she, too, had some of the creepiness he'd put into his portraits of Jennifer.

She was in a wind, running, frightened. A darkness lay behind her. You knew it was in pursuit, yet you could not define what it was. The harder you looked the harder it was to tell it was there. The woman looked right into your eyes. The artist's eyes. Her right hand was just starting the motion of reaching out for help. Her eyes said she knew the person she was looking at knew what was behind her.

It transfixed me. It had the impact of the swamp painting. And this time I couldn't figure out why, because this one couldn't be explained in terms of my own past.

I blew my nose again. I got another whiff of that odor. This time I recognized it.

Smoke!

The damned stable was on fire! No wonder the horses were excited!

I scrambled out of there, to the edge of the loft.

Flames roared at the end where Peters had been working. The animals had gotten out and run. I heard shouting outside. The heat was savage.

I wasn't trapped—yet. If I moved fast I could get clear.

I knew the mileage Morley would get out of the gesture as I dove into the hole leading to Snake's cache. He'd be on me for a year, risking my life over some daubs on canvas.

I slapped a dozen of those daub-hickeys into a pile as big as I could manage and dragged them out. The fire was spreading fast. Flames were almost to me when I burst out. The heat beat at me. I felt my eyebrows curl, my eyes dry out. I staggered away. The flames came after me.

"Damned fool," I muttered to myself. The heat seared the back of my neck. Now my eyes watered, nearly blinding me. My chances were slim enough without the damned paintings.

I couldn't let them go. They were that important. They were worth risking a life. Part of me already mourned those I'd had to leave behind.

The fire had spread below faster than it had up

top. It was ahead of me now, at the end where Snake had lived. I wasn't going to get out that way.

I could see daylight through cracks between the vertical boards that formed the outside wall, rough-cut timber that had shrunk with the years till some of the gaps were half an inch wide. It was like looking through the bars at the gates of hell. From the inside. That close. And so far.

As panic closed in, I threw myself that way.

The stable was old and damned near falling down, and, if it was half as rotten as it looked, I might be able to bust out. I hit the wall with my shoulder, low. Both creaked. Neither broke but I figured the wall had the edge. I got down on my back and shot my feet out. One board gave an inch. That gave me hope and maybe some manic strength. I let fly again. An eight-inch-wide board tilted outward, then fell away under its own weight. Mad as I was, I flipped Bradon's paintings out before trying to make the hole wide enough for me.

The smoke almost overcame me first, but I made it. I jumped.

I lay around panting a while, vaguely aware that I was out there alone, away from the hollering on the other side of the barn. I climbed a fencepost and got myself upright, looked around, counted limbs to make sure I hadn't left any behind. I was still alone. I gathered my priceless salvage.

If there are gods, they agreed with me about those paintings. They hadn't been damaged. I got them together, limped over to the cow barn, hid them in the hayloft. My fuddled sense of humor told me that was appropriate. Then I stumbled back around the far side of the stable.

The whole gang was running around like chickens,

doing the hopeless, bringing buckets of water from the wellhouse. Only the General and Peters were absent.

"Garrett!" Jennifer squealed. "What happened?"

I'm such a handsome devil, they just go to pieces when they see me. "I was taking a nap in there," I lied.

She got a little pale.

I gave her my heroic grin. "Not to worry. I just busted through a wall and here I am." A coughing jag hit me. Great timing. Damned smoke. "Can't stop the true of heart."

"You could've been killed."

"I could have. But I wasn't. Too light on my feet."

Kaid said, "Somebody tried to kill you, boy," as he staggered past with a five-gallon bucket.

I looked at the growing inferno. That hadn't occurred to me, though it should have.

No. You don't kill somebody by setting a barn on fire. Too easy for him to get away. Maybe you start a fire to flush him out, but . . . That wouldn't have worked here. Too many witnesses.

Even in my fuzzy state, it was obvious the arsonist had wanted to get rid of the stable and whatever contents he'd been unable to find during a hasty search.

Wonderful. Snake's information had escaped me again.

Even Cook was out lugging water. But no Peters. I worked up a case of the suspicions before I recalled why he wasn't around.

Hell. Saucerhead was overdue. I said, "You guys are wasting your time. Just keep it from jumping to the other buildings."

"What the hell you think we're doing, dipshit?"

Chain growled. "If you're not going to help, get the hell out of the way."

Which was just the advice I needed. "I'm going inside to treat these burns." I had a few but didn't know how bad they were. Not too bad, I hoped. I didn't need them distracting me. The cold was bad enough.

I stumbled away. The others didn't pay any attention.

27

I walked straight through to the front of the house, past the dueling champions and all the dead Stantnors. I'd been in that stable longer than I'd thought. Saucerhead was way overdue unless I'd guessed badly about how long it would take to recruit a doctor and jump a couple of fences through hoops.

I stepped out the front door. My burns, not bad, made their presence felt. I hoped that doctor would have something for the sting.

Nothing in sight. "Saucerhead, what's holding you up? How long does it take to twist a guy's arm?"

A few raindrops hit the steps leading to the porch. I glanced at the sky. Old slabs of lead again. I wondered if the Stantnor place ever had any other kind. It was getting to me.

The wind was rising. That wouldn't do the firefighters any good. Maybe their best hope was that the rain wouldn't play around.

It did become a steady fall. Not quite a downpour, but it should help. I guess that took fifteen minutes to develop. The wind started gusting, throwing water onto the porch. I started to retreat. A coach came out of the rain.

That damned Saucerhead. Now it was a hired coach.

It pulled up. People tumbled out. Peters galloped up the steps, followed by a tall, distinguished character whom I presumed to be the doctor. A weasely little character followed him, then Saucerhead and Morley Dotes. I asked Morley, "Where the hell you been? I been trying to find you all morning."

He gave me a funny look. "Home taking care of business."

Saucerhead interrupted, "Let's do it, Garret. This here is Doc Stones." He indicated the weasely guy. Which goes to show you what it's worth, judging by appearances. "He'll get an arm and leg off you for this. That's your fence there. We got an agreement. No names."

"Fine with me. As long as he points a finger. Peters. Let's get upstairs."

Peters wore a puzzled look. "What's happening?"

"Somebody tried to burn the stable down. With me inside. Let's go. Doc, you got anything to take the sting out of burns?"

We moved inside as I asked. Saucerhead asked me, "You want to give him the other arm and leg?"

"What took you so damned long, anyway?" Peters led the way, headed for the stairs.

"Morley. He pooted around finding a doc he thought would look like a fence's partner."

That made sense. "Yeah. I guess I can appreciate that. Morley, I thought you were going to prowl around the house, do the stuff I don't have time to do because I've got to be on stage all the time."

He looked at me funny again, like I was maybe talking too much. So did Peters. Dotes said, "I did what I could, Garrett. But I have a business to run and not a whole lot of time to spend working on the cuff."

"But I heard you come in and go out a couple times."

He stopped. "I roamed around an hour after you hit the sack, didn't find squat, decided I better get back and see if Wedge had robbed me while my back was turned. I didn't go back to your room."

I shuddered. The old cold rats pranced up and down my back. "You didn't?"

"No."

"Oh, my. But I'd swear I even saw you once."

"It wasn't me."

I was sure. I'd gotten up to use the chamberpot. I'd even grumbled a hello and gotten something growled in return. I told him that.

"It wasn't me, Garrett. I went home." Dotes said it in a flat, disturbed voice.

"I'll take your word for it." My voice was just as flat. "So who was it?"

"Shape-changer?"

I'd run into one of those before. I didn't want to do that again. "How? Changers have to kill the people they mimic. Then they absorb their souls, or whatever. And even then they can't always fool people who knew them."

"Yes. And this one had me pat?"

"I was pretty damned tired. There was only one lamp burning. And I just walked through, not paying that much attention. But I'd have sworn it was you."

"I don't like this. It makes me nervous, Garrett. Real nervous."

Me too, yeah boy. All we needed was some villain prancing around able to pretend he was somebody else. That would complicate things real good.

Morley was just concerned about Morley Dotes, not everything else. He had troubles enough in life without having somebody else running around doing dirty deeds in his name and face.

I had a broader perspective on it. If somebody here could fake Morley, he could fake me or anybody else, any time. So none of us could ever be sure who we were dealing with. Which undermined the roots of reality. Some fun coming up.

Morley suggested, "You'd better get out while you still can."

I was tempted. Tempted like I've never been tempted before. But, "I can't. I took the job. If I quit because it's getting tough, it won't be that long before I find some good reason to drop another one. That happens a couple times and I won't get work at all."

He politely refrained from mentioning the fact that I spend most of my energy avoiding work. "Figured you'd say something like that. So. Let's get on with it. I want out of here even if you don't." He started up the final flight of stairs. "You drink much milk, Garrett?"

"No. Beer."

"I sort of figured."

"Why?" The others watched us like we were a road show.

"Not sure what it is about milk. But it's good for the teeth and bones and brain. A man who drinks milk always has a healthy sense of self-preservation. Beer guzzlers get increasingly feeble in that area."

He was dressing up a cautionary message as one of his crackpot dietary theories. That way it was easier to tell me he was afraid I was in way over my head.

Peters said, "I don't know what you're talking about, Garrett. I don't much care. But I do think we ought to get on with it." He stared at the glass at the rear of the house. The glow from the burning stable shone through. He looked like he wanted to rush off and get involved.

"Right. Go get the old man set." I stared at the firelight while the rest moved toward the General's suite.

"Garrett!"

"Coming."

I caught a glimpse of the blonde across the way, behind a pillar. She smiled and looked like she might wave back if I started it.

I growled and headed down the hall.

Her portrait was one I'd saved from the flames. I'd bring it in and ask some questions. And I was, by damn, going to get some answers.

I was getting tired of being nice.

28

Peters moved on into the deeps of the old man's suite. The rest of us waited in the study. I killed time by tossing logs on the fire and exchanging puzzled glances with Morley. Each of us wondered how much the other was pulling his leg.

The General arrived, bundled as though for an expedition to the Arctic. He looked at the fire, at me stirring it around so I could get a few more logs on, beamed approval. "Thank you, Mr. Garrett. Thoughtful of you." He surveyed the crowd. "Who are these people?"

"Mr. Morley Dotes, restaurateur and an associate of mine." Morley gave him a nod.

"Indeed?" The old man seemed startled, like maybe he knew the name. He looked at me hard, reconsidering his estimate of me.

I said, "You've met Mr. Tharpe. The other gentlemen prefer to remain anonymous, but they've agreed to point out your thief."

"Oh." A hollow sound, that. Faced by the imminence, he wasn't that anxious to know. I recalled his instructions: Don't let him evade the truth. He asked, "Where are the others?"

I told Peters to get them. He didn't move till the General agreed. I said, "They're out trying to contain a fire somebody set in the stable."

"A fire? Arson?" He was confused.

The doc and Morley studied him intently.

"Yes, sir. Near as I can figure, whoever killed Bradon was afraid something in the stable could connect him with the murder. The place had been searched. Whoever did it probably thought he didn't have time to do it right so he took second best."

"Oh." Again that hollow sound.

I walked over to the door, peeked out. Nothing out there. "Saucerhead, want to warn us when the mob comes?"

He grunted, came over. I whispered, "Did you rehearse those two?"

He grunted again. He didn't have time to explain. I had to trust his judgment. "General, shall I take the position I did last time? Mr. Tharpe and Mr. Dotes can hold the door."

"I suppose. I suppose." As the fire grew and threw more light, I saw that his color was as bad as it had been the other day.

I took my place. A few minutes later Saucerhead announced, "People coming."

"Let them in but don't let them back out."

"Check."

The doctor retreated into a corner. So did the fence. Morley moved to the side of the door opposite Saucerhead.

They came in looking tired and wary and dispirited. They looked at Morley and Saucerhead like they all thought they'd been caught doing something. Even Peters, and he knew what was happening.

The General said, "Mr. Garrett has some news."

Mr. Garrett looked at the fence. So did Mr. Tharpe, glowering like the man wouldn't get out of the house alive if he didn't point a finger.

He didn't have to. The bad boy gave himself away.

I said, "Somebody's been stealing doodads from around here, about twenty thousand marks' worth. The General wanted to know who. Now we know that, Dellwood. I'm curious why."

He took it pretty well. Maybe he'd figured that being found out was inevitable. "To meet household expenses. There was no other way to raise the money."

The General sputtered through a bad case of not wanting to face the truth. He ranted. His people kept blank faces but I got the feeling their sympathies didn't lie with their employer.

For one second I entertained the possibility that they all wanted to do him in.

Dellwood persisted, "The General provides funds suitable for maintaining a household of ten at the time he left for the Cantard. He won't believe that prices have risen since then. Not one copper has gone into my pocket. Not one has been spent needlessly. Our suppliers refused to extend further credit."

Must be hell to be rich and broke.

The General managed, "You might have told me instead of subjecting me to this humiliation."

"I told you repeatedly, sir. For two years I told you. You had your eyes firmly fixed on the past. You refused to believe that times have changed. I had the choice of doing what I did or allowing you to be hounded by creditors. I chose to shield you. I'll collect my things now." He turned to the door.

Saucerhead and Morley blocked his way. I asked, "General?"

The old man didn't say anything.

"For what it's worth, sir, I believe he's telling the truth."

"Are you calling me a miser?"

"I said nothing of the sort. But you do have that reputation." I was piqued. I've never gone out of my way to cuddle up to a client—of the male persuasion, anyway.

He sputtered some more.

Then he had one of his fits.

For a moment I thought it was a ploy. The others did, too. Maybe he'd cried wolf a few times. Everybody just looked till it was over. Then they all moved in, tripping over each other. I gave Saucerhead the signal to turn the fence loose.

Dellwood led the charge. Nobody hung back. Which did not bode well for my hope that breaking one of the cases within the case would start everything unravelling.

"Back off," I told them. "Give him some air." He was past the worst. "Saucerhead, let Dellwood go, too."

Dellwood managed his exit with considerable dignity. I reflected on the fact that my pay, and Saucerhead's, and everyone else's, was likely being financed by his efforts. I glanced at Cook. She'd told me the old man didn't have a pot to pee in. Here he was, living on his principal without even realizing it.

Was some other helpful soul trying to salvage the estate by hurrying an incompetent, tightwad manager to his reward?

The General got himself under control. "I shan't thank you for what you've done, Mr. Garrett, though I asked for it. Dellwood. Where's Dellwood?"

"He's gone, sir."

"Get him back. He can't leave. What'll I do without him?"

"I have no thoughts on the subject, General. I think we've accomplished all we can here."

"Good. Yes. You're right. Leave me. But get Dellwood back here."

"Everybody out. Peters, you'd better stay. Kaid? Morley, Saucerhead, I want to talk to you." I scooted out first.

29

I caught Dellwood in his quarters. He hadn't bothered to close his door. He was stuffing things into bags. "Come to make sure I don't take the family jewels?"

"I came to tell you the old man wants you to stay."

"I've spent most of my life attending his wants. Enough is enough. It'll be a relief being my own man." He lied. "A man's loyalty will only stretch so far."

"You're upset. You did what you had to do and it brought you trouble. Nobody holds it against you. Not even me."

"Bull. He'll hold it against me the rest of his life. That's the kind of man he is. Whatever my reasons, I rubbed his nose in something. He doesn't forgive, no matter who was right."

"But—"

"I know him. Give me credit for that."

I did. "You walk, you lose everything."

"The bequest never meant much to me. I'm not poor, Mr. Garrett. I had few expenses while I was in service. I saved my money and I invested it well. I don't need his bequest to survive."

"Your choice." I didn't move.

He stopped throwing things into bags and looked at me. "What?"

"The General didn't just hire me to find out who was kyping the family trophies. He also wanted me to find out who's trying to kill him."

He sneered. "Kill him? Nobody's trying to kill him. That's just his imagination at work."

"So was theft when I arrived. Except to you. He was right about that and I think he's right about this."

"Bull. Who'd profit?"

"Good question. I don't think the estate has anything to do with it. I can't supply another motive, though. Yet." I looked at him expectantly. He didn't say anything.

"Any friction with anybody? Any time, ever?"

"I can't give you what you want, Mr. Garrett. We've all had our troubles with the General—none of them the kind you kill over. Matters of discipline, that's all."

"None of these people are inclined to hold grudges?"

"Chain. He's a big, stupid farm boy gone to fat at the hips and between the ears. He can hold a grudge forever, but he's never had one against the General. If you'll excuse me, sir?"

"Not yet. You've known this moment was coming since I got here, haven't you?"

"I wasn't surprised you found me out. I *was* startled that you found the man who bought from me. Will that be all?"

"No. Who killed Hawkes and Snake?"

"I wouldn't know. I expect you'll find out. You're a first-class finder-outer."

"It's what I do. You didn't perchance try to discourage me when you decided I could cause you trouble, did you?"

"Sir?"

"There have been three attempts on my life since I arrived. I wondered if you'd thought you could cover your tracks—"

"That's not my way. I made it through a Marine career without killing anyone. I have no intention of starting now. I told you, I have nothing to lose here."

Maybe. And maybe he was just a convincing liar.

I shrugged. "For what it's worth, I don't think you did wrong and I don't feel that proud of rooting you out."

"I bear you no ill will. You were only the agency by which the inevitable arrived. But I would like to get on the road before dark."

"You won't reconsider? I don't think the old man will last without you."

"Kaid can handle him. He should've been all along, anyway."

"Do you know who the blonde woman is?" He had nothing to lose by telling me now.

"A figment of your imagination, I suspect. There's no blonde woman here. No one but you has seen her."

"Bradon did. He painted her portrait."

That stopped him cold. "He did?"

"He did."

He believed me. He didn't get much push behind his "Snake was crazy."

I was pretty sure he knew nothing about any blonde. Which made her that much more interesting an enigma.

I moved out of the doorway, indicating he was

free to go. I said, "You can't tell me anything that might keep somebody else from getting killed?"

"No. I'd tell you if I could."

He picked up his bags. I suggested, "Catch a ride with my associates when they go."

He wanted to tell me to go to hell. He didn't. "Thank you." It was raining and those bags were heavy.

I asked, "One more thing. What happened to Tyler and the draug from out front?"

"Ask Peters. I don't know. My duties confined me to the house."

"The draug that tried to get in the back isn't accounted for. It didn't go back to the swamp. Where could it hide out during the day?" Assuming, like story draugs, that it didn't dare hazard daylight.

"In the outbuildings. I really must go, Mr. Garrett."

"All right. Thanks for talking to me."

He headed out, back stick-straight, unapologetic. He'd done what had to be done. He wasn't ashamed. He wasn't going to be talked out of leaving, either.

Another one down, I reflected.

Now there were six heirs. The cut for the minority people was up near a half million apiece.

Morley, Saucerhead, and the doctor awaited me beside the fountain. I didn't approach in any hurry. I was trying to figure out how to launch a draug hunt.

Cook came out as Dellwood headed for the front door. They went into the entry hall arguing. She didn't want him to go, either.

30

I joined Morley and the others. "What's the verdict?"

Morley shrugged. "He didn't shake enough or have trouble enough talking for it to be what I thought. He show any of those symptoms earlier?"

"Some shaking. No real trouble talking. What about the fit?"

"I don't know. Ask the doc."

I did. He said, "I don't quite know. I should've had a closer look and a chance to interview the patient. But from where I stood it looked like you need an exorcist more than a doctor."

"A what?"

Morley was as startled as I was. I'd never seen his eyes bug before. The remark had caught him from the blind side.

"An exorcist. A demonologist. Maybe a necromancer. Possibly all three. Though the first step should be a physical exam to make sure I'm not imagining things."

"Start over. You've got me all turned around."

"Between us, Mr. Dotes and I have a comprehensive knowledge of poisons. We know of none that produce the combination of symptoms the man shows. Not without affecting him more dramatically, physically, leaving him unable to control his speech and extremities—if he stayed alive at all. Disease is more probable than poison. Who knows what he brought home? I spent eight years down there. I saw a lot of strange diseases, though nothing quite like this. Is he taking any medication?''

"Are you kidding? He'd die first." I had a thought. "How about malaria?" I'd been one lucky Marine. I'd never contracted malaria. "Or some kind of yellow fever?"

"I thought of that. A virulent strain of malaria, with massive quinine treatments, might produce most of the symptoms he shows. Tainted medication might account for the rest. But you said he'd die before accepting medication. I really must know his medical history before I hazard a guess."

"Why that business about an exorcist?"

"My chief suspicion lies in the supernatural realm. Several varieties of malign spirit could produce the symptoms we see. My advice would be to examine his past. You might find something there to explain what's happening. You might also look for an origin in unfriendly witchcraft. An enemy may have sent a spirit against him."

Black Pete showed up in time to catch most of the discussion. I asked, "You make anything of that? The General have enemies who'd off him that way?"

He shook his head. "The answer is here, Garrett. I'm sure. He doesn't have enemies who'd want to kill him. The worst ones he does have are the kind who'd send somebody like your friend." He twitched a hand toward Morley.

"There's no sorcerer around here. Unless you count Bradon, who's gone. Doctor, could an amateur necromancer have sicced something on him, say accidentally, that would stick after the spirit-master died?"

"An amateur? I doubt it. Somebody really potent, maybe. If they stuck around themselves, as a ghost. Hatred is the usual force animating spirits that devour a man from within. And I mean hatred strong enough to bend the laws of nature. Hatred that wants its object to suffer for all eternity. But I'm no expert. Which is why I suggested a demonologist, an exorcist, a necromancer. You must discover the nature of the spirit, then banish it. Or raise it up, find out what animates its hatred and appease it."

Peters said, "This is crazy, Garrett. The General *never* made that kind of enemy."

"We're talking possibilities. The doc says the whole thing could be physical. He needs to do a hands-on physical exam. And he needs a detailed medical history. What're the chances?"

He looked at me, at the doctor, glanced at Morley and Saucerhead. "Better than you think." His voice turned hard. "The old bastard can only threaten so much. We don't have to give him a choice. I'll be back in five minutes." He strode toward the kitchen.

Morley settled on the fountain surround, in the shadow of the dragon's wing. "Now what?"

"Let's wait. He'll talk to Cook. If she goes along, you'll get to look at Stantnor." Cook might not be mother to the world but she was queen of the Stantnor household. "Doctor. Can you suggest any experts who might help?"

"Let's see if we get to examine the patient. If I find no physical cause, I'll provide referrals. They won't come cheaply, though."

"Does anybody but me?"

Morley had a big yuk. "This is the man who paid cash for a house with the take from one case."

"And for every one of those, I have fifty where I give Saucerhead half my fee to get them to pay up. You know anything about the art world?"

"That's a change of subject. I know something about everything. I need to. What do you need?"

"Say I discovered an unknown painter genius whose work deserves display. Who would I see to get things moving?"

He shrugged, grinned. "Got me. Now if you had some hot old masters I could help. I know people who know morally flexible collectors. If you have something like you're talking about, you should see your friend with the brewery."

"Weider?"

"He's got fingers in all the cultural pies. Honorary director of this and that. He has the contacts. You *don't* have some old masters, do you?" He glanced around. I'm sure he'd been inventorying potential plunder.

"You won't find anything here but portraits of old guys with whiskers who scowl a lot, all painted by people you never heard of."

"I noticed the welcoming committee. I wondered how long it takes the Stantnors to train their young not to smile."

"Might be hereditary. I've never seen Jennifer do more than fake it."

"Your buddy's coming."

Peters was coming from the kitchen under a full spread of sail. I knew what he'd say before he said it. He said it anyway. "We don't give the old man a vote."

"He'll cut you out of his will."

"Ask me if I give a damn. Let's go." But he hung back, gave me a look that said he wanted a private word. I let the others move upstairs a flight.

"What?"

"That crack about the will. In all the excitement I plain forgot to tell you before. The copy the General burned wasn't the only one. He always made two of every document. Sometimes three."

"Oh?" Interesting. That meant nothing had changed, if the killer knew. "How many are there?"

"One for sure. He gave it to me to give to you. Like you asked. I put it in my quarters, then got distracted till I was talking to Cook and she said the same thing you did, about getting cut out."

"It wasn't that important to you?"

"No. I did you a favor, then forgot to carry through. Till it hit me what that copy could mean."

"It could mean the killer won't back off. If he knows about it. Who knows?"

"Dellwood and Kaid. They were there. And everybody else knows the General made copies of documents."

"Where'd you put it? Give me your key. I'll grab it now. You go ahead and get after the old man."

He gave me a nasty look. I knew what he was thinking. I wanted to toss his quarters. I told him, "I don't think you've got anything to hide."

"You're a bastard, Garrett. Put me in a spot where I'm damned whatever I do."

"You do have something to hide?"

He glared. "No!"

"Then get it yourself. I'll take your word." I recalled the fire, for which he could have been responsible. I hung in there, taking a chance on my guts. "But hurry."

He gave me the key. "In the drawer of my writing table."

Cook came rumbling up, the stair shuddering to her tread. "We going to do this?" she demanded. "Or we going to gossip?"

Smart woman, Cook. The old man couldn't dismiss her. If she went in and sat on him, all he could do was cuss and take it. "Thanks," I told her.

She gave me half a sneer. "What for? He's my baby, ain't he?"

"Yeah." I watched them hurry to overtake the others. The General would be in the worst tactical position of his life. He couldn't do anything to Morley, Saucerhead, the doc, or Cook. And he'd be damned stupid if he did anything about Peters. If he ran Black Pete off, he'd be damned near out of help. He had to think survival in more than personal terms. He had to think about keeping the estate in shape.

I suspected its value was dropping fast.

I fingered Peters's key, glanced around. I had the feeling I was being watched, but I saw nobody. My blonde again, I thought. I wondered where the others were. At work, presumably.

A vampirous spirit, eh? On top of draugs? What a lovely place to live.

31

Something wasn't right. Black Pete's door wasn't locked. He wasn't the sloppy type.

It worked before, so I grabbed a shield and stormed inside. And didn't find anything this time, either.

The damned place was haunted by practical jokers. I tossed the shield against the doorframe, put up my head-knocker, went to the writing table. The room was a mirror image of my sitting room. I sat down at an identical table.

I guess I heard a sole scuff the carpet. I started to turn, to duck. That's all I did, started.

Something hit me like a monument falling. I saw shooting stars. I think I howled. I lurched forward. My face met the tabletop. It wasn't a friendly meeting.

It's pretty hard to knock somebody out. You either don't hit hard enough, in which case your victim gets after you, or you hit him too hard and he croaks. If you have any idea what you're doing, you don't bash him up top the head. Unless you want to smash his skull.

This blow was aimed at my skull. I moved that much. It hit the side of my neck and bounced off my shoulder. It didn't put me out—not more than ninety-nine percent. It paralyzed me. For half a minute I was vaguely aware of a shape in motion. *Then* the lights went out.

Got to stay away from the hard stuff, I thought as I came around. Getting too old for it. The hangover isn't worth it.

I thought I was slumped over my desk at home. The truth dawned as I tried to get up. I saw unfamiliar surroundings. My head spun. I fell, banged my jaw off the edge of the table, curled up on the floor, and dumped Cook's lunch. When I tried to move, the heaves started again.

Sometime during the fun somebody ran past, headed for the door. All I saw was a flash of brown. I didn't much care.

Concussion, I thought. That scared me. I'd seen guys with their brains scrambled after getting hit on the head. I'd seen them paralyzed. I'd seen them go to sleep and never wake up.

Got to stay awake, Garrett. Got to stay awake. That's what the docs say. Get up, Garrett. To hell with the heaves. Take charge, Garrett. Make the flesh obey the will.

Trouble was, there wasn't much will left.

After a while I got my knees under me and crawled to the door. I fell down a few times during the trek. But the exercise did me good. I arrived so chipper, I was afraid I wasn't going to die. I worked up so much ambition that I swung the door open and moved out a yard before I collapsed and passed out again.

Gentle, delicate fingers slid lightly over my face, feeling my features the way a blind woman once did.

I'd turned over somehow. I cracked one eyelid a millionth of an inch.

My sweetheart in white had come to succor me. At least she looked concerned. Her lips moved but I didn't hear anything.

Panic. I'd heard of guys who'd lost their hearing, too.

She jumped away. Not that she needed to. I was in no shape to run down a brigand snail. More, Black Pete's door had closed on my legs. I was caught like a mouse. I managed a feeble "Don't go. Please."

The investigative mind was at work. It wanted to know.

She came back. She settled onto her knees, resumed massaging my head. "Are you badly hurt?" Her voice was the ghost of a whisper. She sounded concerned. She looked concerned.

"Only in my heart. You keep running away." We investigator types are tough. We keep our eye on the prime objective. "You're the loveliest woman I've ever seen."

That put a light in her eyes. Strange how women like to be told they're pretty. Strange like a rock falling when you drop it. She even smiled for a hundredth of a second.

"Who are you?" I thought about telling her I loved her, but that seemed premature. I'd give it ten more minutes.

She didn't tell me. She just massaged my forehead and temples and sang something so softly I couldn't make out the words.

Who was I to question the will of the gods? I closed my eyes and let it happen.

The song got a little louder. A lullaby. A hush-my-love kind of thing. Fine by me. The hell with business. This was the life.

Something brushed my lips, light as falling eiderdown, warm. I cracked my eye. She was an inch away, smiling.

Yeah.

Then everything drained out of her face. She jumped up and fled. Bam! Before I overcame inertia and turned my head, she was gone.

Feet pounded up the hallway, businesslike, then hurriedly. "Garrett! What happened?" Peters dropped to his knees. He wasn't nearly as attractive as his predecessor.

I managed to croak, "Somebody in your room. Bopped me on my bean."

He jumped up and shoved inside. I had smarts enough left to drag my legs out before the door closed. That's all I did. Seemed like a good day's work.

Peters bounded out. "They tore the place apart." He had something in his hand. "Here's the will. What else could they have been after?"

"Probably was that."

He scowled at me. "Did you have to puke all over?"

"Yeah. A man's got to do what a man's got to do."

"Why didn't he get it, if that's what he wanted?"

"I fell over the desk. He couldn't get at it without moving me and maybe having me wake up. Lit out when I did start coming to. Who could have heard us talking?"

"Couldn't have been Cook or Kaid. They were upstairs with the old man. Wayne's out burying Snake, Hawkes, and Tyler."

I let him help me into a sitting position. "Where were they?"

"In the wellhouse. It's cooler in there. What difference does that make?"

"That leaves Chain, doesn't it? Or Dellwood, if he doubled back."

"Chain's supposed to be out keeping an eye on what's left of the fire and trying to salvage something from the stable."

"Wasn't any ghost. And it wasn't a draug. Did we find the third draug?"

"Nobody's had time to look."

"He'll find us, then." I lifted a hand. He helped me up. Between him and the wall, they managed to keep me upright. "What was the verdict on the old man?" My head hurt so much, I no longer felt my burns. The old silver lining.

"They were looking for you to tell you."

"You tell me."

"He fired me and Kaid, too. We told him to go to hell, we're not going anywhere."

"I guess you aren't going to tell me."

"I don't want to say it. Not something that's easy to believe."

That told me enough. But I let him help me downstairs, to the fountain, where I perched on the fountain surround and tried to work out which way was up till Morley and the others showed. I said, "I take it that I'm shopping for a demonotogist."

"Don't look at me like that," Morley said. "I didn't do it."

"You look spooked."

"Spooks spook me, Garrett. Even a vampire or a werewolf, I can do something about. I can't get ahold of a spook."

"Yeah." He didn't want to believe we had a haunt here. I wasn't quite ready to buy it. It would be easier to swallow without a legacy at stake. It wouldn't be the first fake ghost used to cover a little bloodletting.

It sure wasn't any spook who offed Hawkes and Bradon. No spook tried to trap me, ax me, burn me, knock a hole in my head.

Everybody stood around looking at me like I was in charge. So I said, "My head's killing me." And, "Morley, you want to stay over tonight? Give me a hand?"

"I was afraid you'd ask."

Just his sweet-natured way of saying yes.

"Cash money," I promised.

"How are you going to get cash when that old man doesn't have any?"

I didn't tell him I'd grabbed it off going in, though the expenses had about devoured their allowance. "I'll figure something. How'd he take it?"

"He wasn't pleased. To put it mildly."

I looked at the doctor. "You couldn't find a physical cause?" Oh, please. Please?

The weasel shook his head. "Not saying it isn't something I don't recognize. Or a combination. But bring in a demonologist. Hell, I'll send one. Eliminate the mysterious first. If there's no supernatural cause, send for me. Be an interesting challenge."

Morley grinned slyly. "You two work it right, you could have careers here. Him trying to root out an unknown disease and you trying to find a killer who's smarter than you are."

I grumbled, "My part's easy. I just stay alive till there's only one suspect left." My head was killing me. That didn't do wonders for my temper. "Doc, you got something for a headache?"

"What happened?"

I told him.

He insisted on examining me and offering the usual advice about concussions. Maybe he wasn't a pure thief. I have a low opinion of professionals, notably doctors and lawyers, supported by experience.

He gave me a dose of the old standby, syrup heavily laced with nasty-tasting stuff boiled out of the inner bark of willow branches. With that perking in my stomach I decided to get on with getting on. "Peters, it'll be suppertime soon. These guys might be hungry. Square it with Cook, if they want to eat. I'm going to drop in on the General."

Peters grunted, asked if anybody wanted supper. Saucerhead and the doctor were all for that. And Morley was staying anyway.

As I climbed the stairs, I recalled that I'd told Dellwood he should ride into town in the coach. Was he out there waiting, freezing with the coachman?

It was still raining. I felt for Wayne and Chain, too. Though Chain not so much. I had him. All I needed to do was push him into a box and put a bow on him.

"Throw him out," Stantnor rasped at Kaid, when I invited myself in.

Kaid eyed me. "I don't believe he'll let me, sir." He said it with a straight face. There was a twinkle in his eye. He turned to the fire to hide a smile.

I asked, "Did you hear the diagnosis, General?"

"Mr. Garrett. I didn't employ you to interfere in my life. I employed you to find a thief."

"And a killer. And a would-be killer who wants your scalp. And that implies that part of the job is to keep you alive. And to do that I need to know how they're trying to kill you. The assumption was poison. The assumption was wrong."

He appeared surprised. Maybe they hadn't told him. Maybe he'd become so obnoxious, they'd just walked.

"Mr. Dotes is an expert on poisons. Likewise the doctor, who's also an expert on tropical diseases." Could it hurt to exaggerate? "They say you're not being poisoned, unless it's a poison so exotic they've never heard of it. And you're not suffering from any known disease, though the doctor says you're anemic and jaundiced. Have you had malaria, General?"

I think he was secretly touched that people cared enough to look out for him in spite of himself. "Yes. Hard to avoid it in the islands."

"Bad?"

"No."

"You taking quinine on the sly? The doctor says impure quinine might explain some of your problems."

"No! I won't . . ." He suffered one of his spasms. Was it his heart?

It was a minor one. He'd begun to recover before Kaid reached him. He croaked, "No, Mr. Garrett. No medication. I'd refuse if it was offered."

"I thought so. But I had to make sure before I tell you what they think."

"Which is?" He was coming back fast.

"You're haunted."

"Eh?" That blindsided him. He looked at Kaid. Kaid just looked baffled.

"Your problem is supernatural. Your enemy is a ghost. Or somebody who can send a spirit against you. Peters says you don't have that kind of enemies. The doctor says look at your past for somebody."

I wouldn't have believed it possible, but his color worsened dramatically. He damned near turned gray.

There *was* something. Some dark past moment unknown to anyone else, so dreadful someone might reach out from the grave to restore the balance. Hell, a place like the Stantnor shack wouldn't be complete without a horror in its past, without a curse.

"We'd better talk about it," I said. "We'll have to hire experts." I gave Kaid a meaningful look. The old man wouldn't want to confess ancient evils in front of a crowd. "A demonologist. An exorcist. Possibly a medium or necromancer to communicate with the spirit." Kaid was as thick as a brick. He didn't move.

The General said nothing till he was sure he'd say only what he wanted to be heard. And that was, "Get out, Garrett."

"When you're ready to talk, then."

"Get out. Leave me alone. Hell, get out of my house. Get out of my life . . ."

He had another fit. This was a big one. Kaid yelled, "Get that doctor up here!" His expression lacked any forgiveness for having gotten the old man so excited.

Strange people, every one.

32

I joined Cook in the kitchen. We were alone. "Can you use a hand?"

"Come to try sweet-talking me out of something, eh? I see right through you, boy. You ought to know by now I don't run my mouth. I don't tell nobody nothing that ain't none of their business."

"Of course." I rolled up my sleeves, eyed the heap of dirty stuff distastefully. Not much I hate more than washing dishes. But I stole a pot of hot water off the stove, prepared a sink, put more water on to heat, dug in. Ten minutes of silence passed. I waited till I felt her curiosity becoming palpable.

"You were up there when they looked at the General. What did you think?"

"I think that croaker is as crooked as the General says." She didn't sound convinced. She sounded worried.

"Know what he thinks is wrong?"

"I know what he said. He's crazy if he believes it. Ain't no haunts around here."

"Three draugs."

She grunted. There lay the core of her doubt. If

those draugs hadn't come, she wouldn't have given the doctor's idea a glance.

"People keep telling me, the General doesn't have enemies of the killing kind. And there's no incentive here for anyone to hurry him along, despite the size of the estate."

"What'll be left after he lets it wither. I swear, his damnfool sickness has infected the whole place." Her voice was weak. She wasn't the woman she'd been. Things were going on inside her head. She had no attention to spare.

"If nobody from today wants to kill him, to torment him with slow death and the hell between when he passes, who in his past might? My gut feeling is, it goes back to before his move to the Cantard."

She grunted and threw utensils around and didn't say anything.

"What happened? The only trauma I know of is his wife's death. Could that have something to do with it? Her parents . . . Jennifer says she thinks they were a firelord and stormwarden but she doesn't know who. Is this a legacy from them? A delayed curse?"

She still didn't have squat to say.

"Were they involved in the Blue cabal that went after Kenrick III?"

"You put a lot together out of nothing, boy."

"That's what I do. I get paid for it. I think the grandparents *were* involved. I think Jennifer's mother came here partly to hide from reprisals if the plot failed. Lucky her. It did. And Kenrick devoured everyone remotely related to it. I wonder if the doctor who administered an incorrect drug was on the royal payroll. Maybe Jennifer survived only because he couldn't murder a newborn."

"You do put it together."

I kept quiet, hoping she'd fill the vacuum.

I washed, set stuff out to dry. There was enough work for me to make me a new career when I got tired of the old one. I was tempted.

"The missus's mother called herself Charon Light. Her daddy was Nightmare Blue."

"One fun-loving guy." Nightmare Blue had put the Blue plot together. He'd been as mean-spirited and vicious as they came. The story was that only the threatened defection of key conspirators forced him to confine his scheme to the King. He'd wanted to scrub Kenrick's whole house. The bad blood between the men stemmed from a mysterious childhood incident.

Charon Light, supposedly, was as innocent as a wife could be. She'd apparently been ignorant of the plot till the last hours. There was reason to suspect she'd been responsible for its failure, in the penultimate moment warning the King.

We'll never know—unless someone raises the dead to ask. None of those people survived. I doubt anybody would try. Raising a sorcerer is a fool's game—unless you're a more powerful sorcerer.

"Eleanor's mother brought her here to hide her?"

Cook grunted, having second thoughts about talking. She kept her peace for a few minutes. I got more hot water.

"Her mother brought her. In the middle of the night, it was. A devil's own night, thunder and lightning and the wind howling like all the lost souls. She was some distant relative of the Stantnors' was Charon Light. Don't recall her born name. Something

Fen. She brought the child in so frightened, she wet herself. As bad as Jennifer, she was, never been out of her own house before. Such a pretty young thing, too."

"Like Jennifer."

"She was more retiring than Jenny. Jenny can work herself up. She's an actress, our Jenny. She puts on a role like a dress, that child. Not young mistress Eleanor. Scared of her own shadow, that one."

I grunted this time.

"The old General and Charon Light, they worked it out right here in this kitchen. I was here, serving tea. They'd marry the child to young Will, in name only, so she'd be safe. This was only a couple days before the storm broke. Kenrick couldn't do nothing to upset the old General. He was the only rock between Karenta and defeat in the Cantard in those days."

"The war hadn't meant much to me back then. My father had been dead for years, killed down there, and I wasn't old enough to worry about going. But I did recall that, at about that time, Karenta's fortunes had been at low ebb and there'd been talk about the elder Stantnor being the only man who could handle the Venageti of the day."

"You want the benefit of my suspicion, I think Charon Light was going to deal. Going to sell the plot for immunity. I don't know if that's how she went. She didn't survive."

I told her, "I'm starting to get confused. I thought Jennifer was born about then. And she had an older brother."

"Half brother. His mother was the General's first wife. Have-to wedding when he was sixteen. Daughter of a serving woman. But you don't need to know that."

"I need to know everything if I'm going to make sense of what's happening. Hidden things kill. What happened to the first wife?"

"They stayed married till the boy was old enough for tutors and nannies. Then he put her aside. The old General sent the family away."

"Hard feelings involved?"

"Plenty. But the old General bought them off. He reminded young Will every day. Especially if he spent a night out wenching. A terror, he was, when he was a lad. Obsessed, you might say." She didn't sound like she'd thought him an amusing rake. He didn't sound like somebody I'd have liked.

For fifteen minutes I tried to get her to tell me more. I got only enough to guess the young Stantnor was a crude ass, a driven philanderer whose life had gained direction and meaning only after his permanent move to the Cantard.

"So he wasn't a nice guy. Who from those days hated him enough to—"

"No." There was no equivocation there. "That's life, Garrett. The hurt don't hang on. Everybody does stupid things when they're young."

Some don't ever stop.

"Everybody grows out of them. You don't laugh at them when you look back, but you don't take a killing grudge to your grave, neither."

I don't know. The Stantnors seemed pretty skewed. If that extended to their circle, someone in contact might hold a grudge over something normal people would call bad luck.

"Then you tell me. Who's haunting him?"

She stopped working, looked at me. She'd remembered something she hadn't thought about in years. For a moment she teetered on the brink of telling me. Then she shook her head. Her face closed down. "No. It wasn't that way."

"What wasn't?"

"Nothing. Some cruel gossip. Nothing to do with us today."

"You'd better tell me. It might have some bearing."

"I don't repeat no lies about no one. Wouldn't have nothing to do with this, nohow."

I got my third pot of hot water. I was tearing them up. I bet she hadn't seen so many clean dishes in years. I'm good for something. Can't keep people from killing each other, but I'm a wiz at washing dishes. Might be time to consider a career change.

After a while, she said, "What goes around comes around. He sure fell for Missus Eleanor. She was his goddess."

We all want what we're not supposed to have. I tried an encouraging grunt. When that didn't get any response I tried a direct question. She said, "I think I done talked too much already. I think I done said things I shouldn't have said to no outsider."

I doubted that. I thought she'd weighed every word and had told me exactly what she wanted me to know. She'd give me another ration when she thought I was ready.

"I hope you know what you're doing. I'd bet there're things in your head that could save lives."

Maybe I pressed a touch too hard there. She didn't have to be told what she already knew. She resented it. She gave me a dirty look and clammed up till dinnertime. Then she only growled and gave orders.

33

After supper, having finally gotten the doctor and Saucerhead off, Morley and I headed for my suite. As we climbed the stairs, I said, "I guess old Dellwood got tired of waiting." He'd abandoned the coach hours earlier, according to the coachman, who wasn't pleased with his own lot. It hadn't occurred to anyone to ask him in out of the cold.

Morley belched. "That woman tried to poison me. That mess wasn't fit to feed a hog."

I chuckled. He'd made only one oblique negative comment and had gotten invited to cook his own meals.

His presence didn't thrill the natives. His charm, stoked to a white heat, had been wasted on Jennifer. His feelings were hurt. He wasn't used to being looked at like something from the underside of a rock.

They didn't know who and what he was, only that he was somebody who had invaded their weird little world. Me, I'm not such a sensitive guy.

"A lovely bunch, Garrett. Truly lovely. The girl should work at an icehouse. Where do you find these people?"

"They find me. People who aren't troubled don't need me."

He grunted. There was a lot of that going around. "I understand that."

I suspect his clients are weirder than mine. But he doesn't have to deal with them on an extended basis.

I checked the telltales at the door. There'd been no sloppy visitors. We stepped inside. I said, "I'm going to take a nap. I had a hard night last night. Don't turn into a spook again."

He gave me a sour grin. "Not this time." He started unwinding a piece of cord he'd scrounged up while I was helping Cook clear supper dishes.

"What's that for?"

"To measure with. You say somebody's getting in and out without using the door, there's got to be a way." He measured off a foot of cord, tied a knot, folded the cord, tied another knot. Not a perfect ruler but it would do.

"I was going to do that myself. When I got time."

"You never get time for detail work, Garrett. You're too busy bulling around, trying to make things happen. What do you expect tonight?"

I'd hinted that we could expect some excitement. "I figure that one draug will come back. What else, who knows? Getting so I think anything can happen here. While you're fiddling around, think of a way to get Chain to give himself away."

"The fat guy with the garbage mouth?"

"That's him."

"He the baddie?"

"He's the only one I can line up who had opportunity with Hawkes and Bradon and the attempts on me."

"Turn you into bait. Catch him in the act."

"Thanks a bunch. He's screwed it up three times already. Maybe four. How many shots should I give him?"

"Take your nap. You're safe. Morley's here."

"That's not the comfort you think it should be." I went into the bedroom, shucked my clothes, and slithered in between the sheets. There was something sinful about being naked in such comfort.

For about thirty seconds I listened to Morley putter, measuring and talking to himself while rain tippy-tapped on the windows. Then the lights went out.

The lights never came on. Not quite.

But there were fires to light the night. Well, there was the threat of fire, anyway.

I woke up no longer alone. My blonde friend was back. Checking my head, touching my face, all that. This time she didn't move fast enough. But she was leaning way over, off balance, and I didn't think before I grabbed. I got her wrist and gave her a come-hither tug. She fell on top of me.

It was dark. She'd have been invisible if she'd been a brunette wearing dark clothing. Still, from four inches her face was visible. She wore a sort of smile, like she wanted to look kittenish and playful. The rest of her couldn't fake it. She shook like she was terrified.

"Talk to me," I whispered. "Tell me who you are." I put an arm around her, caressed the back of her neck. Her hair felt fine as spider silk, light as down. I did it to keep her from getting away, but it took only about four seconds for me to start having trouble keeping my mind on business.

She kissed me instead of answering me.

Man, oh, man. It had the kick of straight grain

alcohol. It got me repeating mantras just to remember who I was.

Shaking like she was running naked through a hailstorm, she turned up the heat. She worked her way under the covers. This was what the old man needed to keep him warm. Boy, could he save on firewood.

Then I lost my mantra and kissed her back. About twenty seconds later she forgot about shivering.

Morley pounded the door. "Hey! Garrett! You going to nap all night?"

I sat up so sudden I made myself dizzy. I felt around. Just Garrett, all by his lonesome. What? I've got a vivid imagination and a rich fantasy life, but . . .

"Bring a light in here."

"What about your booby trap?"

What about it? "It's not set."

Morley found me on the edge of the bed draped in a sheet, looking croggled and feeling four times as croggled as I looked. "What happened?"

"You're not going to believe it."

He didn't. "I never left the other room. Well, only long enough to use the pot. Nobody could've gotten past. You had a dream."

Maybe. But, damn! "I could use more dreams like that. If it was. I don't think so. I've never had one like that."

"Man gets on in years, he starts living his adventures in his head." He grinned a big one full of pointy elf teeth.

"Let's don't start. I'm too flustered to keep up my end. You find anything? What time is it?"

"Yes. Your cloak closet is two thirds as big as it should be. It's about midnight. The witching hour."

"I could probably make it through the night without cracks like that." I got up, dragged the bedclothes with me.

Morley got a funny look, stepped over, picked something up.

It was the red belt my blonde always wore, even in Snake's painting.

He looked at me. I looked at him. I maybe smiled a little. "Not mine," I told him.

"Maybe we ought to get the hell out of here, Garrett."

I pulled my clothes on. I couldn't think what to say. I agreed, mostly. Finally, I just muttered, "You ever back out on a job once you took it?"

He got him another funny look and said, "Yes. Once."

I couldn't picture that. That wasn't Morley Dotes. He delivered. He wouldn't back down from the kingpin or from a nest of vampires. I'd seen that with my own eyes. "I don't believe it. What were you up against? A herd of thunder-lizards?"

"Not exactly."

He didn't like talking about his work. I dropped it. "Let's look at that closet."

The situation had him more spooked than he let on. He said, "A man hired me without telling me anything about the mark, just where he'd be at a certain time. I had the biggest surprise of my life when I got there."

I opened the closet door. "All right. I'll bite."

"You were the mark."

I turned slowly. For about ten seconds I had no idea where I stood. Had we reached a moment I'd prayed would never come?

"Easy. That was six months ago. Forget it. I wasn't going to mention it."

He wouldn't have unless he'd gotten so rattled most bets were off. I tried to recall what I'd been working on back then. Nothing significant. One missing person thing that had smelled from the start, but that had petered out when I found the missing guy dead.

"I owe you one."

"Forget it. I shouldn't have mentioned it."

"You forget it. Let's see where the missing space went." I thought I got it. That missing person thing had smelled because I'd thought there was more to it than the client would admit. She'd seemed vindictive when nothing in her story indicated a reason. Looking for a man she'd claimed was an associate of her late husband.

Pieces toppled into place belatedly. The guy she was looking for could have been blackmailing her over the husband's demise. She hadn't needed me once she knew the guy was dead.

The guy might have hired Morley if he'd heard I was after him.

Hell with it. Water under the bridge. Nothing to do with what we were into now.

But I owed Morley. That more than balanced the stunt with the coffin full of vampire.

"On this side," Morley said.

It was obvious once you knew it was there. On the right the closet was twenty inches smaller than it should be. "Give me the light."

I examined the wall inside. Nothing out of the way. No door, nothing to release one or open one. "Has to be out there somewhere."

I went out, examined the wall, looked for some hidden device, cunningly disguised, like those I'd seen before. I didn't find any such beast.

"I got it," Morley said.

He tipped a two-foot section of wainscotting outward like a kitchen flour bin. Bam. No sign it was there when it was in place. "Clever," he said. "Every secret gizmo I ever saw leaves marks on the floor or something if it's used much." The section didn't quite drop to the floor. A leather strap kept it from falling all the way.

We eyed each other. I said, "Well?"

He grinned. "We can either stand here and stare at it or we can do something. I vote we do something."

"After you, my man."

"Oh, no. I'm just the hired help. I hand the knight his lance when he's ready to charge the Black Baron. When I'm in a real helpful mood, I polish a few rust spots off his armor. But I don't stomp into traps for him."

"I love you too, boy." He was right. It was my game to play.

Didn't hurt to try, though.

I got another lamp, made sure both were full, started to crawl into the opening. "Stay close."

"Right behind you, boss. All the way."

"Wait." I backed out.

"Now what?"

"Equipment." It seemed like a good time to arm up. Just in case.

Morley watched me ferret stuff out, grinned when he saw the colored bottles. "I wondered if you kept those."

"Smart man never throws anything away. Might come in handy someday." Loaded for thunder-lizard,

I returned to the passageway. This time I kept going. Morley had less trouble in there, being a foot shorter and a half ton lighter. I kept banging my head. The passage ran straight ahead fifteen feet. It ran under the counter in the dressing room.

We emerged in a two-foot-wide dead space behind the bedroom and dressing room. It was claustrophobic in there. It was dusty and cobwebby, too, and there was nothing to be seen but studs, lathing, and plaster. The wall at my back was identical. It was the wall of the suite next to mine.

There were peepholes. Of course. A couple for the dressing room and three for the bedroom. The thought that I might have been watched left me real uncomfortable.

Morley said, "Here's how you get out."

At the end of the dead space, against the wall of the hallway, there was a two-by-two hole in the floor. Wooden rungs were nailed to the studs.

I sneezed ferociously. The dust and my cold were ganging up.

My head hurt from being banged. My skin burns gave me no respite. I had no reason to be amused. I chuckled anyway.

"What?"

"No way I'm going to get past you. You have to go first."

"Think so?" He ducked into the passageway from my sitting room. "After you, my man."

"You're so slick, you'll slide out of your casket." I tested the rungs. They were solid.

Ever go down a vertical ladder carrying a live fire? Lucky I'm a paragon of coordination.

The third floor was identical to the fourth except for the cover over the hole opening on the second.

"There's a big open storage loft below here," I told Morley. And sneezed so hard, I almost killed my lamp. I listened for movement below. Nothing. I lifted the cover. It swung to the side on hinges.

How would we get down? I'd seen no ladders when I'd explored the storage area.

Crafty builders. Right under the hatch was the end of a rack. The shelf supports made neat rungs.

I dropped to the floor. Knowing what to look for, I spotted trapdoors that would take me to every room in the wing.

"Pretty simple," Morley said. "Think it's set up for spying or for escapes?"

"I think it's probably for whatever's to the advantage of the Stantnors. I wonder how it works in the east wing. That layout is different."

"You've already checked this wing, right?"

"Except for the cellar."

"You didn't find any place your girlfriend could be hiding?"

"No."

"You ask the cook about food shortages?"

"No." I should have. She'd have to eat. I thought of her portrait. I'd better get the paintings into the house tonight.

"Let's do this systematically. The cellar first, then the other wing. Seems probable the passages there start in the cellar."

"Yeah." As I recalled the layout, the walls all sat atop one another from the first floor upward.

We descended to the pantry quietly, listened. Nothing. On to the cellar.

It was your typical earthen-floor cellar, deeper than my own, where I have to stoop, but vasty, dark, and dusty, a wilderness of stone pillars supporting beams that supported joists. At first it seemed mostly empty and dusty and dry—though dry wasn't a surprise. The house sat atop a hill. The builders would have arranged good drainage.

As we moved toward the east end we encountered evidence that an earlier regime had maintained a large wine cellar. Only the racks remained.

"Great place to get rid of bodies," Morley remarked.

"They have their own graveyard for that."

"Somebody sank a couple, three guys in that swamp."

He had a point.

We completed a circuit of the east end finding little but the wine racks, broken furniture, and, near the foot of the steps, sausages and stores hanging so mice couldn't reach them. I sneezed almost continuously.

"That's the easy half," Morley said. We started our circuit of the western end.

That end had less to recommend it or make it interesting, except for the supports and plumbing beneath the fountain. Those would have been of interest mainly to a plumber or engineer. There were no entries to hidden passages.

I said, "We just wasted three quarters of an hour." And sneezed.

"Never a waste when you find something out. Even if it's negative."

"That's my line. You're supposed to grumble about wasted time."

He chuckled. "Must be infecting each other. Let's get out before the spiders gang up."

I grunted, sneezed. Interesting. The cellar was almost vermin-free. Other than spiders there was very little wildlife. I'd have expected a sizable herd of mice.

I recalled the cats. "Can you smell anything? I'm deaf in the nose here."

"What am I supposed to smell?"

"Cat shit."

"What?"

"No mice. If there aren't any, the cats must be on the job. The only cats I've seen are out in the barns. If they're getting in here, there's a way into the basement from the outside."

"Oh." His eyes got a little bigger. He started watching the edges of the light more closely. There was still a draug around somewhere.

He said, "We're not going to find anything here. Let's do the west wing." He was uncomfortable. Usually he's cool as a rock. That creepy house really worked on you.

I was about halfway up to the first floor when I caught the end of a cry. "Oh, damn! What now?"

Don't ever try to run through unfamiliar territory in the dark, even with a lamp. Between us we nearly killed ourselves a half dozen times each before we made it to the great hall.

34

We burst into the light of the hall, where the Stantnors spared no expense on illumination. "What was it?" There was nothing shaking.

"Sounded like it came from here," Morley said. "Looks like we're first to arrive."

"Oh, damn! Not quite. Damn! Damn! Damn!"

Chain had beaten us there. The dragonslayer and his victim had masked him from us at first. He was on the floor, crumpled in a way no man should be. He'd bounced once, some, and had left a big smear. Blood still leaked out of him.

"Looks like he came from the top balcony," Morley said, with an artisan's dispassion. "Tried to land on his feet and didn't quite make it." He glanced up. "He didn't jump. And I'd bet you he didn't trip over the rail. If I was a betting man."

"Wouldn't touch the bet at a thousand to one." The fall wasn't much more than thirty feet. For Chain it must have seemed like a thousand.

Thirty feet is a bad fall, but people have survived it. If they have themselves under control or they're lucky. Chain hadn't been either.

I glimpsed movement on the opposite balcony,

whirled. I expected to see my mystery blonde. I saw Jennifer instead, in her nightclothes, at the rail at the end of my hall. She looked down in a sort of daze. She was very pale.

Peters appeared right above us a moment later. "What the hell?" he bellowed, and came bounding downstairs.

"Stay with him," I told Morley. "I'm going up there." I indicated Jennifer.

Black Pete galloped up to Morley as I trotted away, mouthing questions too fast for anybody to shove an answer in sideways.

I was puffing my lungs out when I reached Jennifer, swearing that, when this one was over, I was going to work out every day. Right after I spent a week catching up on my sleep.

She was flushed now, so red she looked like she'd run a mile. She snapped, "Where were you? I've been trying to wake you up for ten minutes."

"Huh?"

She stared at the floor, shivering. "You said . . . I thought you wanted me to . . ."

Hell. I'd forgotten. Damned good thing she hadn't come earlier. Especially damned good thing I hadn't given her a key.

Standing there shy and shamefaced and looking vulnerable, in nightclothes that did little to hide the fact that she was one gorgeous hunk of woman, she made me react after all. I got all set to howl at the moon. Only Peters's chatter downstairs kept my mind on business. Part of my mind on business. A small part of my mind.

"What do you know about this?" I jerked a thumb at Chain.

Her eyes got big. "Nothing."

"Come on. You had to see or hear something."

"All right. Don't bully." She eased a little closer, still shivering. Business, boy, mind on business. "I sneaked out of my room about thirty minutes ago. When I got to the end of my hall, Chain and Peters were down by the fountain. They were just sitting there. Like they were waiting for something to happen. I couldn't get to the stairs without them seeing me. So I waited. The more I waited, the more scared I got. I was ready to chicken out when Peters said something to Chain and started upstairs. Chain turned his back, so I hurried up to the fourth floor, before Peters saw me . . .

"Chain must have seen me when I was sneaking toward the loft stairs. He yelled. I went up and over. When I got to your side he was on the fourth floor, going into the hall to my father's suite. I ran down your hall to your door and tried to get you to answer. You didn't. I kept trying. Then I heard that yell. I didn't know what to do. I was scared. I tried to hide in the shadows at the end of the hall until I heard your voice."

"You didn't see anybody but Peters and Chain?"

"No. I told you."

"Huh." I thought a moment. "You'd better get back to your suite. Before anybody else comes out. Peters's questions will be troublesome enough."

"Oh!"

"Yeah. Let's go." I followed her to the stairs, up to the loft and across. The darkness there didn't bother her a bit. We parted at the head of the stair to the third-floor balcony. I said, "I'll come talk to you as soon as we've settled things down."

"All right." A quavery mouse voice. She was scared as hell. I didn't blame her. I was scared myself.

Chain was dead. Helped along. My favorite suspect. My almost certain killer. Gone. Out of the picture. Meaning I'd wanted to nail the wrong hide to the wall. Unless he'd tried to do unto another and got it done to him in self-defense.

I walked along the balcony to the point where, I guessed, he'd gone over. Morley and Peters were quiet now, watching me.

"He got wool pants on?" I asked.

"Yes," Morley replied.

There were strands of wool on the rail. There were scratches and flecks of skin, too, like he'd tried to grab hold as he'd gone over. Minute scraps of evidence but they made me certain he'd been shoved. I pictured him standing there, looking down, maybe talking to somebody, when he got a sudden boost with barely enough oomph on it. Maybe he'd even needed a little extra help after he'd started going.

Sometimes I suffer too much empathy for men who die untimely deaths. I picture the thing and conjure the feelings they must have felt as the realization hit them. Falling scares hell out of me. I had more than the usual ration of compassion for Chain.

What would it take, about a second of free fall? All of it intense with fear and wild desperation and vain hope, trying to adjust to take the fall and maybe, just maybe, survive?

I shuddered. This one was going to haunt me.

Trying hard not to think about it, I clumped down to the ground floor. I hurt everywhere. I wasn't in a good mood at all. "What's your story, Sarge?"

He was taken aback by my intensity. But he excused it. "We were waiting for the draug." There was a collection of instruments of mayhem lying in the fountain. I hadn't noticed before. "Kaid and Wayne were going to take the next watch, in about an hour. I had to take a leak. I didn't want to go outside so I headed for my room."

"You took a long time taking a leak."

"Found out I had to do more once I got there. You want to check? It's still warm."

"Take his word for it, Garrett." Morley isn't your dedicated investigator, willing to stir fouled chamberpots in search of damning evidence. I'm not that devoted myself. Anyway, I believed Peters. He'd have come up with an alibi less dumb if he was going to toss somebody off a balcony.

I was about out of suspects.

Which meant I had to open the whole thing up and suspect everybody again. Even the unlikelies.

Shares of the legacy were worth over six hundred thousand now. If the value of the estate wasn't falling faster than the murderer could expand his share.

Peters. Cook. Wayne. Who? For no sound reason I gave Wayne top billing. And Cook was starting to look better, though she had pretty good alibis. But alibis aren't everything.

"I guess the killer knows there's a copy of the will," I told Peters. "That means the General could be in double jeopardy."

"What?"

"After last night the killer has to worry about the other copies going, too. They do, all his risks have gone for nothing. So maybe he'll want the old man to check out before the last copy of the will does.

Better find out exactly how many there were and where they're at now." I tapped my shirt to make sure I had my copy.

Not that it was particularly safe with me, considering I was no more immortal than Chain, Hawkes, or Bradon.

Snake popped into mind, and after Snake, his paintings. I had to get those inside.

But it was pouring out. Maybe headed for something worse. There was the occasional flash of lightning. I said, "Getting around to the kind of weather that suits this place. All we need is something howling and ghost lights puttering around outside."

Peters snorted. "You get the next best thing. A frisky draug." He pointed.

There it was, back at the rear again, trying to get in. A lightning flash illuminated it. I got my first good look. It was more decomposed than the others.

Peters selected a few items from the stockpile in the fountain. "Shall we take care of it?"

"That's my old sergeant, Morley. Cool in the face of the enemy."

"Uhm." He went through the arsenal himself. Here was something he could get a hold on.

"All right. I guess we should take care of it. Get it out of the way." I checked their leavings. They'd taken all the best stuff already. "Hell with this." I went and disarmed a retired knight.

I had to be getting close to the end. There weren't many suits of armor left for me to vandalize.

35

Morley sat on the fountain surround hugging cracked ribs. Peters was curled up on the floor in a pool of vomit, clutching his groin. He did his manly best not to whimper. Me, I'd been luckier. All I'd come up with was a shin bruise and a badly stomped foot. Not on the same leg. "Maybe next time I'll save myself some grief and let whoever wants kill me."

Morley gasped, "Why didn't you say the man was a hand-to-hand specialist when he was alive?"

"Don't look at me! I didn't know anything about him. Not even who he was."

Pieces of draug were scattered all over. Some still moved.

"What now?"

"Eh?"

"You burned the other two. Right?"

"One of them, I know."

"Both," Peters groaned. He got onto his knees, his forehead on the floor. His knuckles were bone white. He'd gotten hit bad. "They dumped the other one into the stable fire when they saw there wasn't no stopping it." He didn't say that in one chunk but in little gasps, a word or two at a time. The effort cost him a spate of dry heaves.

I felt for him, though not as much as I would have if I hadn't been hurting myself.

I got up. "Better make sure we got the job done." The thing looked like it was trying to get itself back together. The pieces were trying to get to a central point. I hobbled, pitching random limbs back.

"What the hell's going on down there?"

I looked up. Wayne and Kaid had appeared for their shift, at the third-floor rail. "Come on down. We're in no shape to finish this."

Wayne beat Kaid by a floor. He looked at what was left of Chain, at the pieces of rotted corpse, at Chain again. "Man. Man, oh, man. Man." He didn't say anything else till he asked, "What happened?"

I told him. Kaid arrived in time to get it all.

"Man. Man, oh, man." Wayne was scared. For the first time since I arrived I saw one of those people convinced of his own mortality.

"Hell. You're all a hundred thousand richer now."

"Man. I don't care about that. I don't need it. It ain't worth it. I'm out of here soon as it's light enough that nothing can sneak up on me."

"But . . ."

"Money ain't everything. You can't live it up if you're dead. I'm gone." The man was almost hysterical.

I glanced at Peters. He was preoccupied, though he'd made it to the fountain surround. He hoisted himself up and perched with his misery. He had no attention left for anything else.

Morley was no help. But he couldn't be. He didn't know the people.

I looked at Kaid. He was as pallid as a man could get, as shaken as Wayne, equally eyeball to eyeball with death. It had come home. The field was so narrow, each knew he might be next.

He swallowed about three times, then managed, "The General. Somebody's got to take care of the General."

Wayne snarled, "Let that bastard take care of himself. I'm gone. I ain't dying for his money or for him."

Pain will distract you some, but mine wasn't so all-devouring that I couldn't spend some effort trying to figure out what the hell would happen next. I wondered which of the three was acting and how he'd gotten so good.

I wondered some about Cook, Jennifer, even the old man, and how I could figure one of them for the killer. Or more than one. That was an angle I hadn't given much thought. Maybe there was more than one killer. That would take care of alibis.

And my ivory lover. What of her? The mystery woman suddenly looked like a top bet for the villain.

Who the hell was she?

I plunked myself down on the fountain surround, as nimble as a quadraplegic dwarf. Kaid and Wayne came out of shock enough to start thinking and doing. Kaid went to the kitchen, got some big burlap sacks. He and Wayne stuffed them with pieces of draug and tied them shut. They gagged while they worked. My cold was that much of a blessing. I didn't have to take the smell.

Morley was three feet away. I asked, "How you doing?"

"Be running windsprints in the morning." He grimaced, spat on the floor, winced again as he leaned to look at it.

"What?"

"Wanted to see if I was spitting blood."

"Come on. You rolled with it."

He flashed me a down-under smile. He was putting on a show. He wanted folks to think he was hurt worse than he was. Might be an edge for him later.

I shut my mouth.

Peters managed to say, "What now, Garrett?"

"I don't know."

"How do we stop this before we're all dead?"

"I don't know that, either. Unless we just scatter."

"In which case the killer wins by default. Wayne walks tomorrow, it's the same as if he got killed."

Morley said, "Makes your job easier, Garrett." He did a grimace. He was overacting.

"Eh?" I was at top form.

"Shortens the list by another name."

Black Pete grunted out, "Garrett. How're you going to catch him?"

Him? I wasn't so sure now. If Wayne walked and Peters was clean, the crowd was so small I'd have to lynch Kaid. But I thought Kaid was too old and feeble to have done all the killer had.

"I don't have a clue, Sarge. Don't press me. You people know each other better than I know you. You tell me who it is."

"Shit. It isn't anybody. Logically. One way or another you can discard everybody. Except maybe your phantom blonde, that nobody sees but you."

"I saw her," Morley said. I looked at him, puzzled. Was he lending moral support?

Hadn't he said something about seeing her last night? Or was that the other Morley?

I'd forgotten that. The thing that could be somebody else. Probably the spook that the doctor was sure was here.

It didn't get any easier.

"Your picture," Morley whispered.

I frowned.

"Get it and find out who she is. Besides a hot tumble."

Maybe he was right. Maybe. I wanted to say the hell with it for now. We were out of the woods for a while. That draug had been cared for. The killer wasn't likely to make another move for a while. I hurt everywhere. I just wanted to slither upstairs and finish what I'd started before I'd been interrupted.

But I'd put off seeing Bradon for a few minutes and look what that had cost. Not just Snake but Chain. Not to mention the stable, those paintings, and however many horses had vanished into the sunset because there was no one to round them up.

I got my feet under me. "Peters. Any rain gear handy?"

Morley got up, too. He scrunched over, held his side with his left arm.

"Rain gear? What the hell you need to go outside for?"

"Got to get something while it's still there."

He looked at me like he thought I was crazy. Probably right, I thought. "To your left at the end over there, through that arch. The old guest restrooms." He still wasn't talking in big gobbling chunks.

Morley and I went to the arch, which was barely five feet wide. A crack of a doorway for this place. It opened on an alcove, eight by eight. There was a door in front of me and one to my left. "Check that one," I told Morley, and opened the one in front of me.

Mine was the women's, the only pissoir I'd seen in the house. I hadn't noticed any plumbing downstairs. Maybe it wasn't there anymore. The place was dried up, used only for storage.

There were no raincoats.

I went to check on Morley.

His room was the men's. Surprise, surprise. One wall was all marble that fell to a trough. The flush pipe whence water ran, at eye level, had rusted out. I spied the rain gear but not Morley. "Where are you?"

"Here." His voice came from beyond a copse of brooms and mops and whatnot in the left-hand rear corner. He'd found another movable panel. He was halfway up the narrow stairway behind it.

"We can check it out later." I spied a lantern amongst the junk on the marble four-holer. It smelled like it had been used in the modern era. When Morley came down I was getting it lighted.

Morley said, "If there weren't people hanging around, you'd think the place had been abandoned for twenty years."

"Yeah." I shrugged into an oilcloth coat so big it hung long on me. "Let's get with it." While Morley tried to find something smaller than a circus tent, I snapped up a few extras to wrap Bradon's artwork. We put on hats and dashed out into the storm.

Actually, we stumbled. I wasn't getting any friskier. Neither was Morley. I had to spend most of my energy keeping the lantern from blowing out.

There was a brisk wind blowing, throwing barrels of water around. It came from every direction but up. The thunder banged away. Lightning, over the city, carried on like a battle between hordes of stormwardens. We reached the barn in spite of all.

"Thank heaven we found rain gear," Morley said. "We might have gotten soaked."

Sarky bastard. I was wet to the skin. I rooted through the place where I'd squirreled the paintings. "Damn me! Something's gone right."

"What?"

"They're still here."

"Watch out for a booby trap, then."

I almost took him seriously. That's the way my luck runs.

I shook the water off the extra coats. Morley held the lantern and cursed and dodged bats. "Those coats aren't going to be enough. Let me look around." He scurried off, leaving me halfway convinced I'd never see him again.

He came back with a couple of heavy tarps. We wrapped the paintings in two bundles. We took one apiece and slogged into the storm. I got soaked all over again. I had mud up to my knees when we reached the house, but the paintings arrived dry.

We shed our gear.

"Guess we better take these up to the suite," I told Morley. He was looking at the paintings. "What do you think?"

"The man was disturbed."

"And good, too. That's her."

"I'm in love." He stared at the portrait like he might dive in.

"Let's admire her upstairs."

But we had to pass Kaid, Wayne, and Peters to get to the stairway. Black Pete asked, "What's all that?"

No reason not to tell the truth. "Some of Bradon's paintings. I saved them from the fire."

They wanted to see. They hadn't seen Bradon's work before. The man never had shown it.

"Yech!" Kaid said after a couple of war scenes. "That's sick."

"It's good," Wayne said. "That's how it felt."

"But it doesn't look like—"

"I know. It's how it *felt*."

"Man," Peters said. "He didn't like Jennifer much, did he?"

Somehow I'd managed to save four portraits, the blonde and three Jennifers. Just as well I hadn't salvaged any of these guys. They wouldn't have appreciated them. I'd gotten more than one Jennifer by accident. It had gotten hurried toward the end.

Peters lined the portraits up against the fountain. The third and probably most recent Jennifer stood out from the others. It was the ugliest. Jennifer was radiant yet something horrible about her made you doubt the artist's sanity.

Kaid said, "He was crazier than we thought. Garrett, don't ever let Miss Jennifer see these. That would be too cruel."

"I won't. I took them by accident more than anything. I was just grabbing. But the blonde, now. I took that one on purpose. That's the woman I've been seeing. Who is she?"

They looked at me, at the painting, at me again. Their studied blandness said they were unsure about my sanity. They thought I'd let my imagination attach itself to the first thing handy.

Peters played it straight. "I don't know, Garrett. Never seen her before. You men?"

Wayne and Kaid shook their heads. Wayne said, "There's something familiar about her, though."

That seemed to cue something in Kaid's head. He frowned, moved a step closer. I asked, "You know something, Kaid?"

"No. For a second . . . No. Just my imagination."

I wasn't going to argue with them till I could produce physical evidence. "Let's get these tucked away, Morley."

We started gathering the paintings. Now Peters was frowning at the blonde, something perking in the back of his head. He was a little pale and a whole lot puzzled.

He didn't say anything, though. We collected the paintings and headed for the stairs.

Maybe intuition nudged me. When I reached the fourth floor I went to the rail. Peters and Kaid had their heads together, yakking away. They kept their voices down but were intense.

Morley's ears are better than mine. He told me, "Whatever they're talking about, they're determined to convince each other it's impossible."

"They recognized her?"

"They think she looks like somebody she couldn't be. I think."

I didn't like the sound of that.

36

Morley perched the mystery woman on the mantle in my sitting room, contemplated her intently. I misread his interest. I seldom do that because his interest in the female tribe is definite. "Can't have her, boy. She's taken."

"Be quiet," he told me. "Sit down and look at the painting."

He wouldn't be sharp if it wasn't important. I planted myself. I stared.

I began to feel like I was part of the scene.

Morley got up and snuffed a few lamps, halving the light in the room. Then he threw the curtains open, apparently so we'd get the full benefit of the storm. He settled and resumed staring.

That woman came more and more to life, grabbed more and more of my being. I felt I could take her hand and pull her out, away from the thing that pursued her.

The storm outside intensified what was going on in the painting's background. That damned Snake

Bradon was a sorcerer. The painting, once you looked at it awhile, was more potent than the swampscape with hanged man. But this one was more subtle.

I could almost hear her begging for help.

Morley muttered, "Damn her. She's too intense. Got to block her out of there."

"What?"

"There's something else there. But the woman pulls your attention away."

He'd lost me. The rest of the painting was decoration to me. Or arrows pointing out the crucial object.

Morley got paper from my writing table, spent ten minutes using a small knife to trim pieces to cover the blonde. "You damage that thing, I'll carve you up," I told him. I had a notion where it ought to be displayed. There was a big bare spot on the wall of my office at home.

"I'd cut my own throat first, Garrett. The man was crazy but he was a genius."

Curious, Morley calling him crazy without having met him.

Morley killed another lamp. He hung his cutouts over the canvas.

"I'll be damned." The painting was almost as intense without the woman. But now the eye could rove.

Morley grunted. "Let your mind go blank. Just let it sink in."

I tried.

The storm carried on outside. Thunder galloped. Swords of lightning flailed. The flashes played with the flashes in the painting. The shadow seemed to move like a thunderhead boiling. "What?"

It was there for just a second. I couldn't get it back. I tried too hard.

"Did you see the face?" Morley asked. "In the shadow?"

"Yeah. For a second. I can't get it back."

"Neither can I." He removed the cutouts, settled again. "She's running from somebody, not something."

"She's reaching out. You think Bradon has her reaching for somebody particular?"

"Running from somebody to somebody?" he asked.

"Maybe."

"Him?"

"Maybe." I shrugged.

"You? You're the one who—"

"You said you saw her."

"I saw somebody. Just a glimpse. The more I stare at this, the more I think it could have been the other one."

"Jennifer?"

"Yes. They look a lot alike."

I tried to see Jennifer in the blonde. "I don't know. There's a lot of Stantnor in Jennifer but I don't know about this one."

I guess I squeaked. He asked, "What?"

"That face in the background. There was a lot of Stantnor in it."

"Jennifer? Bradon did her bad."

"I don't think so. I got the feeling it was male."

"Around thirty and stark raving mad."

The lightning had fits outside. I shuddered, jumped up, started lighting lamps. I couldn't shake the chill. "I'm spooked," I confessed.

"Yes. The more I look, the creepier it gets."

The chill stayed with me. I wondered if we were being watched. "Think I'll start a fire."

"Whoa! What did you say?"

"I'll start a fire. I'm freezing my—"

"You're a genius, Garrett."

"Nice of you to notice." What did I genius? It went right by me.

"Fire in the stable. You figured right, too. Not for you at all. For something Bradon had hidden. What did you find hidden? The paintings." He gestured at the blonde. "*The* painting."

"I don't know—"

"I do. What were the others? Crazy stuff. But people we've seen and places in the Cantard."

So I looked at the painting again.

Morley said, "There's the key to your killer. That's why Bradon died. There's why the stable burned. That's your killer." He laughed. It was a crazy noise. Hell. Everything was crazy in this place. "And you slept with her." He started to say something else, caught himself, reflected. "Oh, man." He came and put a hand on my shoulder.

He could have slept with a mass murderer and thought nothing of it. Maybe he'd have smiled and cut her throat afterward. A lovable rogue most of the time, but there's a cold subterranean stream inside him.

He knew how it would hit me before it hit. He was there when I started to rattle.

It wasn't as bad as I feared, but the idea did shake me. "I've got to pace."

He let me get up and try to walk it off. That didn't do much good. The whoopee-making noises outside didn't help. The thunder ripped at my nerves like cats howling at midnight.

Then I recalled promising Jennifer I'd see her later. The old mind fixed on that, telling me I could clean out a whole bird's nest with one stone.

"Where you going?" Morley demanded.

"Something to do. Promises to keep. Almost forgot." I got out before he pressed me, sudden as that, not quite sure I was thinking right.

37

I glanced over the rail. Kaid and Wayne were seated on opposite sides of the fountain, not talking. They'd cleaned up Chain. Peters had gone. I wondered why they bothered. Maybe they couldn't sleep. I couldn't see me getting much sleep despite exhaustion and hurting everywhere.

I made it to the loft, crossed, slipped down to the third floor without attracting attention. It was a great house for sneaking. I tiptoed to Jennifer's door. I tapped. She didn't answer. I shouldn't have expected her to, as long as it had been. I tried the door. Locked.

Only reasonable. Any fool would have taken that precaution. I tapped again and still got no response.

"So much for that idea." I started for home.

And stopped. And without understanding why I turned back and went to work on the lock. I had it undone in moments.

Jennifer didn't like the darkness. Half a dozen lamps burned in a sitting room identical to her father's. Not knowing the layout of these end suites, I decided the best place to find her would be behind the same door the old man used to make his entrances. I locked the hall door and headed that way.

I don't know what you'd call the room beyond. It wasn't a bedroom. It was more a small, informal sitting room with only a few pieces of furniture and one big window facing west. It was gloomy, lighted by a single candle. Jennifer was there, in a chair facing the window. The drapes were open wide. She'd fallen asleep despite the excitement outside. I doubted she'd have heard my knock had she been awake.

Now what, bright boy? Make the wrong move and they'll turn you into a eunuch.

Hell. It'd been tried before. I shook her shoulder. "Jenny. Wake up."

She shrieked and jumped and stumbled away and . . . The gods were kind. One of those barrages of thunder absorbed her cry. She recognized me and got herself under control—more or less.

She held her hands over her heart and panted. "You scared me to death. What're you doing here, Garrett?"

I fibbed a little. "I told you I'd come by. I knocked. You didn't answer. I got worried. I fiddled the lock and came to see if you were all right. You looked so pale I just reached out to shake your shoulder. I didn't mean to scare you."

Did I sound sincere? I poured it on. I do sincere pretty good. Been studying Morley's technique. She relaxed some, moved a little closer.

"Gods. I hope I didn't wake the whole house yelling like that."

I apologized some more. Then it seemed only natural to hug her to comfort her. A minute after that, when she'd stopped shaking so bad, she found a little girl voice and asked, "You're going to ravish me now, aren't you?"

For me it was the perfect thing for her to say at the moment. I busted out laughing. It took the built-up pressure out of me. It took almost too much. I had to fight it to control it.

"What's so damned funny?"

Her feelings were bruised. "No. Jenny. Honey. I'm not laughing at you. I'm laughing at me. Honest. I really am. No. I'm not here to ravish you. The condition I'm in, after today I couldn't ravish a chipmunk. I've been burned, bludgeoned, and kicked half to death. I hurt all over. I'm so tired I could pass out on the spot. And I'm totally upset about Chain. If there's anything I'd want from a woman now, it would be for her to comfort me, not for me to ravish her."

You slick talker. Pay attention. Talk like that, it's eight to five you'll wind up getting comforted by a vestal virgin. Just be harmless, helpless, and in need of mothering, and pour on the sincere.

Well, what with one thing and another, I talked myself right into something without consciously planning it. Fifteen minutes later we were in her bed. Fifteen minutes after that I was trying hard to stay harmless, helpless, and in need of comfort.

There's something reassuring about just lying around holding somebody after you've been bruised and abused and treated like a wolf treats a fox that isn't fast on its feet. But there's also something about being comforted by somebody put together like Jennifer that makes you forget they shoved you through the meat grinder sideways—hide, hooves, and all.

We'd been whispering, mostly just talk, innocent enough but she couldn't lie still. She was relaxed enough now, considering. She moved, seemed startled, asked, "Is that what I think it is?"

Body pressure left no doubt what she meant. "Yeah. Sorry. Can't help it. Maybe I'd better go." I didn't make any move to leave, though. Not me.

"I can't believe it. No. It's impossible."

It wasn't impossible at all.

For a while I forgot the painting, the storm, all my aches and pains. I even got to sleep some. Though that was more like catnaps between tests of the limits of possibility.

I knew I was going to hate myself in the morning.

It was just my body that hated myself in the morning. It felt about a hundred and two years old. My head was fine, not counting my cold. I kissed Jennifer on the forehead, nose, and chin, headed for my own quarters while it was still early enough that I might not be noticed.

Wayne and Kaid were on duty still. Sort of. Kaid was nodding. Wayne was sprawled on the fountain surround, snoring. Cook was in the kitchen cursing. I heard her all the way to the fourth floor. I wondered what was bothering her. I was sure we'd all know before long, what with her closed-mouth, stoic ways.

I went up, through the loft, down. I glanced across as I started into my hallway. The blonde stared at me from the hall to the General's suite. I waved feebly. She didn't respond. "Oh, boy." I headed for my door.

For a second I thought she'd gotten there before me. Then I realized it was the painting. It seemed so creepy, I turned it to face the wall.

"You have a nice time?"

Morley was in a big overstuffed chair. He looked like he'd been asleep.

"Ghastly."

"That's what puts that smug look on your face. I'll remember that. Get cleaned up. It's almost time for breakfast."

Him eager for one of Cook's breakfasts? "I'll give it a skip and take a nap instead."

"You're working, Garrett. You don't take time off to nap whenever you feel like it, do you?"

"That's the beauty of being your own boss." He was right. More right than he knew, really. I could go get some sleep, sure. And if somebody got killed while I did, I'd be haunted for years. "Yeah. All right."

Now he looked smug. Bastard. He knew right where to poke me. I went into the dressing room, threw some water on my face, mixed up some lather, hacked and slashed. Morley planted himself in the doorway. He watched the show awhile, then said, "I'd better move on the cook fast. Or you'll have every woman in the place wrapped up."

"You're out of luck. She was my first conquest."

He snorted.

I said, "I had to move fast because I knew you'd head for her like a moth to a candle." I wiped my face. "On the other hand, I won't stand in your way. She's definitely your type. I'll sing at your wedding."

"Don't think you can provoke me into a battle of wits with an unarmed man."

"Huh."

"I know it's your diet talking. Maybe I ought to talk to the cook about that. Dietary improvements could do your General more good than squadrons of doctors and witches."

"Got you on the run already?"

"What?"

"Last recourse, old buddy. You start talking about red meat and celery juice and boiled weeds."

"Boiled weeds? You ever actually *buy* a meal at my place? I mean, pay for it out of your own pocket?"

I was tired enough to forget how well he does sincere. I made the mistake of offering an honest answer. "I don't recall doing that. Every time it's been on the house." And not that bad, but who was going to admit that?

"And you complain about free meals. You know how much it costs to gather those 'weeds'? They're rare. They grow wild. They aren't cultivated commercially." He put on a lot of sincere. I wasn't sure if he was yanking my leg or not. I know it isn't cheap to eat at his place. But I'd always figured that was part of the ambience. Make his customers think they were buying class.

"We're getting too serious," I said, by way of ducking possible issues. "Let's go see how she'll poison us today."

"Not the best choice of words, Garrett, but let's."

38

Sometime back a hundred years ago, Cook whumped up one big breakfast and she'd been rewarming leftovers ever since. The same old greasy meats and biscuits and gravy and all that, so heavy it would founder a galleon. Your basic country breakfast. Morley was in pain.

He concentrated on biscuits and muttered, "At least the storm passed."

It was quiet out. The rain had fallen off to a drizzly mist. The wind had died down. It was getting colder, which I didn't interpret as a positive omen. I figured it meant the snow would be back.

Jennifer didn't show, which I didn't find mysterious and nobody else mentioned, so it must not be unusual. But Wayne wasn't around either and he wasn't the kind who missed his meals. "Where's Wayne?" I asked Peters, who looked groggy, crabby, and like he still hurt plenty.

He gave me the answer I was afraid I'd hear. "He pulled out. Soon as there was enough light, just like he said. Kaid said he had his stuff all packed and at the front door. He was raring to go."

I looked at Kaid. Kaid looked like I felt. He nodded, which seemed to take all the energy he had. I muttered, "And then there were three."

Peters said, "And I'm having a hard time talking myself into sticking."

Cook rumbled, "What are you boys on about now?" I realized she probably hadn't heard. I told her about Chain. And when I thought about Chain I wished I hadn't, because Wayne the gravedigger was gone and that meant either Peters or I or both of us would have to hike over to the graveyard and wallow in the mud till we got Art Chain planted. I knew Morley wouldn't do it. He hadn't hired on for that, as he'd remind me with a shit-eating grin while he kibbitzed my digging style.

Eight hundred and some thousands apiece now. And all the survivors improbable suspects.

I thought about burning my copy of the will right there. But what good would that do if they didn't know it was the last copy? Then I had a terrible thought. "Was the will registered?" You can do that to keep your heirs from squabbling. It means filing a copy of the document. If Stantnor's was registered, then the villain did not have to worry about my copy or about the General having torched his.

They all looked at each other, shrugged.

We'd have to ask the General.

I started to say I wanted to see him, but a racket out front cut me off. It sounded like a cavalry troop arriving.

"What the hell is that?" Kaid muttered. He shoved himself off his stool, started moving like he was forty years older than his seventy-something. Everybody but Cook toddled along behind. Cook didn't leave her bailiwick for trivia.

We swarmed onto the front porch. "What the hell?" Peters demanded. "Looks like a damned carnival caravan."

It did. And the mob with the garish coach and wagons boasted every breed you could imagine.

None of the vehicles were pulled by horses or oxen or even elephants, which you sometimes see with a carnival. The teams were all grolls—grolls being half giant, half troll, green, and from twelve to eighteen feet tall when they're grown. They're strong enough to tear out trees by their roots—*big* trees.

A pair of those grolls waved and hollered. Took me a moment. "Doris and Marsha," I said. "Haven't seen them for a while."

A skinny little guy bounced up the steps. I hadn't seen him for a lot longer. "Dojango Roze. How the hell are you?"

"A little down on my luck, actually." He grinned. A strange little breed, he claimed he and Doris and Marsha were triplets born of different mothers. I'd given up trying to figure that out.

"What the hell is this, Dojango?" Morley asked. I've never been sure but I think Dojango is some distant relative of his.

"Doctor Doom's medicine show, carnival, and home spirit disposal service, actually. Friend of the Doc said you had a bad spirit needing handling." He grinned from ear to ear. His brothers Doris and Marsha boomed cheerfully, not giving a damn that I didn't understand one word of grollish. They and the other grolls and all the oddities with them got to work setting up camp on the front lawn.

I glanced at Peters and Kaid. They just stared. "Morley?" I raised an eyebrow about a foot high. "Your doctor friend's referral?"

His smile was a little weak around the edges. "Looks like."

"Hey!" Dojango said, sensing my lack of enthusiasm. "Doc Doom is the real thing, actually. Real ghost tamer. Exorcist. Demonologist. Spirit talker. The works. Even does a little necromancy, actually. But there ain't much call for those skills, really. Not when you're not human. How many you humans would think of using a nonhuman to call up your uncle Fred so you can find out where he hid the good silver before he croaked? See? So Doc has to make a mark here and a mark there some other way. Peddles nostrums mostly, actually. Hey. Let me go get him, bring him up, let you judge for yourself." He spun around and headed for the coach, which hadn't disgorged any passengers yet.

He ran halfway down the steps. I muttered, "I don't believe this. The old man would foul his drawers if he saw it."

Morley grunted. His eyes were glazed.

Roze came back. "Oh. Doc Doom is kind of a quirky guy, actually. You got to give him some room and be a little patient. If you know what I mean."

"I don't," I told him. "Better not be too quirky. I've got quirky enough right here and no patience left over for more."

Dojango grinned, managed to leave without using his favorite word again. Actually. He dashed down to that ridiculous coach, which was so brightly painted it would have blinded us on a sunny day. Breeds swarmed around it. A couple got up a giant parasol. Another one brought a set of steps. Somebody else laid out a canvas dingus from those steps to the steps to the house.

Morley and I exchanged glances again.

Dojango opened the coach door and bowed.

Meantime, grolls set up a circus on the lawn.

I asked Morley, "You heard of this guy?"

"Actually, yes." He smiled. "Word is, he's the real thing. Like Dojango says."

"Actually."

Kaid sputtered and went back into the house.

A figure seven feet tall and maybe six hundred pounds wide descended from the coach. What it was wasn't immediately obvious. It was wrapped up in so much black cloth, it looked like a walking tent. The tent was covered with mystical symbols in silver. A huge hand came out and made a benevolent gesture to the troops. One of the taller breeds dragged something out of the coach and planted it atop Doctor Doom's head. It added three feet to his height. Priests should wear something so bizarre and ornate.

He came toward us as though the star of a coronation processional.

"You Doc Doom?" I asked when he arrived. "Give me one good reason why I should take you seriously after that clown show."

Dojango, bouncing around like a puppy, seemed stricken. "Hey. Garrett. You can't talk to Doctor Doom that way, actually."

"I talk to kings and sorcerers that way. Why should I make an exception for a clown? You better pack your tents and get rolling. The nitwit who sent you made a mistake."

Morley said, "Garrett, don't get excited. The man is for real, he's just kind of into drama and maybe has a little bit of a puffed-up notion of his own importance."

"I'll say."

Doom hadn't spoken yet. He didn't now. He gestured. A breed beside him, female, about four feet tall who looked like she had a lot of dwarf and ogre in her—she was *ugly*—said, "The Doctor says he'll excuse your impertinence this once because you were ignorant of who he is. But now you know—"

"Bye." I turned. "Sarge, Morley, we got work to do. Sarge, maybe you better see if you can find a horse. We may have to send for the garrison." There isn't much law anywhere in Karenta, but guys like the General have access to a little. Somebody irritates them, they can always get a hand or two hundred from the army.

Dojango had a fit. He pursued us into the hall, where he lost the thread of his thoughts as he looked around at the paintings and hardware and bellicose scenes in glass. He mumbled something about, "He's desperate for work, actually."

Cook strode onto the scene, as formidable as a war elephant. Now I knew where Kaid had gone. She damned near trampled Roze. I said, "I don't think we'll need the army."

Morley said, "You're being too hard, Garrett. One more time. The man is the real thing."

"Yeah. Right." I went back to the door to watch Cook in action.

The action was over, essentially. She stood in front of the marvelous doctor with hands on ample hips looking like she might breathe fire. He was out of his wonderful hat already and getting rid of the tent.

Like I thought, the guy inside went more stone than I had fingers to count, but I had to revise his tonnage downward. He didn't go more than four-fifty in his work clothes.

He had some troll in him and three or four other

bloods; once you saw him without the costume, you figured maybe he was smart to wear it. He made his little mouthpiece look gorgeous.

"Mr. Garrett. I'll dispense with the showmanship. As my good friend Dojango has assured you, I am the genuine article." His voice was down a well's depth below bass. Somewhere along the line somebody had popped him in the Adam's apple. That added a growly, scratchy character to his voice and made him hard to understand. He knew that and spoke slowly. "You have a problem with a malign spirit, I'm told. Unless it's of a class two magnitude or greater, I can deal with it."

"Huh?" I'm not up on the jargon. I try not to hang around with sorcerers. That can be hazardous to your health.

"Will you reconsider and allow me a preliminary examination of the premises?"

Why not? I'm an easygoing guy when people don't shuck me. "As long as you knock the horse apples off your boots and promise not to wet on the carpets."

He was so ugly his expression was hard to read. I don't think he appreciated my humor, though. I asked, "What do you need from us?"

"Nothing. I brought my own equipment. A guide, perhaps, to show me those places where the spirit most commonly manifests."

"It doesn't. Leastwise, not when anyone is looking. The only evidence we have that there is one is the doctor's opinion."

"Curious. A spirit of the sort he suspected ought to manifest frequently. Dojango. My kit."

Morley asked, "Could it appear to be somebody familiar?"

"Explain your question, please."

I told him about having a Morley in my room who wasn't.

"Yes. Exactly. If it wanted, it could cause a great deal of confusion that way. Dojango, what are you waiting for?"

Roze scampered off to the Doctor's coach. Meantime, Doom said, "Perhaps I should apologize for distressing you with my arrival. The sort of people who usually employ me won't believe I'm real unless they get a show."

I understood that. Sometimes I have that problem in my business. Potential clients look at me and wonder, especially when they catalog the marks on my face. I have to remind them that they should see the other guys.

Dojango staggered up the steps with four big cases. They probably outweighed him. His face was frozen in a rictus of a grin.

Cook seemed satisfied that everything was under control. She headed into the house. Never said a word to me. My feelings were hurt.

But not much.

Dojango arrived panting like he'd run twenty miles. Doctor Doom said, "Shall we begin?"

39

Once the good doctor stopped clowning, he impressed me as quite professional.

He started at the fountain, about which he made several remarks, suggesting he thought it one of the great sculptures of the modern age. He asked if it might be for sale in the foreseeable future.

Peters and I exchanged glances. Peters was way out at sea, encountering a side of the world about which he'd only heard before. He said, "Unlikely, doctor. Unlikely."

"A pity. A great pity. I'd love to own it. It would make a wonderful prop." He shuffled through his cases as Dojango popped them open, took out this and that—and nobody else knew what they were. For all I could tell they had no use at all and were just stuff to impress the peasants.

Three minutes later he said, "A great many traumatic events have occurred in this house." He looked at something in his hand, drifted to the spot where Chain had made his exit from this vale of tears. The boys had cleaned up good. I guessed Chain was taking his ease in the wellhouse till planting time.

"A man died here recently. Violently." Doom looked up. "Pushed, I'd guess."

"On the money," I admitted. "Maybe an hour after midnight last night."

He wandered around. "The dead have walked here. Zombies . . . No! Worse. Not under control. Draugs."

I looked at Morley. "I guess he knows his stuff. Unless he's got a friend on the inside."

"You're suspicious of everything."

"Occupational hazard."

The spook hunter spent fifteen minutes just standing by the fountain with his eyes closed, holding some doohickeys to his ears. I'd begun to wonder if we weren't getting shucked after all when he came back from wherever he'd been. "This is a house of blood. The very stones vibrate with memories of great evils done." He shuddered, closed his eyes for another three minutes, then turned to me. "You're the man who needs my help?"

"I'm the guy the General hired to straighten out a mess that only gets more tangled by the minute."

He nodded. "Tell me what you've learned. There have been so many evils done here that it's impossible to separate them."

"That'll take awhile. Why don't we get comfortable?" I led him to one of the rooms on the first floor west where, I presumed, in better times the business of the estate had been managed. We settled. Peters went off to sweet-talk Cook into providing the next best thing to refreshments in a household where alcohol was banned.

"A twisted place indeed," Doom said when he learned that. I decided maybe he wasn't so bad after all.

I told him what I'd learned, which wasn't that

much when you came down to it. Mostly a catalog of crimes.

He asked no questions till I finished. "The spirit seems content to victimize your principal? The other deaths are the work of other hands?"

"Hell, I don't know. The longer I'm here, the more confused I get. Every time somebody dies or emigrates, the list of suspects gets more improbable." I explained how I'd had Chain locked in as the villain—till he took his tumble.

He considered. He reflected. He took his time. He was one guy who didn't get in a hurry. He said, "Yours isn't my field of expertise, Mr. Garrett, but I would, as a disinterested layman, suggest that you may be following false trails because you began with faulty assumptions."

"Say what?"

"You think you're after someone who wants a greater share of the estate. Have you considered another motive? The heirs keep demonstrating a lack of interest in the legacy. Perhaps there's another cause for murder entirely."

"Perhaps." I'm not exactly a dummy. I'd considered that. But I couldn't come up with anything to connect these people any other way. Only the legacy offered any normal basis for bloodshed. I told him that. "I'm open to suggestions. I'll tell you I am."

He did some reflecting. "How separate are your separate investigations?"

I explained it the way I saw it. Morley fretted, thinking my perspective too narrow.

"Good heavens!"

"Huh?"

Doom was staring past my shoulder. I had my back to the doorway. I turned.

Jennifer had appeared.

"Good heavens," I said.

She looked like death warmed over.

Doom said, "Come here, child. Instantly."

I got up, put an arm around her waist. She was almost too weak to walk. She hadn't had strength enough to dress herself properly. "Garrett . . ." There were tears in her eyes.

That's all she said. I led her to the seat I'd vacated. The light was better. What it showed me wasn't. She'd taken on the color the old man showed. "It's after her," I croaked. "The spook."

Doom looked at her a long time before he said, "Yes."

Morley looked at her, too. Then he looked at me. "Garrett, let's take a walk. Doc, see what you can do for her. We'll be back."

Numb, I didn't say anything till Morley started leading me upstairs. "What are we doing?"

"That spook's been gnawing on the old man for a year, right? It never bothered anybody else. Right?"

"Yeah." We were headed for my suite.

"Something changed that between last night and this morning."

We reached the fourth floor, me puffing and renewing my vow to get in shape. "I guess. But what?"

He unlocked the door with my key, held it for me. Once we were inside, he took down the portrait of my mystery blonde. "Where'd you spend the night, Garrett?"

I looked at her. I looked at him. I recalled seeing her as I wandered home. I said, "Oh." That's all I had to say. It was a lot to swallow.

Morley went back into the hall, me tagging along.

He said, "Time to get an opinion on this from everyone."

"Morley, this isn't possible."

"Maybe not. I hope not." He has no mercy sometimes. His tone was a hot flensing knife.

We returned to the room where Doom and Jennifer were. Doom was disturbed. Jennifer looked a lot better, though. He'd done something for her. She had strength and attention enough now to put herself into better array. Morley placed the portrait on a table nearby, face down. "Peters. Would you get everyone in here? Garrett has something to show everybody."

Peters had been hovering over Jennifer. He looked at me. I said, "Please?"

"The General, too?"

"We can do without him for the moment."

He was gone longer than I expected. I found out why when he came back. "Cook and Kaid were up feeding the General. Garrett, he's damned near gone. Can't even sit up. Can't talk. It's like he's had a stroke. Or had all but the last ounce of life sucked out."

Doom listened but said nothing.

"How soon will they be here?"

"Soon as they get him cleaned up. He fouled his bed. He's never done that before. He always got hold of Kaid or Dellwood. Most times he had enough strength to make it to his chamberpot."

After that there wasn't much to say. I watched Doom fuss over Jennifer and Jennifer continue to improve. I tried not to dwell on what Morley had said without saying it in so many words.

There are things you just don't want to believe.

*　　*　　*

Kaid and Cook came in, Cook grumbling steadily about the interruptions in her schedule. Morley said, "Sit down, please. Garrett?"

I knew what I had to do. I didn't want to, for some reason that seemed almost outside me. But Garrett's got willpower. I looked at Jennifer. Too bad Garrett don't have a little more won't power.

"Snake Bradon was a remarkable artist but it seems he never showed his work. Which is a damned sin. He was able to capture the essence of what it felt like in the Cantard. He painted people, too. With a very skewed eye. This is one of his portraits. I managed to save it from the stable fire. It could be the key to everything. I want you all to look at it and tell me about it."

Morley brought a lamp closer so there'd be more light. I lifted the painting.

Damn me if Jennifer didn't let out a squeak and faint. And Cook, who hadn't deigned to seat herself, collapsed a moment later.

"Hell of an impact," I said.

Doc Doom stared at the blonde. He got the look Morley had last night. He shook himself loose, said, "Lay it down again, please." Once I had, he said, "The man who painted that had one eye in another world."

"He's got both of them there now. He was murdered night before last."

He waved that off. It was irrelevant.

Morley asked, "You see what was in the background?"

"Better than anyone with an untrained eye, I suspect. That painting tells a whole story. An ugly story."

"Yeah?" I said. "What is it?"

"Who was the woman?"

"That's what I've been trying to find out since I got here. Nobody but me ever sees her. The rest of these people say she doesn't exist."

"She exists. I'm surprised you're sensitive . . . No. I did say she'd manifest frequently. Sometimes they will attach themselves to a disinterested party, gradually trying to justify themselves before an impartial court."

"Huh?"

Morley said, "I get it. I was wrong, Garrett. She's not the killer. She's your ghost. She didn't need secret passages to get in and out."

"Morley! Morley. You know damned well that's impossible. I told you about . . ." Some sense wormed through my confusion. There was a crowd here. Was I going to be dumb enough to tell them all I'd fooled around with a spook?

Was I dumb enough to believe it myself?

"She's the haunt," Doom agreed. "There's no doubt. That painting explains everything. She was murdered. And it was the culmination of a betrayal so immense, so foul, that she stayed here."

I had it. "Stantnor killed her. His first wife. The one he got rid of. Supposedly he bought her off and sent her away. He murdered her instead. Maybe there is a body in the cellar, Morley."

"No."

"Huh?"

That was Cook, getting up off the floor. "That's Missus Eleanor, Garrett."

"Jennifer's mother?"

"Yes." She moved to the table. She lifted the painting. She stared. I was sure she saw everything Snake Bradon put there, maybe stuff Morley and I missed. "So. He did it hisself. He's lived a lie all these years because he can't give up that alibi. It wasn't no fumble-fingered doctor at all. That lousy bastard."

"Wait a minute. Just wait a damned minute—"

"The story is there, Mr. Garrett," Doom said. "She was tortured and murdered. By an insane man."

"Why?" My voice was in what you'd call the plaintive range. I wasn't calming down any. I couldn't get last night out of my head. That hadn't been any spook . . . Well, if it was, it was the warmest-bodied, friskiest, most solid spook there ever was. "Doc, I need to talk to you in private. It's critical."

We went into the hallway. I told him. He went into one of his reflections. When he came out a week later, he said, "It begins to make sense. And the child? Jennifer? Did you sleep with her, too?"

Well, hell. They say confession is good for the soul. "Yes. But it was kind of her idea. . . ." Stop making excuses, Garrett.

He smiled. It wasn't a salacious grin; it was a eureka kind of grin. "It falls together. The old man, your principal, whose life she's been leeching slowly as she sets his feet upon the path to hell, is drained this morning. She'd have had to do that to assume solid form with you. Then the other—her own daughter?—wounds her by taking you to her bed. You, the focus she's chosen to justify. You've been tainted. That has to be punished." He got reflective again.

"That's crazy."

"We're not dealing with sane people. Living or dead. I thought you understood that."

"Knowing it and *knowing* it are two different things."

"We have to talk to the troll woman. It would be wise to know the circumstances of those days as well as possible before we take steps. This isn't a feeble haunt."

We went back inside. Doom asked Cook, "What reason would General Stantnor have had for doing what he did? From what Mr. Garrett tells me, she was frightened of everything, had almost no will of her own. It would take great evils to animate her to the point where we'd have the situation that exists here now."

"I don't tell no stories—"

"Cook. Can it!" I snapped. "We have the General nailed here. He murdered Eleanor, evidently in extremely traumatic fashion. Now she's getting even. That doesn't bother me too much. I kind of like the idea of retribution. But now she's started on Jennifer. I don't like that. So how about you just puke up some straight answers?"

Cook looked at Jennifer, who hadn't yet recovered.

"I kind of hinted at it but I guess not strong enough. The General . . . Well, he was obsessed with Missus Eleanor. Like I told you. But that never stopped him from rabbiting around hisself, tumbling every wench who'd hold still while he threw her on her back. He wasn't discreet about it, neither. Missus Eleanor, naive as she was, figured it out. I can't tell you what she felt for him. She wasn't never one to talk or show much. But she had to be his wife. She didn't have nowhere to go. Her parents was dead. The king was out to get her.

"She was hurt bad by the way he done. Real bad. Maybe, because she was the way she was, lots more hurt than a deceived wife ought to be. Anyway, she told him if he didn't straighten up, she'd see if what was good for the gander was good for the goose. She wouldn't never have done it. Not in a million years.

She didn't have the nerve. But that didn't make him no never mind. He thought everybody worked inside like he did. He beat her half to death. Maybe would've killed her if I hadn't of got between them. Anyway, he just went crazy after that. Poor child. Only time she ever stood up to him. . . ."

I wanted to tell her to make the long story short, but it might not be smart to interrupt while she was puking her guts.

"Well, the poor child was pregnant with Miss Jennifer. She didn't know it yet. Naive child. Once she did figure it out, it was a day too late. I like to pounded his head for him but he wouldn't believe he was its dad. Not till she was gone. Him thinking that poor child was as loose as him! With who? I asked him. Was there anybody around the house? Hell, no. Not but him. And the child never went outdoors. Half the time she didn't even come out of her room. But try to convince a fool with logic."

"He put her through hell. Pure hell. Tormented her. Tortured her, I think. She had bruises all over. Trying to get her to tell him the name. I done what I could. That wasn't never enough. Only made him worse when I wasn't looking. And it got worse when the old General passed." She looked at me. There were tears in her eyes the size of larks' eggs. "I swear, though, I never thought he killed her. I never believed that even when there was some whispers. If I'd of known it then, I'd of plucked off his fingers and toes and arms like plucking feathers off a chicken. How *could* he have killed her?"

"I don't know, Cook. But I'm going to ask." I looked at Doctor Doom.

He asked, "You intend to confront him?"

"Oh, yes. I sure do." I grinned like a werewolf.

"He hired me to unravel his troubles no matter how much he didn't like what he learned. I'm going to give him apoplexy."

"Take it easy," Morley said. "Don't get so upset you can't think straight."

Good advice. I've been known to gallop around like a beheaded chicken when I'm excited, doing more damage to myself than to the bad guys. "I've got it under control." I glanced at Jennifer. She'd begun to recover while Cook was talking. She looked a little goofy, still, as she stared at the portrait of her mother. She seemed amazed and puzzled. She mumbled, "That's my mother. That's the woman in the painting in father's bedroom."

I looked at Peters. "Why didn't you tell me that last night?"

"I didn't believe it. I guessed, but this painting doesn't look anything like that one. I thought I had to be wrong. That it was just a coincidence. Snake never saw her, anyway."

Cook said, "That's not true."

"That's right," I said. "He came from the estate, didn't he? I should have thought of that. Did he know her at all?"

Cook shook her head. "He never came in the house even back then. She never went out. But he would have seen her from a distance."

Peters just shook his head. "I didn't believe it."

I recalled him and Kaid arguing after Morley and I left. Now I knew why. They'd been trying to make up their minds. "What do we do about the ghost, Doctor?" At the moment I was on her side, despite what she'd done to Jennifer.

Not hard to understand. Last night she'd added adultery to the punishments visited upon Stantnor, twenty years after he'd convicted her. Then Jennifer and I had . . . But why shouldn't she consider Jennifer my victim, the way she'd been Stantnor's? Was there more to it than I knew? I supposed Doom could explain but I couldn't ask.

I shrugged. Go try to unravel motives and you'll drive yourself crazy. In my line you're better off dealing with results. That's much more straightforward.

Doom said, "She has to be laid to rest. Her staying here and walking the night . . . That's far more cruel. That's more punishment that's undeserved. She needs peace." He paused, apparently expecting comment. When he got none, he added, "It's not my place to be judgmental. I suspect the man who killed her deserves all he's gotten and more. But my own ethics don't let me let the victimization go on."

He was starting to look like a right guy despite his clown show. Most of the time that's the code I follow myself. *Most* of the time. I've been known to get involved and consequently stumble into some homegrown justice sometimes. "I agree. Mostly. What next?"

Doom worked his ugly face into a smile. "I'm going to work a constraint on the shade that will keep it from draining any more substance off the living. The principal will begin to recover immediately. Once he regains some strength—this is just a suggestion—I'd like to call her up to confront him. A direct confrontation will leave her less reluctant to go to her rest, I think. And I have a feeling that an exorcism against a hostile shade would be very difficult here."

"Yeah." I reckoned he knew what he was talking about. And a confrontation sounded good to me.

"You can't do that," Jennifer protested. "That might kill him. He might have a stroke."

Nobody else much cared if he did. At the moment there was very little love for Stantnor around that place. Cook looked like she was considering ways she could help him across to the other shore. She'd raised him like her own but she was less than proud of him.

She said, "I got to get back to work. Lunch is going to be late as it is." She stomped out.

"Keep an eye on her, Sarge," I suggested. "She's pretty upset."

"Right."

40

Doom didn't need help doing his constraint thing. In fact, he wanted to be alone. "There are always risks in these things. I have a tendency to underestimate ghosts. It would be safer for everybody if you stayed away till I finish."

I said, "You heard him."

The party broke up. Nobody said much to anybody else. There was a lot of thinking going on.

Peters went to the kitchen to ride herd on Cook. Kaid went up to take care of the old man, probably with severely mixed feelings. I had them. It was hard to reconcile the General Stantnor of the Cantard War with the vicious monster we'd uncovered here.

Morley went outside to talk about old times with Dojango and his big green brothers. I took Jennifer up to her suite and put her back to bed, alone, to rest. She was badly shaken, seemed to want to curl up and make the world go away.

I didn't blame her. I'd be the same way if I found out my father murdered my mother.

I didn't tell her why she was in such bad shape physically. She had enough troubles. And I still wasn't sure I could accept that myself.

Nothing much to do till Doom was ready to go. I put my coat on and walked out to the Stantnor graveyard. I stared at Eleanor's marker awhile, trying to make peace with myself. It didn't work. I noticed a shovel leaning against the fence. Wayne had left it behind, as though he'd known there would be more graves to dig and why bother lugging tools back and forth? I found a spot and started digging, trying to lose myself preparing Chain's resting place.

That didn't work very well.

It especially didn't work when, after I was about three feet down, I noticed Eleanor by her tombstone, watching me. I stopped, tried to read something from features that were none too clear in daylight.

She'd been pretty substantial last night—because she'd sucked so much life out of Stantnor. Had she taken on substance at other times, to attack him by eliminating his servants? A ghost could make murder out of even apparently accidental deaths, by maddening a bull or maybe causing heart attacks. "I'm sorry, Eleanor. I never meant to hurt you."

She didn't say anything. She never did, except that once, when she found me outside Peters's room.

She seemed to gain substance. What was taking Doom so long? Was she giving him more trouble than he'd expected? I tried to think about that, the grave I was digging, lunch, the killer still to be caught, anything but the sad, futile, brief life this woman had lived.

It didn't work.

I sat on the edge of the grave, in the muck, and cried for her.

Then she was sitting opposite me wearing that look of concern, the same one she'd worn when she'd found me hurt. She didn't have enough substance not to be transparent. I told her, "I wish it could have been different for you. I wish you could've lived in my time. Or I in yours." And I meant it.

She reached out. Her touch was like the impact of falling swansdown. She smiled a weak, sad, forgiving smile. I tried to smile back but I couldn't.

There are evils in this world. It's the nature of things that there are, though it's a struggle accepting that. Because what Eleanor Stantnor had suffered, through no fault of her own, was an evil beyond ordinary evils. It was the kind of evil that goes beyond Man and rests squarely on the shoulders of the gods. It was the kind of evil that had left me an essentially godless man. I can't give allegiance to sky-beasts who'd let things like that happen to the undeserving.

General Stantnor would suffer in turn but the guilt wasn't all his. Nor did it belong to Eleanor's parents. Her mother had tried to protect her. Nor did it belong to the world as a whole. If there are gods at all, *they* deserved equal pain.

I looked up. Doom must have been finishing up, maybe getting an edge because she was distracted by me. She had little substance left. But she smiled as she faded. At me. Maybe the guy who had been best to her, ever. And you can guess how little that made me feel. I said, "Be at peace, Eleanor."

Then she was gone.

I dug some more, in a fury, like I was going to open a gate to hell and shove all the evils of the world down that hole. When I had a grave a foot deeper than necessary I came to my senses, sort of. I hoisted myself out and headed for the house. I had so much mud on me I feared somebody might mistake me for a draug.

41

I stopped and chatted with Dojango and the boys but my heart wasn't in it. I gave up after five minutes and headed for the house. Morley watched me go, worried. About the time I reached the head of the steps he said something to Dojango, trotted after me. Dojango sighed one of those sighs I recalled meant he felt immensely put upon, hitched up his pants, and started running down the drive.

What the hell?

I went inside. As I passed the dead Stantnors I told them what I thought of them and their ways and especially the last of their line. Morley caught up when I was halfway through. "Are you all right, Garrett?"

"No. I'm feeling about as bleak as I can and still be breathing. But I'll be all right. Just frustration over all the mindless wickedness in the world. I'll come back."

"Oh. Pure essence of Garrett. Wishing he was triplets so he could straighten up three times as many messes."

I smiled feebly. "Something like that."

"You can't take it all on your own shoulders."

You can't, no. But it's a hard lesson to learn. And knowing that doesn't keep it from getting to you.

A tremendous metallic crash came from the main hall, punctuated by a high-pitched scream like a rabbit's death cry. We charged through the doorway, bouncing off one another.

Kaid lay six feet from where Chain had died, smashed by a suit of armor. He wasn't dead. Not yet. He made me think of a smashed bug. His limbs still moved.

They stopped before we got the armor off him. The light went out of his eyes as I knelt beside him.

"And then there was one," Morley whispered.

"And I know which one, now." I hated myself. I should have known sooner. It was there to be had. Doctor Doom had been right. I'd looked at it from the wrong angle all along. But we all miss what we don't want to see. I'd just concentrated way too much on motive, blinded by the one motive I could see. Sometimes the motive doesn't make sense to anybody who isn't crazy.

"Yeah." Morley had it, too. Pretty obvious right now. But he didn't mention it. He said, "Can't do anything for him. Can't do anything about it this minute. You go get yourself cleaned up."

"Where's the point? I've got to dig another grave."

"That can wait. You need to get clean. I'll keep an eye on things."

Maybe he was right. Maybe he knew me too damned well. A bath probably wouldn't help, but it would be symbolic. I went to the kitchen. Cook and Peters had lunch almost ready. They hadn't heard the crash, amazingly. I didn't tell them what had happened. I just swiped all the hot water and headed for my suite. They didn't ask questions. I guess I looked too grim.

I didn't feel any better when I came back down, clean and changed. Some things won't wash off. "Anything?" I asked Morley.

He shook his head. "Except Doom wants to see you."

I went to the room where I'd left the Doctor. He had heard but still was startled when he looked at me. "You look bad."

I told him. He said, "I suspected it. I've done everything I can here, till we bring her up to face her husband."

I told him about my parting with Eleanor. He was a kind soul under that ugly exterior. "I know how you feel. I've been there a few times. Your business, mine, they have their painful sides. You'll get another chance to say good-bye."

"Let's do it."

"Not yet. You're not ready. You need to calm down. Your state is too emotional right now."

I started to argue.

"I don't tell you your business. You don't tell me mine. I'm not thinking about you. We can't operate properly if there's too much extraneous emotion. There'll be plenty involving the key characters."

He was right. I need to learn to separate myself more from my work. "All right. I'll get myself under control."

Morley stuck his head in. "Lunch. You'd better take time to have some, Garrett."

Great. Everybody was looking out for Garrett's mental welfare. I wanted to scream and holler and carry on. I said, "I'll be right there."

*   *   *

I guess I looked a little less ferocious now. Black Pete watched me gobble whatever it was I wasn't seeing or tasting. He asked, "Did something happen?"

"Yeah. Something did. A suit of armor jumped off the fourth floor and squashed Kaid. Dead."

"Huh?" He frowned. He looked at Cook. She looked at him. It took them maybe five seconds each. Then Cook started crying quietly.

I told them, "Soon as we're done here, we're going up to see the old man. We'll wrap it up."

Peters said, "It's almost not worth the trouble anymore. And I'm almost sorry I ever came looking for you."

"I'm sure sorry you did." I finished stuffing my face, never having tasted a bite. Nobody else was in as big a hurry. Morley watched me like he was afraid I was going to blow. I told him, "I've got it under control. Iceberg Garrett. Cucumber Garrett." I'd turned off everything inside. But I didn't look it outside yet. Like the heat going out of a corpse, it would take awhile for the fury and frustration to radiate away.

They ate slower and slower, like kids knowing they were going to get taken to the woodshed after supper. I told Morley, "I'm going up to the room. Be back in a minute." I'd forgotten something, one of Snake's paintings.

When I returned, everybody was done eating. Doctor Doom was there with his tools, Snake's masterpiece under his arm. He was ready to go. He checked everybody over, seemed satisfied with my emotional control. He asked me, "You want to get the girl?"

"Sure. Morley, you carry this."

We trooped across the hall, past Kaid, averting our

eyes. We climbed stairs. I broke away at the third floor and went to Jennifer's room. The door was locked but I had my skeleton key this time. I went through the big room into the sitting room where I'd found her during the night. She was there again, in the same chair, facing the same window. She was asleep. Her face was as untroubled as a baby's.

"Wake up, Jennifer." I shook her shoulder. She jumped.

"What?" She calmed down quickly. "What?" again.

"We're going up to see your father. Come on."

"I don't want to go. You're going to . . . It'll kill him. I don't want to be there. I couldn't handle it."

"I think you can. And you have to be there. Things won't work out unless you are." I took hold of her hand, led her. She hung back, making me pull her, but she didn't fight me.

The rest were in Stantnor's sitting room, waiting. As soon as Jennifer and I arrived, Peters pushed on. The next room was a private sitting room like the one in Jennifer's suite. We trudged through into the bedroom.

42.

The old man looked like a mummy that hadn't gotten the word and kept on breathing. His eyes were closed and his mouth was open. Some kind of slime bubbled out and dribbled down his cheek. Every third breath sounded like a death rattle.

We got to work. I collected paintings. Morley planted himself beside the door. Peters wakened the General and sat him up. Cook started feeding the fire.

The old man looked like hell but his eyes were bright when they focused. His mind hadn't deserted him. He saw how grim everybody looked, knew I'd come with my final report.

I told him, "No point you wasting strength talking, General. Or arguing. It's final report time. Won't take long but I warn you, it's worse than you dreamed. I won't make recommendations. I'll give it to you and you can do what you want with it."

His eyes sparked angrily.

I said, "The man you don't recognize is Doctor Doom, a specialist in paranormal activities. He's been a big help. You don't see Wayne because he quit. He left this morning. Chain and Kaid aren't here because they were taken suddenly dead. Like Hawkes and Bradon. By the same hand. Doctor."

Doom started doing his part. I gave him a little time to get rolling. Lips tightened into a colorless prune, Stantnor watched. Only his eyes moved. They weren't filled with gratitude when they turned my way. There was something behind the anger in them, too. He was worried.

I told him, "First we'll talk about who's been trying to kill you."

Doom let out a howl. Everybody jumped. A flash filled the room. I'm no pro but that didn't feel right. "You all right?" I asked.

He gasped, "It's fighting me. But I'll get it here. Stay out of my way and don't bother me."

It took him a few minutes more.

Eleanor materialized at the foot of Stantnor's bed. But not as Eleanor. Not right away. First she did a good Snake Bradon, then a less credible Cutter Hawkes before surrendering to Doom's will. I compared her to the portrait they said Stantnor stared at all the time. It didn't look much like her and nothing like the woman in Bradon's painting.

Stantnor's eyes got huge. He sat up straight. "No!" he squeaked. He threw up an arm to shield his eyes. "No! Get her away!" He started whimpering like a whipped child. "Get her out of here!"

"You said my job was to make you face the truth no matter how unpleasant that truth might be, General. One truth I've uncovered is this. I'm going to enjoy making you face it. The woman you tortured and murdered—"

Jennifer burst out, "I still can't believe it! My mother!" She staggered.

"Keep her under control, Morley." Morley left the

door, moved to support her. She started blubbering. Words dribbled out but none of them made sense.

Stantnor sputtered like he was going to run a bluff. Spittle ran down his chin. He couldn't talk. He was too rattled. He looked like he might have the stroke Jennifer had predicted.

I faced Eleanor. "Go now. Rest. You've done enough. It doesn't become you. Don't darken your soul any more." Our eyes locked. We stared at one another till the others grew restless. I said, "Please?" And wasn't quite sure what I was pleading for.

"She'll rest easy, Mr. Garrett," Doom said, gently. "That's a promise."

"Turn her loose, then. She doesn't need . . ." I shut my mouth before I said something that might cause me more trouble than I could handle. I closed my eyes, got myself under control. When I opened them Eleanor was little more than a wraith.

She smiled for me. Good-bye.

"Good-bye."

I took another minute before I faced the old man. He was gasping and wheezing but less distressed. "I brought along a little something for you to remember her by, General. You'll love it." I took down the junk portrait of Eleanor, flipped it away, replaced it with Bradon's masterpiece. "Isn't that better?"

Stantnor stared at it. And the longer he stared the more terrified he became.

He screamed.

I looked at the portrait.

I damned near screamed.

I can't tell you what it was. It hadn't changed in any obvious way but it had changed. It told Eleanor's story. You couldn't look at it and not be crushed by her pain and her fear of the thing that pursued her, that mad shadow that wore the face of a young Stantnor.

I tore my gaze away just before Doom did it for me. He told me, "You still have work to do." His voice was soft and calm. It reached way down inside me, like the Dead Man's can, and gentled that part of me about to stumble over the brink.

"What are you doing?" he asked.

"I want him to know he has to spend the rest of his life looking at that."

"Not now. Let's go on."

"You're right. Of course. Peters, get his attention away from the painting for a minute."

Peters turned the old man's head. I watched madness fade from Stantnor's eyes . . . No, it wasn't madness. Not exactly. He'd just been focused on something far away, that only he could see. On his own vision of hell. He was back now. For a few minutes, at least.

"I have another present for you," I told him. "You'll like this one, too." To make sure he paid attention I turned Eleanor's portrait to the wall. I replaced it with Snake's last portrait of Jennifer. "Your lovely daughter, so like her father."

Jennifer screamed. She threw herself forward. Morley caught her. She didn't notice the pain.

Cook stopped feeding the fire, elbowed Morley aside, took Jennifer into her arms, took the knife away from her, controlled her, held her, wept over her, murmured, "My baby, my baby. My poor sick baby." Nobody else said anything. Everybody knew. Even the General knew.

"There's why your stable burned. That painting. She sat for Bradon several times. But Snake Bradon had an eye that could see the true soul. Which is probably why he retreated from the world. A man with his eye would see a lot of awful truths.

"I look for truth but this time I didn't see it soon enough. Maybe I didn't want to. Like so many of the darkest evils, this one came in a beautiful package. Maybe the painting of Eleanor preoccupied me too much. Maybe I should have studied this one more closely."

Stantnor coughed.

"Eight murders, General. Your baby killed eight mostly good men. Four she lured to the swamp on the Melchior place." Once I'd accepted Jennifer as the villain the pieces had fallen together. "Took a while but I finally figured what they had in common. They were all chasers. She pretended she was catchable. She got them out there and killed them and dropped them in. That got her past the stumbling block I came up against whenever I wondered if she might be the killer. How did she move the bodies? I missed the obvious answer, that she got them to move themselves. The heaviest work she ever did was shove Chain off the fourth-floor balcony and drop a suit of armor on Kaid.

"Maybe I was slow because the murders weren't the kind you associate with women. I just didn't face the fact that in a house full of Marines *everybody* might think like Marines and be straightforward and bloody. Who'd picture a woman being daring enough to take on a trained commando with a Kef sidhe strangler's cord?"

I looked at Jennifer, thought of our stroll to the graveyard. She'd planned to kill me out there, I knew now. I'd offered her an unexpected moment of kindness. That had saved my life and had cost her her chance to get away with everything.

"I know who and how. But I sure as hell don't understand why."

She cracked. She laughed and wept and talked a yard a second and never made a lick of sense. It seemed to have to do with a fear that, if there were any heirs but her and Cook, parts of the estate would get sold off and once it was dismembered she'd be forced to leave for that deadly world she'd visited only once, when she was fourteen.

I was wrong about one thing. She hadn't committed eight murders. She'd committed eleven. She'd done in the three men whose deaths had seemed natural or accidental. She admitted it. She bragged about it. She laughed because she'd made fools of everybody till now.

Stantnor stared at her the whole time, aghast. I knew what he was thinking. What had he done to deserve this?

I started to tell him.

"Garrett!" Morley took hold of my arm.

"What?"

"It's time to go. The job's done."

Doom had gone already, his part complete, Eleanor laid to rest. Cook was trying to comfort and control Jennifer and to work out some separate peace with herself. The girl wasn't the daughter of her flesh, but . . . Stantnor had become fixated on his daughter's portrait, seeing deeper than anyone but Bradon had. Maybe seeing the hand he'd had in creating a monster. I had no pity for him. I did try to find it. It just wasn't there.

Then he had one of his fits.

This one went on and on and on.

"Garrett. It's time to go."

The old man was dying. Rough. Morley didn't want to stay for the show.

Peters just stood there, numb, doing nothing. He didn't know what to do. I did pity him.

I shook off the hold emotion had on me. I told Morley, "Stantnor owes me. I spent my whole fee and then some getting him his answers. It don't look like he'll hang around to be billed."

He looked at me weird. That kind of cold remark wasn't in character. "Don't," he said, though he had no idea what I was going to do. "Let's just go. Forget it. I won't charge you for my time."

"No." I snagged the painting of Eleanor. "My fee. An original Bradon." The General didn't argue. He was busy dying. I looked at Peters. He just shrugged. He didn't care.

Morley snapped, "Garrett!" He was sure I was going to do something I'd regret.

"Wait a damned minute!" I still had a responsibility here. "Cook, what're you going to do?"

She looked at me like I'd asked the dumbest question possible. "What I always done, boy. Look after the place."

"Get hold of me if I can do anything." *Then* I followed Morley. I didn't think another thought about the old man. If there'd been a doctor outside who could have saved him, I doubt it would have occurred to me to mention his distress.

Peters was at the vestibule door when Morley and I got there, carrying paintings and my stuff. He was staring at the great hall the way I'd stared at Bradon's painting of the swamp and hanged man. He had a shovel in one hand. He had graves to dig. I wondered if anybody would bother giving Stantnor a marker. He said, "I don't think I can say thanks, Garrett. You came when I called, but I don't think I'd have visited you if I'd known—"

"I wouldn't have come if I'd known. We're even. What're you going to do?"

"Bury the dead, then go somewhere. Maybe back into the corps. They'll need veterans with Mooncalled running amok. And it's all I know, anyway."

"Yeah. Good luck. See you again someday, Sarge."

"Sure." We both knew we'd never see one another again.

A terrible scream came from upstairs. It went on and on till it seemed no human throat could have produced it. We all looked up. Peters said, "I guess he's dead." He said it with a complete lack of passion.

The scream came again. Now it was filled with mad rage. Cook boomed, "Miss Jenny, you come back here!"

The girl had cracked completely. She flew out of the fourth-floor hallway carrying a dagger, screaming. Shocked, I realized she was yelling my name.

"Get moving, Garrett," Morley said. He'd seen berserkers before. Even a ninety-five-pound woman could tear me apart.

She was so far out of her mind, she didn't know where she was. Realization hit her too late. She hit the balcony rail full speed.

The heroic knight caught her in his lap. Broken, she dribbled down off him, wound up at one of the dragon's feet. She looked like the monster's prey. The hero had come to her rescue moments too late.

But this hero had been way too late to save anybody.

I turned and walked. Morley stayed behind me, just in case I did some damnfool thing like try to go back.

Morley and I didn't talk much on the way home. Once I muttered something about finding another line of work, and he just told me not to be a damned fool. I asked if he'd filled his pockets while he was there, or planned to drop back in some midnight. Usually if I ask something like that he just looks at me like he hasn't got the faintest idea what I'm talking about.

"I wouldn't take anything out of that place if you paid me, Garrett. Not if you begged me. There's a darkness in every stone, every thing, in there."

We didn't talk again till we were coming up Macunado Street toward my house. Then he said, "Go in there and get roaring drunk. Falling down, puking drunk. Get the poison out."

"That's the best idea you've had in years."

43

Dean let me in. He looked older and leaner, though it'd been only a few days. "Mr. Garrett. We were concerned, not hearing from you for so long."

"We?" I grumbled. He was going to fuss over me.

"Him." He jerked his head toward the Dead Man's room. "He's been awake since you left. Expecting you to ask for help."

"I handled this one alone." Boy, did I handle it.

"Oh." He'd gotten the sense of my mood. "Guess I'd better draw one."

"I might drink a whole barrel."

"That bad?"

"Worse. Find me a hammer, too." I eased into my office, checked the spot where I meant to hang Eleanor.

Dean went. He moved with a swiftness I should remember next time he went at his customary snail's pace. He was back with a beer, a hammer, and a cup of nails in less than a minute. I drained the beer mug. "More."

"I'll start a meal, too. You look like you could use one."

Old sneak. Going to get something in my stomach

before I started my serious drinking. "I did miss your cooking where I was." I drove a nail into the wall. Dean brought beery reinforcements before I unwrapped Eleanor. This time he brought a pitcher as well as a mug.

I unwrapped the lady and hung her, stepped back. It wasn't the same picture.

Well, yes, it was. But something had changed. The intensity, the passion, the horror weren't there. But it looked the same. Except Eleanor seemed to be smiling. She seemed to be running *to* something instead of *from* something.

No. It was the same. Nothing had changed but me. I turned my back on it. Snake Bradon hadn't been that great a painter.

I glanced over my shoulder. Eleanor smiled at me.

I downed another mug.

Dean scurried off to get something cooking before I downed enough to pass out.

The Dead Man dragged me into his room almost against my will and dragged the story out of me. He didn't criticize, which was unusual. We didn't get into an argument, despite my best efforts. Instead of climbing all over me for my mistakes, for not having recognized that Jennifer was crazy and a killer earlier than I had, he made thoughtful sounds in my mind. When I finished he meandered off on an extended review of the latest news from the Cantard.

I got interested despite myself.

Glory Mooncalled had attacked Full Harbor. He'd postured and threatened too much. He'd had to prove he wasn't all wind. He'd done his damnedest, launching night attacks from the sea and air, using Cantard creatures. He'd tried to capture the city gates so he could get his ground troops inside. And he'd gotten his ass whipped. Just as I'd predicted.

"There goes the myth of his invincibility," I told the Dead Man.

He responded with a huge mental chuckle. *Not at all. Now they will chase after him, to finish him off. Into his country.*

"Oh."

So. If he whipped them out there, there wouldn't be enough defenders to hold the city next time he attacked. Maybe. And our boys would chase him. In a mob. We don't have enough competent commanders. Our last really capable man retired three years ago.

I am curious, Garrett. Why would the woman hit you in the head in the sergeant's quarters? You had rendered yourself immune by plying her with your adolescent charm. He couldn't resist getting in a small needle here and there.

"I don't think she wanted to kill me. She just wanted to get the copy of the will before I did."

Why?

I had the feeling he'd figured it out and wanted to see if I had. "For exactly the opposite of the reason I assumed at the time. She wanted to destroy it. If she could get rid of the copies, she wouldn't need to kill people. There'd be no evidence there were any other heirs. The law would pass the estate to her. No dismemberment, no need for her to leave."

And how did she know where to find the copy?

"I think she was behind the wall listening when I talked to Peters. I think a lot of the time she was supposed to be in her rooms, she was creeping around in the walls, listening in. Look, I really don't want to talk about it. . . . I have one for you. Why did Eleanor pretend to be Morley? And *how* could she do it so slick that I never suspected a thing?"

She did it because she wanted to know more about you. Your fatal charm again. You had caught her eye. How is quite simple. Especially for one with her antecedents. She simply opened your mind and made herself a mirror. She did not have to know a thing about Mr. Dotes, she just had to make you think she did. You did all the work. Almost like a dream.

There was an implication, remote, that I didn't like. If Eleanor had been inside my head, she knew all about why I was there. She probably could have told me about Jennifer any time. She could have saved . . . I didn't want to think about it. "That's a little much to swallow."

Watch.

Suddenly that fifth of a ton of dead meat was gone, and in his place was a guy named Denny Tate who was so real, we talked about things the Dead Man couldn't possibly know.

Solid proof. Rock solid. Denny Tate had been dead more than a year. A good choice by the Dead Man. I couldn't call it a trick. He wasn't somebody who could be sneaked in for a little sleight of eye. And Denny was one of the few people important to me who'd died untimely without violence. The silly sack had fallen off a horse and broken his neck. "Enough, Old Bones. I'm a believer."

Denny Tate vanished. What replaced him was ugly as sin but I didn't tell him so. Not today.

My mood hadn't vanished. I almost asked him to conjure Eleanor.

Man, a guy could set up a hell of a racket faking calling up the dearly departed.

Think about something else, the Dead Man suggested.

"I'd love to, Chuckles. But it isn't that easy." Hell. I couldn't do anything right. Not even get drunk. I was barely light-headed.

You need a distraction.

"Right." So conjure me a miracle, Old Bones.

Somebody hammered on the front door.

The Dead Man *is* dead. In the flesh, anyway. But I swear he looked like he was smiling.

Dean hollered, "Can you get that, Mr. Garrett. I'm right in the middle, here. I've got both hands full."

Muttering, I stomped down the hall and flung the door open without bothering to look first. "Maya?"

"Hi, Garrett." Bright, perky, like she'd never been gone, except maybe to step around the corner. She walked in like she belonged. Which she did.

As I started to close the door I caught a glimpse of Morley Dotes holding up a wall down the street, smiling.

That slick bastard. He'd sent Dojango ahead to set this up. I bet he knew where Maya was all along. Maybe they all had.

From the kitchen Dean called, "Welcome back, Miss Maya. Dinner will be ready in a minute." He never looked to see who it was.

Set me up good, they did.

Maya took my hand and led me down the hall. For a second I resented everybody ganging up on me. But I didn't spend a whole lot of time worrying about it. Maya was there.

I was distracted.

About the Author

Glen Cook was born in 1944 in New York City. He has served in the United States Navy, and lived in Columbus, Indiana; Rocklin, California; and Columbia, Missouri, where he went to the state university. He attended the Clarion Writers Workshop in 1970, where he met his wife, Carol. "Unlike most writers, I have not had strange jobs like chicken plucking and swamping out health bars. Only full-time employer I've ever had is General Motors." He is now retired from GM. He's "still a stamp collector and book collector, but mostly, these days, I hang around the house and write." He has three sons—an Army officer, an architect, and a music major.

In addition to the Garrett, P.I., series, he is also the author of the ever-popular Black Company series.